THE GRAND COMPLICATION

ALSO BY ALLEN KURZWEIL

A Case of Curiosities

THE
GRAND
COMPLICATION

ALLEN KURZWEIL

An Imprint of Hyperion
NEW YORK

Copyright © 2001 Allen Kurzweil

Excerpt from "Unpacking My Library" in *Illuminations* by Walter Benjamin, copyright © 1955 by Suhrkamp Verlag, Frankfurt a.M., English translation by Harry Zohn copyright © 1968 and renewed 1966 by Harcourt, Inc., reprinted by permission of Harcourt, Inc.

Excerpt from *The Letters of Henry James, Volume IV, 1895–1916*, Cambridge, Mass.: The Belknap Press of Harvard University Press, Copyright © 1984 Leon Edel, Editorial, copyright © 1984, Alexander R. James, James copyright material, reprinted by permission of Harvard University Press.

A portion of this work appeared under the title "Slips of Love" in *Granta 54: Best of Young American Novelists, 1996*.

"Roll-Player" patent pending

Library of Congress Cataloging-in-Publication Data

Kurzweil, Allen.
    The grand complication / Allen Kurzweil.—1st ed.
      p. cm.
    ISBN 0-7868-6603-9
     1. Librarians—Fiction.   2. Art thefts—Fiction.   3. New York (N.Y.)—Fiction.   4. Collectors and collecting—Fiction.   5. Bibliomania—Fiction.   I. Title.

PS3561.U774 G73 2001
813'.54—dc21   2001016811

FIRST EDITION

10 9 8 7 6 5 4 3 2 1

For my father

The author gratefully acknowledges the Center for Scholars and Writers at the New York Public Library, the John Simon Guggenheim Memorial Foundation, and the John Nicholas Brown Center for the Study of American Civilization at Brown University for generous financial and intellectual support during the writing of this book.

You have all heard of people whom the loss of their books has turned into invalids, or of those who in order to acquire them became criminals. These are the very areas in which any order is a balancing act of extreme precariousness. . . . And indeed, if there is a counterpart to the confusion of a library, it is the order of its catalogue.

Walter Benjamin, *Illuminations*

1

THE SEARCH BEGAN with a library call slip and the gracious query of an elegant man.

"I beg your pardon," said the man, bowing ever so slightly.
"Might I steal a moment of your time?"

He deposited his slip on the reference desk and turned it so
that the lettering would face me. And if this unusual courtesy
wasn't enough to attract attention, there was also the matter
of his handwriting—a gorgeous old-fashioned script executed
with confident ascenders and tapering exit strokes—as well as
the title of the book he requested. *Secret Compartments in
Eighteenth-Century Furniture* played right to my fascination
with objects of enclosure.

"Let's see what we can do for you, Mr.—" I double-checked
the bottom of the slip before uttering his improbably literary
name. "Henry James Jesson III."

After I had directed him to the tube clerk, curiosity got the best of me, so I rang the stack supervisor and asked that she expedite retrieval. In a further breach of protocol, I pushed through the swing gate and planted myself near the dumb-waiter in Delivery, where I waited for the book to surface.

"This is terribly kind of you," Jesson said as I slid *Secret Compartments* under the brass grille.

"Glad to be of service."

I was professional enough not to mention the uncanny over-lap of our interests—I don't meet many readers keen on letter-ing technique and enclosures. But that same restraint left me mildly disappointed. The call slip was so enticing, our exchange so stilted and brief.

Jesson settled himself at a table near the municipal tax codes. He quickly supplied further proof of a charmingly out-moded manner by digging deep into his capacious trouser pock-ets to extract a roll of paper, a tiny ink pot, and a calligraphy pen. Though he seemed to ignore the stares of nearby readers, he occasionally glanced in my direction, as if to confirm that I'd stuck around. Which, of course, I had. In fact, while he took notes on *Secret Compartments*, I took notes on him, con-vinced that the consonance of our uncommon pursuits de-manded annotation.

He wore billowy trousers of moss-green corduroy that had wale as thick as pencils. These he partnered with a button-down shirt of subtle stripe and a dainty chamois vest tied at the back with a fat purple ribbon. He had an indulgent-looking face and blue-gray eyes that recalled the color of the buckram on my compact *OED*. Despite a bump at the bridge of his nose and teeth that predated fluoridation, he was un-deniably handsome, a scholar who appeared unencumbered by the tattered frugality of most academics I assist. Those, in toto, were my preliminary observations of the elderly man wishing to steal a moment of my time.

When the closing bell sounded, I sifted through the wire basket of call slips kept at Returns. My friend Norton noticed me swapping the calligraphic original for a quickly scribbled substitute.

"A little something for your collection?"

I nodded.

"What is it this time?"

"Just some furniture book," I said, downplaying my interest. Norton and I disagreed about the utility of paper records, and I didn't want to be deflected from inspection by yet another sparring session.

I located Jesson's book without difficulty. *Secret Compartments* was filled with line drawings of card tables, glass-fronted cabinets, and pedestal globes, each image accompanied by a technical description of the mechanism triggering release.

Norton glanced over my shoulder and chuckled. "Let's see here. A book about false fronts and hidden recesses." He paused. "Seems an awful lot like you."

2

AFTER MR. SINGH, one of our more vigilant exit guards, doweled through my satchel with his stick of polished pine, I said good night to Norton and started the long walk uptown.

At a traffic light near Lincoln Center, on a stretch of Broadway that brashly disrupts the city's grid, I withdrew the purloined call slip just as a taxi pulled up to the curb. The driver, compact and neatly dressed, jumped out, popped the trunk, and produced a small rug, which he unfurled with a firm, practiced *snap*. Then, facing a warehouse topped by a miniature Statue of Liberty, he kneeled in prayer. While the cabby, oblivious to the rush-hour traffic, satisfied his devotional obligations, I focused on the slip, noticing for the first time that its lettering leaned gently backward, as if to corroborate the writer's inclination toward the past. When the light

changed, I put the slip back in my pocket, determined to investigate the origins of the beautiful script.

I got home just as the sun was dropping behind the water
towers. Mr. Lopez, wearing his super's hat (he also owned
the corner bodega), was hosing down an old ceramic sign that
said, NO LOITERING OR BALL PLAYING, a wistful reminder of
quieter times—before the spray of fluorescent paint and nine-
millimeter bullets blemished the brick, before teenage crack
dealers hung sneakers from lampposts to advertise their drive-
by business.

"Hey, Mr. Lopez," I called out. "Can we get the landlord
to update that sign?"

"Eh?"

"Maybe it should just say, NO DRUGS."

Mr. Lopez said, "Okay, my friend," his standard response to
all complaints, whether about street crime, boiler malfunctions,
or rats sharpening their teeth against the rotting wallboard. He
turned to admire one of his children, who had just crawled inside the cabinet of a television set abandoned on the curb a week
before. The little boy, discovering that an old paint roller served
nicely as a gun, scanned the block for targets and soon found his
father and me in his sights. As the child squeezed off imaginary
rounds from inside the TV, I took a few quick notes. The natural place to register the scene would have been the "Enclosure"
section of my girdle book, but I'd determined long before to re-
strict that rubric to purely autobiographical entries. I opted for
"Street Views, Misc."

A gypsy cab caught my eye. Once more a driver hopped
out and yanked something from the trunk. This time the object was a black satin jacket that advertised *Les Misérables*.
The cabby beckoned Mr. Lopez, who, after careful inspection

of the contraband, peeled a twenty from a fat roll of cash. As he was completing the sale, the nightly drug trade started revving up.

"We gots blue." . . . "Blue's doin' it." . . . "Blue's out."

The super grabbed his child from the TV cabinet and bundled him into the building. I followed close behind but stopped when I felt a crunch underfoot. I bent down and picked up an inch-long torpedo of plastic used to package crack cocaine. *This isn't blue*, I found myself thinking. *There's too much purple in the mix. Periwinkle, maybe, or cornflower.* Suddenly I had a vision of the guys on the corner shouting, "Periwinkle's doin' it!" and "We gots cornflower!" Maybe I could scrounge up an offprint of "A System of Color Identification for Bibliographical Description" and convince the dealers to refine their patter.

My attention shifted when an ebony BMW pulled up to the curb. A tinted window lowered with an electronic whir.

"*Yo!* You with that fuckin' notebook thing. You gots a problem?"

The challenge was punctuated with a prodigious gob of spit. Sensing there was little dividend in direct response, I smiled and ducked inside, taking the stairs two at a time. At the front door of our apartment, I tripped over the size 16EEE sneakers my wife keeps around to scare off intruders.

I hung up my jacket and satchel and checked the mail: credit card bills, the Dewey Circle quarterly, and a course bulletin from House of Paper, the arts center where Nic taught the odd course on pop-up design. There was also a letter from a library-school classmate I never much liked, announcing his appointment as head cataloger for the central branch of a "very posh" township in New Jersey. To his boastful update he added a newspaper clip showing a "Map of Murder" that confirmed graphically the dangers I'd just been annotating downstairs. The map displayed my section of the Upper West Side obliterated by a cluster of dots marking instances of violent crime. In the margin, my classmate had written, "Wow! You live there??!!"

The punctuation bothered me more than the jibe. After I dashed off a reply on the back of a catalog card from my collection, for a novel called *Death in Suburbia*—"Wow is right!!!" I wrote—I added his offensive letter to the scraps of paper already heaped on the hallway carpeting. I kicked a path to Nic's studio and found her perched over her drafting table, bare feet hooked on the rungs of a stool.

"*Pardon*," she said preemptively.

"About?"

Without looking up, she waved an ink-stained hand at a riot of paper, paint pots, glue brushes, and cardboard.

I lowered the sound on an Edith Piaf CD. "Who's the project for?"

"Club Med," she said unenthusiastically.

"How'll you use those?" I pointed at some photos pinned above the table: palm trees and sunsets, sandy beaches, a couple in rapturous embrace.

Nic reached for a cleverly hinged pop-up that made the palm trees sway when the brochure was opened.

"And the couple?" I asked.

She swiveled around to face me. "They will do what lovers are *supposed* to do, Zander—if I can get them to stay together."

My stomach rumbled. The walk home had made me hungry. "Want to hit that new Malaysian place on Broadway?"

"*Pas ce soir*," Nic said, turning back to her work. "Deadline."

"Then let's order in."

"But we are broken."

"The expression is 'broke,' Nic . . . I still have some coupons for those satay skewers you like."

"No, I must work."

"Okay. Can you at least take a look at this?" I fished out Jesson's call slip. "Have you ever *seen* such lettering?" Before I could show her, Nic stretched out an arm and raised the volume on the CD player, effectively ending the exchange.

I retreated to the kitchen and made do with a bowl of Shredded Wheat. Irritation kicked in again when I saw the sink; it was so filled with dishes it resembled a library book drop at the end of a long weekend. And the recyclables! Their consolidation showed a total disregard for the nuances of plastic. Yet what really got me was the fridge.

Nic and I had talked through our organizational differences more than once and had, I thought, reached an understanding. The upper rack was to be reserved for tall objects, with smaller items claiming the narrow spaces below. So why did an aggressively horizontal platter of apples and nectarines now dominate the topmost shelf? True, Nic had put together a composition worthy of Cézanne, but that hardly negated the fact that we'd agreed fruit belonged in the compartment designated to hold it, namely the one marked FRUIT.

I told myself to let it go, which only accelerated the swirl of petty thoughts. How could a woman skilled enough to create exquisite pop-up cards and books leave a mountain of greasy dishes in the sink? How could her sense of style coexist so peaceably with a capacity for clutter? I tried to repatriate the apples and nectarines, only to find that the fruit bin had been packed with high-speed film, tarot cards, and various herbal remedies Nic's mother had sent from Toulouse. A catalog started running through my head: messiness, homeopathic medicine, sexual voracity . . .

I shifted the Cézanne one level down. As I was attempting to relocate a stick of butter—whose color, I took pleasure noting, resembled that of Jesson's yellow vest—to the dairy compartment, a clip of imported French suppositories bearing the all too evocative name Ammorectol clattered to the floor. Unable to cram the foil-wrapped bullets back behind the plastic door, I yanked open the vegetable bin. There I discovered further proof of Nic's relentless subversion of order.

From under a rotting cabbage I pulled a small package of "Big Boy Brew," the humiliating residue of her most recent effort to restore my virility. After tossing the cabbage and twigs and shoving the butter back where I'd found it, I halted the reconnaissance, determined to calm down by researching the source of Jesson's distinctive lettering.

My facsimile edition of *The Universal Penman* contained nothing remotely resembling the calligraphy on the call slip, nor did *The Scribe's Companion*. But I hit pay dirt with *The English Writing Master*. The anatomical structure of the penmanship—specifically those parts of the *b*s and *h*s that rose above the waistline—matched precisely a round hand taught during the late eighteenth century.

"Can't you put things back?"

Engrossed in my sleuthing, I hadn't noticed Nic glowering by the door, milk pitcher clutched accusingly. Apparently, I'd left it on the counter.

My first thought was, *This from a woman who uses the fridge as a storage closet.* I didn't have the energy for a fight, so I mumbled an apology. That earned me one of those withering shrugs all French women seem to master, and the suggestion that I go see my "shrimp."

3

THINGS HADN'T ALWAYS been so nasty between us. For nearly three years, Nic and I were well matched, two acid-free volumes bound together as one.

We met during my first year of library school. I was struggling to master the taxonomic inconsistencies of the Anglo-American Cataloguing Rules, conducting research on Melvil Dewey and Samuel Johnson, and starting to collect call slips. Also, I was working as a library technician, which is how I was able to push a book trolley full of reshelves over the foot of my future wife. By way of apology, I offered to help with her research.

Nic introduced herself in halting English and explained that she needed to learn how to make *boules de neige*, those kitschy snow globes so many people seem to love. A skiwear company had commissioned a batch of Christmas cards, and Nic was hoping to adapt the blizzard-in-a-bubble effect to her paper constructions. The problem was she couldn't find the right suspension fluid. She had tested tap water, alcohol, and bleach. None supplied the desired effect; her little hats and ski gloves kept bobbing to the surface.

The novelty of the query, and the seriousness with which Nic presented it, attracted me almost as much as her beguiling Jean Seberg looks. It didn't take more than an hour to track down the required formula—a simple mix of glycerin and antifreeze—and write up the recipe.

Nic thanked me profusely, insisting that no one in any *French* library would ever have shown such finesse. Then she punctured the formality of her appreciation with a devastating wink.

Two days later we bumped into each other again, this time in Periodicals. Nic was poring over a 3-D journal called *Stereoscopy*.

"How's the foot?" I asked.

She stared up at me through a pair of paper eyeglasses fitted with one green and one red lens. "He is fine. Like to see?" She provocatively extended her leg and wiggled a ribboned ballet shoe.

"I should've been more careful."

"*Au contraire*," she countered, staring over the tops of her funny glasses. "Then we would never have meeted."

The very next day Nic handed me a manila envelope containing a "snow card" filled with miniature books. I gave the card a shake and watched the volumes whorl about. "For me?"

"*Évidemment.*"

"It's perfect. I don't know how to . . . Hold on."

I turned to a nearby terminal and searched for a book that would dazzle her. At first I targeted a rare elephant folio with hand-painted planets that orbited the page on a tiny gold grommet, but I had to nix it when the screen indicated the book had been exiled to Conservation. A few more minutes of furious typing led to an even better citation, a facsimile Meggendorfer *Circus*.

"*Extraordinaire!*" Nic shouted when the book emerged from the stacks. My selection hit just the right chord: she adored the carousel-shaped display of sideshow life . . . and me because I'd found it. For the rest of the afternoon, Nic studied the pop-up and sketched its leaping stallions, winged acrobats, and clowns in Vandyke collars. By closing time, the two of us were caught in a flurry of books almost as glorious as the one she'd designed.

I showed Nic's handiwork to my friend George Speaight, the curator of the library's Center for Material Culture.

"A reader *made* this for you?" I could hear the envy in his voice as he shook the card and watched the tiny books settle.

"The blond woman in the harem pants, over there."

He took a long look and said, "You'll certainly want to add her to your holdings." Speaight often talked that way, his lewdness a by-product of the stuff he was sanctioned to acquire.

"You think she'd let herself be added?"

"Come off it, Short. Remember last year? The slave auction

organized for the Book Fund? Who caused a bidding war with the gals in Collection Development? You sold for *three times* what any of us did. Believe me, the woman knows a limited edition when she sees one."

I didn't need Speaight's encouragement to start dating Nic. Within days we were swapping call slips and revealing private ambitions.

"I want to compose lists," I confessed grandly during one of our early, encyclopedic talks.

Nic asked if I meant "compose" musically.

"I hadn't thought of it in that way, but why not?"

"*Parfait.* You make the lists and I will bind them!"

Our first joint effort was probably our best. We gathered up all the call slips we'd exchanged and interleaved them. Then I annotated each one with some of the conversational details the citation had stimulated. Nic, for her part, constructed a cover out of corrugated cardboard and bound the slips together with telephone wire.

The reaction to our register of courtship was flattering. "Pushes the material possibilities of the printed word," cooed Speaight. "You'd better plan on donating it to the center."

"As soon as Nic's done with the cover."

"And what's it called?" Speaight asked.

"*Slips of Love.*"

The first thing Nic did after she moved in was to detonate the apartment with color: tulips in old milk bottles on the windowsills, lamps draped in exotic fabric, platters of tropical fruits at the door. (When Nic caught a mouse gnawing on a mango, she relocated her still lifes to the fridge.)

Initially I was charmed by our differences. The rare moments of discord always seemed to end in laughter or lovemaking or gestures of good-natured rebuke. After one such skirmish, I presented Nic with a copy of *Knife Throwing as a Modern Sport*. She reciprocated by making me a luscious journal inspired by a Benedictine breviary we'd admired together in Manuscripts. I should have guessed she was up to something when she asked why medieval clerics buttoned, or "girdled," prayer books to their robes. "To guarantee a physical connection to God," I had told her.

Using leather from a discarded army boot and some handmade paper with a lovely deckle, Nic produced a stunning replica I could tether to my clothing pretty much the way the monks had done some five hundred years earlier. For the longest time, the beauty of the girdle book kept me from using it. When I finally started to write things down, I tried to generate lists that Nic could turn into books. But after I showed her what I'd produced, she gently suggested removing the inchoate pages, a course of action I instantly endorsed.

The following day, as I trudged off to work with the expurgated notebook laced through the buttonhole of my coat, I had to step over a scattering of crack vials and condoms that testified to a grim barter of goods for services. I couldn't get the image out of my head. That night, I girdled my first decent note. By the end of the week, I had composed a catalog of a tenement hallway, filed under *H*.

After that, subjects sprouted up in quick succession: the

seating choices of notable readers (this is where I documented Jesson before reassigning him to the *J*s), favorite library sounds, a register of Nic's paper creations, observations on forms of enclosure. In short, I was soon attached to the girdle book by much more than a bootlace.

4

TWO HUNDRED AND sixty-four call slips after *Snow Dome Repair* brought us together, Nic and I decided to reclassify our relationship. I'd been out of school for a year and was working overtime at the library when she sidled up to Reference wearing a short leather skirt and a gauzy silk wrap.

"Hey," I said.

Without a word, she handed me a slip for a Victorian instructional treatise called *Hints on Husband Catching, or A Manual for Marriageable Misses*. Then she winked and said she'd wait for my reply at the delivery window.

Her proposal didn't blindside me entirely. Living under the specter of deportation, Nic's visa having expired a couple of months before, we both knew marriage was the most effective countermeasure to the menace of the INS. When I reached

Delivery with my call slip all filled out—I requested a young adult novel titled *Just Say Yes!*—I discovered the area overrun by a tour group from Japan. It was impossible to find Nic, so I convinced a page to flash my response by configuring the numbers on the indicator board to blink I DO! I DO! I DO!

Explanations for the light show spread quickly, triggering applause that stretched from the Reading Room to the office of my boss, Emil Dinthofer, whose congratulations took the form of a memorandum about unacceptable noises. And lest there be any doubts as to the reason for the snide posting, Dinty circled violation No. 12 ("Percussive Laudation") to direct attention my way.

Fifteen call slips later, Nic and I married quietly down at City Hall. Neither of our families could afford a big wedding and that suited us both just fine. Nic's father, a poster hanger, had little to show for thirty-five years of labor besides forearms made of rock. His meager pension was only nominally supplemented by the five- and ten-franc coins his wife earned selling homeopathic remedies at a local market outside Toulouse. My parents were slightly better off, having retired to a one-bedroom condo outside Tampa. When told about the marriage, they mailed us a voucher for a weekend package at a swank New York hotel. (The neighbors two palms down apparently had a son whose girlfriend was a travel agent.)

It was in that hotel room that Nic and I had our first fight as husband and wife. At issue was a headboard bearing an oversized image of Vermeer's pensive lacemaker. As an art student in Paris, Nic had studied the original; there was no way, she announced, she'd make love under the grotesque gaze of a silk-screened reproduction.

"What if we drape a sheet over it?" I suggested.

Nic shook her head. "*Pas question!*"

Since our "suite" wasn't much bigger than a study carrel and the offending headboard was bolted to the wall, I ended up sliding the mattress off the box spring and dragging it to the channel between the bathroom and the closet. When it came time for the conjugal act, our heads were positioned six inches from a stainless-steel toilet, the sight and proximity of which instantly caused me to wilt.

In the weeks and months that followed, Nic did all she could to cure my wedding-night failure. She tried exciting me with a variety of herbal potions, and when those failed, she created a moveable book designed to ignite dormant lust.

I will say this: Nic's pop-up *Kama Sutra* was a marvel of paper engineering; the loins of the cardboard lovers slapped together like majestic elephant ears. Sadly, our attempts to replicate the *Kirtibandha*, or Knot of Fame, failed every time. That's when Nic urged me to consult a shrimp.

Dr. D. was the first to attach psychoanalytic significance to my growing need to girdle. He labeled my graphomania (to quote his bloated diagnosis) "a buffer against shame offering the precarious semblance of order to an emotionally blocked, obsessive young adult male."

Talk about buffers! *Of course* the annotations were compensatory. Sure I used them to offset frustration, fear, disappointment, and who knows what else. And yes, I was blocked.

But none of that drivel remedied the situation. I saw no point paying someone to lump me together with the guy who counts the windowpanes in the Reading Room or the woman who turns the pages of her romance novel only when the second hand on the wall clock passes the twelve.

Which is not to deny I had problems. When life was a hassle, whether at work or at home, I did reach too quickly for my notebook. And how to explain my embrace of tachygraphy, a shorthand technique I learned while studying Dewey? I told myself that the contractions and el-hooks allowed me to squeeze more words on the page, and, better still, prevented snooping. But that only underscored the weirdness of the habit.

Nic continued to make me gifts in the hopes they'd stir up the flurries of affection that had started to settle. For my twenty-fifth birthday she built me a small book house inspired by a scholar's library I'd seen in a slide lecture on bibliomania. When I described the closet-sized room to Nic, she said, "*Tu le veux?*"

"Want it?" I said with a laugh. "Who wouldn't?"

"So then? We will make you one."

Working from a grainy black-and-white photograph of the Dublin library of Narcissus March, Nic constructed my "cage" in under three weeks. I tried to get her to simplify the design, but she refused. At the downtown demolition site of a gobbled-up savings and loan, she salvaged a couple of solid-brass teller windows and some oak that was perfect for shelving. She then reconstituted a half dozen card catalog trays (tossed when my library went online) to create special storage drawers for an ever-growing collection of call slips. To one wall she chained the second edition of Dewey's pugnaciously spelled *Decimal Classification and Relativ Index* and Lindsley's shorthand treatise *The Note-Taker*—even though theft of those volumes seemed unlikely.

Nic had hoped the placement of the cage below our loft bed would encourage intimacy, but it did no such thing. The space became my private refuge from the fights and demands and the paper scraps that spread through the apartment like spore growth.

"A tribute to Monsieur Narcissus," Nic had announced when she showed me to my cage. Alas, she was right.

5

JESSON APPROACHED THE reference desk soon after I came on, and requested another book close to my heart.

"Boswell's *Life of Johnson*? That's a favorite of mine, too," I volunteered. "The preface to the *Dictionary* was required reading for a seminar I took on lexicons."

"Splendid," he said. "That makes you an ideal agent of inquiry. At the moment, I'm looking into the irony of influence in late-eighteenth-century literature."

"I'm honored. But actually I'm not allowed to provide that kind of help." I handed back the call slip. "The tube clerk can send this straight down."

"I see." Jesson seemed disappointed. "And suppose it were missing the proper references? Could you help me then?"

"It's not. You've completed the slip perfectly."

"Have I?" Jesson produced his lettering pen and blotted out the call number.

"Excuse me," he then said. "Might I steal a moment of your time?"

I scanned the altered request, amused by his subversion. "This slip isn't complete," I said. "You'd better come with me." At a distant terminal, I downloaded a few dozen citations.

"Superb," he said, scanning the list. "I've studied *Rasselas*, naturally. Imagine my not knowing about the Rusher edition. Did the printer actually remove all descending letters from the text?"

"Never underestimate the hubris of publishers," I said.

"But it's Johnson they're tampering with! No writer who uses *adscititious* and *equiponderant* in the same sentence deserves such disrespect."

Our banter continued for several minutes before Jesson got down to business. "Young man," he said, "I cannot restrain myself any longer. My work would benefit immensely from your continued assistance. Must you really return to that miserable desk?"

"Unfortunately. We have query quotas that need to be met."

Rejecting my excuses, Jesson got me to promise I'd approach my boss about the possibility of providing personalized help.

Dinthofer was chalking up the schedule board when I made the pitch. His response was swift.

"Are we a private research firm, Short?"

"No, of course not. It's just that his interests mesh amazingly with my own."

"Well, that does change matters, doesn't it?"

"I only meant—"

"Perhaps you'd be willing to judge the worthiness of *all* our visitors, hmm? Help weed out the ones pursuing research at odds with yours?"

"I'll just tell him no, Mr. Dinthofer."

"That would be prudent, Short. Do you have any notion what your proposal would do to our query quotas? Need I remind you that you already drag down the department mean?" To reaffirm his displeasure, Dinty assigned me to a double shift of phones.

A reader waylaid me as I was about to give Jesson the news. "The *Physician's Desk Reference*. It's not on the shelf!"

"Can this wait, Mrs. Boyd? I'm—"

"But my blood count!"

Having nursed Mrs. Boyd through a malaria scare a week earlier and sleeping sickness the week before that, I wasn't inclined to view her current condition as pressing.

"Do something, *please*," she pleaded. "I may not have much time." I got down the *Merck*, only to have her yank it from my hands. (And Conservation wonders why the manual requires a complete rebind every few months.)

Jesson was waiting patiently where I'd left him. "I trust you have squared things away," he said.

"Afraid not. My head turned me down."

"I see." He sounded despondent. "You would have been such a help . . . have been already. I called up that variorum Johnson you urged me to consult. It's so vastly superior to my Croker."

I sighed. "Sorry, Mr. Jesson, but I've got to go."

He must have sensed my regret. "Young man," he said. "How shall I put this? . . . Could I override your head and hire you after-hours? I suspect you're paid far less than you deserve."

"I better be. My salary's pretty poor."

Jesson leaned over and said, "Two hundred dollars a day—plus prorated compensation for any work done during library hours."

"Wow. And what exactly would this moonlighting involve?"

"Research and transcription—two skills I know you have mastered. That little book, the one you keep on a string, suggests a certain enthusiasm for note taking."

"Does the project involve Johnson or secret compartments?"

"No, it concerns a case."

Mrs. Boyd ambushed me again, now worried she might have contracted dengue fever.

"I do not believe it's endemic to Manhattan," said Jesson, his tone frosty enough to cure us of Mrs. Boyd. He turned back to me. "Now, do say you'll accept my proposal."

"I'll have to talk it over with my wife."

"Fine," he said. "Let's reconvene tomorrow at one."

Norton was at a computer in the staff lounge when I crept up and shouted, "Freeze!"

He jerked forward to block the screen, relaxing when he saw who it was.

"Up to no good again?" I said.

"Trying my best. Just got rid of a couple of *Gooks*, three

Chinks, and a 'see also' linking *Homosexuality* to *Perversion*. Care to help me eliminate the *Jewish Question*?"

"If Dinty catches you dickering with the database . . ."

"He won't. I've taken precautions."

"Spare me. Something urgent's come up."

"What could be more urgent than wiping out bigotry in our lifetime?"

"Henry James Jesson III."

"Mr. Secret Compartments?"

"He wants to hire me."

Norton smirked. "Did I call it or what? You and this character *are* two pages from the same cube of wood pulp. What's the subject field?"

"A case of some kind."

"Murder? Blackmail?"

"I doubt it. But I still want to do a background check. That's where you come in, O Maestro of the Modem. The guy intrigues me. Ever since he showed up, I've regained a bit of the old enthusiasm. I'm no longer feeling like I want to stick my head between the compact shelving and hit the button marked COMPRESS."

"Just remember what happened with Sharansky."

"All I did was help him finish his Johnson concordance."

"Red light. The man exploited you. You deserved joint authorship, not a passing mention in the acknowledgments."

"Spilt milk. Right now I need to know about Jesson. Dig up something robust and I'll spring for lunch at the Automat one last time before it closes down."

"You're on."

"It'll have to be early. Dinty stuck me with double phones and I'm meeting Jesson at one."

6

A PUNGENT MIST and a Piaf lament greeted me when I got home. I kicked my way through the scrap paper blocking access to the kitchen and found a stockpot boiling on the stove.

"Nic, we've been through this. The love potions don't work. It'll take more than your mother's twigs to fix things between us, and the steam is hell on the books."

I turned off the flame and went to the studio, where I found Nic smirking and clutching a poster tube.

"Can we talk before you show me what you're up to? You know that call slip I've tried to get you to look at? The man who wrote it offered me a job."

"Doing . . ."

"Research, transcription. The details are still fuzzy."

"What about our projects, Zander? My images, your words. *Slips of Love* was supposed to be our *début, non*?"

"Your images don't need my words, Nic." I pulled out the girdle book and flipped to a list of the ingenious things she had made.

"Put that away."

"You gave it to me."

"I thought it would bring us closer, not make you a slave. Concentrate on this." Nic presented the poster tube.

Reluctantly I popped off the cap and scissored my fingers against the inside wall to extract the contents. The tube contained a hand-tinted topographical map of an unidentified island. There was no key, nor were there legends or place-names of any kind.

"Is this for that Club Med commission?" I asked, weighting the corners of the map with four snow globes.

Nic shook her head.

"At least give me a hint. Have I been there?"

"Not recently, *malheureusement*."

As I looked up from the map, I saw Nic pull off her cotton smock, using a mysteriously female cross-armed technique I've never understood. As soon as the smock fell to the floor, one of her hands moved to a mountain range. The other cupped an exposed breast.

"You mean it's . . . Christ! How did you do it?"

Nic pointed to a call slip for a cartography text called *The Representation of Relief*.

We both knew what was supposed to happen next. I was expected to move from two dimensions to three, from map to body, from the representation of relief to relief itself. Nic grabbed my hand and placed it on a portion of the island that correlated with the precipitous drop of her belly button, an innie of unusual depth. When I failed to respond with a corresponding gesture and instead began to girdle, Nic snatched my notebook and threw it to the ground. The bootlace interrupted its fall.

I reached down. "One quick entry."

Nic caught my hand and redirected it more explicitly. "*Vas-y*," she said bitterly. Go on.

The situation deteriorated until a snow dome whizzed by my head, suggesting it was time to leave.

From the pay phone at the corner I called Norton and got a busy signal. He was probably online, I decided, harvesting facts about Jesson. I headed for a cash machine, where I typed in my PIN—1755, the year Johnson released his *Dictionary*—and waited. By the time the self-described Timeless Teller turned me down, my mood was so low that I thought the ATM had accused me of "insufficient fun."

Again I called Norton and again I couldn't get through, so I tried Speaight, who answered on the first ring.

"Can we talk?" I blurted into the receiver.

"I was about to take a run."

"Oh."

"No need to sound so gloomy. I was employing the term curatorially. Actually I'm off to the Crystal Palace. You're welcome to come along. My treat—the center has a budget surplus that needs spending down."

7

BUDGET SURPLUS IS not a phrase commonly spoken in the library world, but then, George Speaight's Center for Material Culture was not your typical collection. Though affiliated with our research division, the center received its funding externally, from a publisher and collector of pornography who supported freedom of speech in all its lewder forms.

Our director, when asked about the center, usually compared it to the Private Case maintained by the British Museum or the licentious materials filed under the Delta call mark at the Library of Congress. If pressed, he'd mention an impeccably pedigreed document—a Cocteau sketch or a letter from Anaïs Nin—and mumble banalities about the literary merits of erotic curiosa. Never did he detail the full scope of the holdings, knowing as he did that even the library's most unwavering supporters would have questioned the merits of the massive photo archives of buttocks and breasts and the document boxes filled with sex-trade realia.

Because its funding remained beyond the reach of the administration, the center was enviably immune to criticism. An independent endowment enabled Speaight to pursue what he pleased, and what pleased him fit the mandate of the center to a T. Hence the Cocteau and the Nin, Nic's pop-up *Kama Sutra*, and our coauthored *Slips of Love*. Officially Speaight may have held the title Curator of the Center for Material Culture, but colleagues and friends knew him as the Librarian of Sexual Congress.

"So what's up? Why the long face?" Speaight had already seated himself at the bar.

"Just had a fight with Nic."

"About?"

"A strip joint seems the wrong place to discuss one's weakened libido, but here goes." I told Speaight about the relief map and the tussle it had provoked.

"She surveyed her naked body, and all you did was take notes? You're—"

Pop! Pop! Pop! Gun blasts from the other end of the bar drowned out Speaight's words. I asked him to repeat what he'd said.

"I was saying you should give your wife as much attention as you give that blasted book."

Pop! Pop! Pop!

"What *is* that?"

"Pistol range," said Speaight nonchalantly.

A waitress wearing a Stetson and an open vest approached. "What can I get you boys?"

Speaight glanced up at the drinks board. "Give my friend here a Continental Screw." After the cowgirl left, he belabored the joke. "Get it? With Nic being French and all?"

My drink arrived with a coaster depicting a naked woman in silhouette; a bull's-eye zeroed in on her genitals. "Two years ago the big thing here was Super Soakers," Speaight said. "You know, those pump-action water guns. Patrons got to aim them at the dancers. Nowadays it's six-shooters and these." He fiddled with the coaster. "I should take one for the center archives."

"Here," I said.

"No, you'll need it for the firing range. Might relieve some tension."

"Doubtful. Don't you ever tire of this stuff?"

"Why would I? I don't have a wife sketching relief maps of her breasts."

The cowgirl returned to say that her shift was over and that she had to cash out. "Can I give you boys anything else?" Her hand brushed my thigh.

"I'm fine," I said.

"Change your mind, y'all know where to find me."

Speaight paid and, adding a hefty tip, whispered something in the cowgirl's ear. She whispered something back, which prompted him to hop off his stool. "Care to join us, Short?"

"I'll pass."

By the time I noticed the brass token near my coaster, the cowgirl had guided Speaight behind a beaded curtain.

"That gets you six shots," said the bartender when I presented the token. He thumbtacked my coaster inside a small enclosure and handed me an air pistol.

I squeezed off one-two-three-four rounds, paused, and pulled the trigger twice more.

The bartender retrieved the untouched bull's-eye. "Distracted, eh?"

When he asked if I'd like to keep the target as a memento, I said no. But then I remembered Speaight wanting to add the coaster to the G-strings and tasseled pasties archived at the center, so I shoved it in my pocket before leaving the bar.

Back at the apartment, I stepped over the decoy sneakers and the cracked snow dome and nervously headed for the loft, the dank odor of boiled herbs still hanging in the air. Nic was half asleep when I crawled in next to her.

"I'm sorry," I said, grasping her hand.

She pulled herself closer and arranged the comforter over my chest. "*Moi aussi.*"

Nic nodded off quickly, while I tossed and turned. Six times I had fired at the pinup and six times I had missed, not that accuracy was the issue. The issue was aiming a pistol at the silhouetted crotch of a naked woman.

8

NORTON AND I met as planned at the Automat, a soon-
to-be-shuttered restaurant with a décor I'd always loved.
The chrome-framed cubicles containing cellophane-wrapped
sandwiches and the brightly colored desserts so carnivalized
the act of eating that it didn't much matter that the food
stunk.

"Last days of Pompeii," I told Norton, as he extracted a
tuna sandwich from a tiny glazed cubby. "Enjoy it while you
can."

"What's happening to all the hardware?" he asked, helping
himself to coffee from an urn with a dolphin-head spigot.

"The *Times* said some guy named Stolz bought it."

"Frederick Stolz?"

"Could say."

Norton shook his head. "You sure you're a reference librarian? Stolz is the guy building that Arcade of Obsolescence over in New Jersey. Come to think of it, he could make you one of the side shows."

"Let's stick to the real throwback. What'd you find out about Jesson?"

"Not much. I got a few hits on one of the social science databases. Seems he's a scholar of sorts. 'Contemporary Roots in Historical Fiction' by H. J. Jesson. 'Doggerel and Ditty in Johnson's Grub Street' by H. J. Jesson. 'Pygmalionism and the Narrative Life of Things' by H. J. Jesson. The pieces all appeared in the *Journal of European Studies*. Periodicals has the whole pathetic run."

Once we'd settled in a booth, Norton rummaged through the plastic grocery sack he used as a briefcase and pulled out some papers. "I downloaded this from a genealogy site." He dropped a printout on the table and gave it a flick. The page sailed into my lap.

"A family crest?"

"Can't be a hundred percent sure it's relevant," he cautioned.

I inspected the shield, which included an imaginary beast clutching an open book that had another book inside it. A blurry Latin motto was ribboned underneath. "Anything else?"

"The guy belongs to a chichi racquet club in the East Fifties."

"Hard to imagine him hitting an overhead."

"Could be a prestige thing. At least you know he can pay the hired help." Norton assembled the rest of the printouts in a pile and handed them over. "This is everything I got on Jesson comma Henry, Jesson comma H, and Jesson comma H. J."

"He puts a three after his name. Was there anything on Jessons one and two?"

"Not per se, though I did get a hit for a defunct company called Jesson Secondary Metals, but again there's no reason to assume a link. There was a hit for a Jesson who took four hostages in a 7-Eleven outside Tacoma, only his first name was Durrell. Now, if I could dig up a social security number or a date of birth . . ."

"Don't. I want to keep the privacy violations to a minimum."

As soon as I got back from lunch, I called down to Periodicals to have the Jesson articles pulled and set aside. While that was happening, I stopped in at Genealogy.

"Fin, could you help me with a crest?"

"They're not called crests, Short."

"Shields, then."

"Tut-tut. How long have you worked here? The preferred term is coat of arms."

The world of books has no shortage of prigs, which may be why Finster Dapples decided to distinguish himself by slip-casing commonplace pretension in Anglo speech. (How many native New Yorkers say "Tut-tut"?) Finster, far from tracing his roots to a twelfth-century Lincolnshire leasehold, grew up in a Brooklyn housing project. His own coat of arms might well have been crossed stickball bats and cockroaches rampant on a field of cracked concrete.

After I acknowledged my error, he resumed the interrogation. "By the by. The coat in question, would it be blazoned or in trick?"

I handed him the printout, hoping to avoid further censure.

"Is this the best you can do?"

"Afraid so."

Grouchily, he inspected the image. "You see this wavy line?" he said. "It's a mark of illegitimacy. Your coat is the coat of a bastard, or of someone with bastardy in his past. There's a rather good article in the—"

Fin interrupted himself when he caught me looking at my watch. "If you're pressed, Short . . ."

"Sorry."

Fortunately, professional interest outweighed irritation. "See this cockatrice?" he continued, his pencil tapping the imaginary beast. "A creature of extreme malice, dangerous to all but the weasel. Quite a common icon. What perplexes me is the device in its talons."

"The book inside the book?"

"Haven't come across anything like it."

Fin started pulling references: Burke's *General Armory*, Papworth's *Ordinary of British Armorials*. Nothing he consulted helped. The nested image had him stumped. "Where exactly did you get this, Short?"

"Are you suggesting it's a fake?"

"Not at all. Unrecognized by the College of Arms, to be sure, but that's a far cry from falsification. Unfortunately, I lack the time to check further, and it would appear you are similarly constrained."

Ignoring the dig, I asked if the Latin was significant.

"Heraldically speaking, no. Mottoes are not part of the grant proper and can therefore be changed at will."

"Do you know what it means?"

"*Sapere aude*. I believe the line is most famously associated with Kant. I would render it thusly: 'Dare to know.'"

I thanked Fin for the help and hurried over to Periodicals, where a small stack of quarterlies awaited inspection. With less than half an hour till my meeting, I could only skim Jesson's writings.

The first article, "Contemporary Roots in Historical Fiction: A Case Study of the Eighteenth-Century French Novel," turned out to be an uninspiring meditation on literary appropriation, elevated stylistically by an epigraph Jesson had plucked from a letter written by the *other* Henry James:

> The "historic" novel is, for me, condemned, even in cases of labour as delicate as yours, to a fatal *cheapness*. . . . You may multiply the little facts that can be got from pictures and documents, relics and prints, as much as you like—*the* real thing is almost impossible to do, and in its essence the whole effect is as nought: I mean the invention, the representation of the old CONSCIOUSNESS, the soul, the sense, the horizon, the vision of individuals in whose minds half the things that make ours, that make the modern world were non-existent. . . . [Y]ou have to simplify back by an amazing *tour de force*—and even then it's all humbug.

Hard to disagree with that. Historical fiction always did strike me as little more than costume-party antics. Jesson unwisely tried to extend the indictment of his "allonym"—that's the fifty-cent word he applied to his namesake—but failed to improve on the pitch-perfect original. Inclusion of a second quotation hampered the article further. Jesson wrote (and I girdled): "If, as Thomas Mann claims, 'Time is the medium of narration, as it is the medium of life,' should we not do everything in our power to turn back the clocks that govern literature?"

The rhetorical question so confused me I started to have doubts about working for its author. I was just trying to decide whether to skim "Doggerel and Ditty in Johnson's Grub Street" or "Pygmalionism and the Narrative Life of Things" when a hand grabbed my shoulder. I twisted around.

"You caught me off guard."

"Did I or was it my writing?" Jesson reached over and closed the journal.

"So you and H. J."—I tapped the cover—"you're one and the same?"

"Hardly. The author of those pieces was young and arrogant, whereas the man standing here now . . . well, at the very least, he's no longer young." Jesson's embarrassment came as a relief, and though I wanted to say something to diminish his discomfort, he didn't give me a chance. "Time is of the essence," he announced brusquely. "I really do need to know whether or not you plan to work on the case."

"Does the job come with a deerstalker?"

"It's not that kind of case, Alexander. Well?"

"I never got an answer from my wife."

"Let's consider that a yes, then." From the fob pocket of his vest, Jesson removed another call slip. On the author line he had written our names, followed by his address. The words *six o'clock, Monday next* filled the date/volume box.

"You left the title blank," I said.

"Any suggestions?"

"How about *The Case of the Lapsed Librarian*?"

"Does that mean you accept?" Jesson asked.

Placing the call-slip invitation in my girdle book, I smiled and gave a nod.

9

I HAD HOPED to confirm our rendezvous, but as Norton had discovered online (and I subsequently corroborated by opening the phone book), there was no listing for a Henry Jesson living in Manhattan. It made sense. Everything I'd seen so far suggested a man happier in the heretofore, with its ink pots and chamois vests, than in the here-and-now world of laptops and cell phones. I wouldn't have been surprised if he planned to greet me at the door wearing knee breeches and frock coat, candlestick in hand.

The call slip directed me to an elegant town house—actually two town houses conjoined—in the middle of a quiet side street on the Upper East Side. Ivy covered the brickwork, the vines meticulously pruned to expose an oval nameplate engraved with the word *Festinalente*.

At the stroke of six, I pounded a brass door knocker shaped in the form of a fist missing one of its fingers. A postcard-sized judas hole slid open and a man with muttonchop whiskers gave me the once-over. He shut the window and opened the door.

"You are expected, Mr. Short. This way, if you please."

The butler, whose imperious manner would have given Finster Dapples a run for his money, took me through a stunning domed vestibule and pointed toward an open pair of pocket doors. "Make yourself comfortable inside the salon. Mr. Jesson wishes to apologize for the delay."

"No problem," I said, eager to take in the extravagant setting before getting down to work.

The salon, an oak-paneled room that ran the length of the residence, was so packed with antiques that it nearly over-whelmed my taste for inventory. I tried to resist the impulse to girdle, until I remembered that Jesson was aware of my propensity and had even praised it. I decided he probably *wanted* me to snoop about. More likely than not, the "delay" was intended to get the ogling out of the way.

Items I listed during that first, bug-eyed survey included: a harpsichord, seven apples lining a carved mantelpiece, a paw-footed globe, a three-paneled Louis-something screen depicting a devotional encounter between father and son, and an ivory-and-tortoiseshell chess table. Everything in the salon seemed to be set just where it belonged. Yet there was none of the stifling perfectionism that often infects professionally decorated homes. The apples on the mantel were withered and released a tangy odor. Candle wax speckled the rugs underneath the gilded wall sconces. Sheet music—a reduction for four hands of Haydn's Symphony no. 101 in D—fanned over the top of the harpsichord, Jesson's distinctive writing embellishing the margins. The chess set was left in midplay.

The black king gave me a start. A bump on the nose, imperfect teeth, crow's-feet around the eyes . . . Swap the robe for a vest and the chessman was a dead ringer for my host. I took a closer look and discovered that the white king, too, rendered Jesson in miniature. It seemed even the man's games played games, though by what rules I couldn't imagine.

The violins started in almost imperceptibly, a restrained arrangement performed over a subtle tick-tock. My grasp of classical music is weak at best, but the reduction on the harpsichord clued me to the fact that I was listening to a recording of Haydn's famous *Clock*.

A sudden tapping from the other end of the salon broke the spell. I turned and tried, unsuccessfully at first, to locate the source of the noise. Eventually I noticed Jesson standing on the far side of a pair of French doors; he was rapping his knuckle on the glass. Framed by the casement window, he looked like a museum specimen.

He entered and advanced to the globe at the center of the salon. "Early sixteenth century," he said, spinning it gently with his palm. "And to my mind every bit as enticing as the Blaeus that fill the Vatican, Ptolemaics of this quality being so much harder to find. Come take a look."

He stopped the revolving globe and pointed to a small island shaped like a kidney bean.

"*Pairidaeza*?" I said tentatively, unsure of the pronunciation.

"The word's Persian and translates as 'enclosed park.'

When this globe was constructed, geographers and clerics were actively debating the locus of paradise."

"The only Paradise I've known is a movie theater a couple of blocks from where I grew up."

"No longer standing, I take it."

"Long gone."

Jesson gave a knowing nod. "The Eden was my refuge as a child. It, too, was demolished."

"At least you've got this place."

The compliment prompted a smile. "Festinalente is a haven."

"About the name . . ."

"It means 'Make haste slowly.' A private challenge to the fast-paced mediocrity society teaches us to worship."

"You're not too keen on interactive technologies, I take it."

"Interactive, my eye! Judging from the bovine stares of the computer users in your library, 'intrapassive' seems more apt. To risk stating the obvious, I much prefer books to those glowing glass-and-plastic boxes."

I took a risk of my own. "A Jesson legacy, I take it."

"Excuse me?"

"The book in a book. I looked up your family shield."

"You *are* diligent," said Jesson, giving the globe another spin. "Truth be told, that coat was a fairly desperate attempt to reinvent the past." He nervously twisted his foot. "An attempt I'd rather not discuss just now."

His butler reappeared.

"Andrews, coffee—and use the Mandheling beans." As soon as we were alone again, Jesson turned to me and said, "I really should go back."

"Back?"

"To Sumatra. Unfortunately, such trips are no longer practical given my antipathy toward flying. Have you ever visited
that part of the world?"

"Never. The closest I've gotten is *Gulliver's Travels*.
Doesn't Swift set Lilliput around there?"

"He does indeed," said Jesson. He crossed the room and
dropped into one of two lounging chairs, then gestured for me
to take the other. After arranging his trousers, he stretched
out his foot and repeated the awkward twisting motion.

His butler hurried back in.

"The *Gulliver*, Andrews. It should be next to that Hakluyt
I had you pull last week."

When the requested book was found and delivered, Jesson
grabbed it firmly and applied enough pressure to fan the
pages.

"A fore-edge painting!" I exclaimed as soon as I eyed the
extraordinary watercolor that emerged from under the gilding,
an image of Gulliver tied down on Lilliput.

"Do you know the scene?"

"Know it? I can list each of the items pulled from Gulliver's
pockets."

Jesson flipped through the book till he reached the passage
in question. "Begin," he said.

I closed my eyes. "Okay, for starters, there's the huge silver
chest."

"That would be Gulliver's tiny snuff box . . ."

"And a length of timber affixed with iron rods."

"The pistol. Keep going."

"There's a reference to an engine, I'm pretty sure, but I
can't remember what kind."

"Need a hint? A half-silver, half-transparent globe."

"Oh, right," I said. "The watch."

"The object Gulliver famously calls his 'oracle.'"

Talk of timekeepers made me suddenly aware of the hour. "This is fun, Mr. Jesson. But shouldn't we be discussing the actual project?"

"Coffee and fore-edge paintings first, project after," he said. Andrews entered the room and set down a tray of cookies and a glass coffeemaker that looked like something from Lavoisier's chemistry lab.

Jesson said, "A friend once accused me of Paracelsian habits when he saw how I serve coffee. At the time, I took offense. I don't any longer. I've learned to admit my distrust for the alleged conveniences of the late twentieth century. That's one reason I need someone like you." He reached for a cookie and gobbled it up with unself-conscious delight. "Still, I do compromise. I have a phone, albeit with an unlisted number, and I did get these installed." Jesson twisted his foot back and forth as he had twice before. "Recessed buzzers," he explained. "You might say my toes keep Andrews on his."

I dragged my shoe over the rug until I felt a small protuberance. "You do a good job keeping your devices from view, Mr. Jesson."

"I try my best," he said with a smile. He placed two rough-hewn cubes of sugar on a spoon and lowered them gently into his cup. "Now, suppose I tell you what's expected. To begin with, you will be responsible for a certain amount of transcription. Everything that emerges from our research should of course be included. Is that clear?"

"Elementary," I said.

"Please dispense with the Holmes-Watson analogy. I see you

as more than an amiable sidekick. You must function as an investigator, amanuensis, confidant, and sounding board."

"Boswell to your Johnson?"

"A much finer comparison. I need someone to research and record all aspects of a special case." Jesson put down his cup and fidgeted with his armrest until it clicked open to reveal a hidden compartment.

"Does your library research always find such practical application?"

He was too busy rooting about in the hollow of his chair to answer. "Are you able to handle this thing?" he asked after he produced a microcassette recorder.

"Sure, nothing to it."

He dangled the machine between two fingers as if it were a rotting fish. "My opinion precisely. But it will be useful when we begin our work in earnest. Can you make it back next Saturday?"

"Saturday's fine."

"Splendid," said Jesson placing the recorder on the table and snapping the armrest shut. Then, after some rocking motions and a few failed takeoffs, he pulled himself up and shuffled toward the French doors.

"Is that all?" I said, startled by the abrupt end to our talk.

"For today."

I caught up with him at the globe. "I'm going to enjoy my visits to paradise," I said.

"I hope so."

"You don't sound convinced."

Jesson paused before responding: "I only know what the sages say about paradise. That it can depress, oppress, and sadden—and has even been known to betray."

10

MR. SINGH HAD to flick his parcel probe three or four times to catch my attention the following morning. "Greetings, Alexander. Late for the staff meeting?"

"Is it today?" We were standing near the foreign language reference shelf. The guard's turban bobbed.

"Indeed it is. And it is imperative that I tell you Mr. Dinthofer, he is most unhappy. And Mr. Grote is most unhappy also."

"I'll get up there as soon as I'm done." My consultation of a Persian-English dictionary (to check Jesson's etymology of the word *paradise*, which turned out to be flawless) agitated the guard. He seemed relieved when I finished jotting down the citation and headed for the great staircase.

Dinty stopped in midsentence to glower before refocusing on his clipboard. "Where were we? Ah yes, the homeless man obsessed with ancient Rome. Any thoughts?"

My colleagues remained silent, all except Irving Grote, the head of Conservation.

"His oral emissions make him a liability," said Grote as he fussed with the white cotton gloves he never seemed to remove.

"Point taken," Dinty said.

"C'mon, he's not that bad," said Speaight. Departmental independence and an external budget allowed him to express views the rest of us could not. "Remember the Sniffer?"

Grote bristled. "If you spent less time satisfying your questionable proclivities and more time on desk duty you would know this one's *far* worse."

Dinty weighed in. "I must concur with Mr. Grote. He's a horrid nuisance. The staff is to employ all necessary expedients, as spelled out in my 'Memorandum on Loitering, Lewdness, and Larceny,' to keep the fellow in check."

"He doesn't loiter," said Speaight.

"You are mistaken," Dinty countered. "Check the New York State Penal Code if you have any doubts. Section 240.35."

"What's criminal is that the man probably got prematurely released from some psych ward. The Reading Room and the collected works of Gibbon are all he has."

"We're not social workers, Mr. Speaight, and the library isn't a halfway house. We cannot compromise the efforts of *legitimate* researchers for the benefit of some rank-smelling noisemaker who's a few volumes shy of a complete set."

"Here, here," said Grote. "Do any of you realize that the man *dog-ears*? I happened to be walking through Periodicals—"

Speaight cut him off. "Give me a break. You were spying on him."

"And if I do feel an obligation to monitor our patrons, what of it? My mandate's clear: to preserve and protect the printed word. The Gibbon man defiled a copy of the *American Spectator*."

"Are you kidding?" interjected Abromowitz, the head of Judaica and a well-known lefty. "Defacing that rag should be a cause for celebration."

Dinty rapped his clipboard against the table. "Thank you, Mr. Abromowitz, for the ideological intercalation. Unfortunately, we have little time to debate either matters of politics or issues of mental health. Library policy is clear. Mr. Singh or one of the other guards should be called in next time the man causes a ruckus. Now, I understand Mr. Grote wishes to make an announcement."

Dinty's ally nodded. "It's come to my attention that some of you have been taking liberties with unopened leaves." Grote targeted me with a scowl. "All such books, repeat, *all* such books, are to be sent directly to Conservation for inspection and treatment."

I cleared my throat. "Is this about the hymnal?"

"If the shoe fits, Short."

"We've been through this twice already. Mea culpa. The reader was only in town for the day, and we both know how overworked you are. I thought I'd be saving the lab time. Besides, how long would it have taken to get the book back?"

"Three months, perhaps four," said Grote.

"And what was the guy supposed to do in the meantime?"

"Wait. You lack the skill to open books."

Norton rose to my defense. "It's not brain surgery. Obtain sharp knife. Insert knife between pages. Cut."

"Wrong!" the conservator bleated. "I would never employ a knife, not even a dull one. A knife cuts much too cleanly. An index card or, better still, a bone folder, properly angled— which is to say, almost but not quite parallel to the plane of the paper—effects the desired serration. Our friend Short butchered that hymnal. One glance was enough to see that he moved at an *inward* angle, instead of out and away. Plus there's the whole issue of whether the gatherings should have been opened in the first place."

As Norton and Grote argued back and forth, my thoughts drifted to Jesson's cryptic parting words. *Paradise can depress, oppress, and sadden* . . . Maybe. But it couldn't be as oppressive as a library staff meeting.

Dinty thwacked his clipboard on the tabletop. "Time to wrap things up. There's still the matter of the fund-raising video. The board of trustees is very keen on this happening. I've been informed it's to be called"—he checked his notes— "*The People's Palace.*"

The title sparked widespread groans.

"I for one quite like it," said Dinty. "True, the moat and drawbridge have been replaced by sensor screens. And our security guards use parcel probes instead of pikestaffs. Nevertheless—"

"What security?" Norton called out. "This place could be looted in a nano."

"You think so? I shall be sure that Mr. Singh knows how you feel. Expect to be searched with particular care." Dinty concluded the meeting by reading the names of those selected for the video—thankfully, I got passed over—and said, "Now, off to the ramparts, all of you!"

The tape's title stayed with me as I walked to the schedule board. Dinty had actually overlooked some of the more interesting parallels between palaces and libraries: the overburdened pages scurrying this way and that, the rival factions plotting their intrigues and gossip-fueled deceptions, the shameless attempts to curry favor with an inaccessible king. Here, however, the comparison breaks down, for no king I've ever read about made a name for himself by courting rich dowagers and getting photographed holding up donation checks the size of beach towels. Still, Dinty did serve as a kind of lordly eminence, and Speaight was, in his own way, a would-be procurer. Norton, given his skill with electronic formulas, could easily have worn the wizard's hat, and as for the job of court jester, the place overflowed with qualified candidates.

"Short!"

"Mr. Dinthofer?" I resisted the impulse to bow.

"Late again."

"Track fire on the downtown local."

Dinty frowned. "I wish you answered desk queries with the speed you respond to mine. And where the devil's your badge? You know policy. 'Clipped and visible.'"

I patted my pockets. "Must have left it home."

"Shape up, Short. If you don't, you'll find yourself driving a bookmobile through Amish country. Now get down to the gift shop. I've scheduled you for a student tour."

Clearly, the South Bend High School football team hadn't come to New York for the libraries. Their varsity jackets, appliquéd with a head, in profile, of a growling jungle cat, and their newly purchased caps, advertising a restaurant chain fronted by aging rock stars, suggested passions unrelated to books.

To be fair, the script that Dinty forced tour guides to recite wasn't intended for younger visitors. Who in his right mind would expect a teenager to care about shelving capacity, Beaux Arts architecture, and our hybrid use of Dewey and Library of Congress classifications? The only time the team seemed to perk up was when I mentioned that the Reading Room measured three feet shy of a football field.

A pimply kid wearing a button that read TEENAGER WITH ATTITUDE decided to stir things up.

"Wow," he said after I'd described the marble frieze of Clio. "An entire half ton of Vermont limestone just to make her!"

I smiled and asked for the chaperone, only to be told she'd stayed behind in the gift shop. As the tour progressed, Teenager with Attitude grew bolder.

"A bas-relief of Dante? Holy Toledo!"

I did my best to ignore him by sticking to the Authorized Version of the script. "Those cautionary words—'All hope abandon, ye who enter here!'—were the architect's idea of a joke. The door below the quotation leads directly to the stacks, thought by some to rival Dante's hell."

Teenager with Attitude rattled the doorknob.

"Don't bother," I said. "It's locked. Even the reference staff can't get in without written consent."

"That's bogus."

"You're right, it is." I was hoping agreement would put a stop to the sarcasm, but the kid continued to interrupt with snide queries and quips. By the time we reached Rare Books he'd notched up to slander. "Who's the towel head?" he asked as Mr. Singh passed by.

Enough was enough. I filled out a request for a manuscript.

"Like, what's so special about this?" the troublemaker demanded as he fingered the document suspiciously.

"It dates back to 1664."

"Yeah . . . *So*?"

"The author died before he could finish it. See how it ends midsentence?"

"What made him croak? Boredom?"

"*Bacillus pestis*, actually. Bubonic plague. When the writer composed the account you're holding, he had pus-filled sores the size of golf balls popping out of his groin."

Horrified, the kid dropped the manuscript.

"Of course, contagion needs a host. The manuscript is no longer infectious."

His buddies roared. "Busted." "Burned." "Snagged."

As the snickers subsided, I said, "You guys don't give a damn about the shelving capacity or marble friezes, do you?"

Silence.

"Tell you what. Suppose we tweak policy and I give you a *real* tour?"

Calling up a small collection of rock memorabilia donated

by a music executive in need of a tax write-off, I showed them Jimi Hendrix's report card from the fifth grade, the original cover art for a Grateful Dead album, and some lyrics bound in cannabis leaf, which the kids all wanted to sniff.

As we were leaving Rare Books, a member of the team stopped at a display case. "What's that?"

"An illuminated breviary, circa 1450."

He bent over the glass. "What is the button thing for?"

"To tie to a monk's robe so that the word of God would remain close at hand."

"People carried books around like *that*?"

"Some still do," I said, reaching into my jacket.

The students closed in as I held out the journal for inspection.

"You've got your own secret language?" said the reformed delinquent. "Cool."

When the unofficial tour continued, I offered up some sinister stories about library life, explaining how, before pressure plates were inserted under the compact shelving, a member of our stack crew had been crushed to death by a closing wall of books. Bringing my hands together slowly to reinforce the image, I said, "Make no mistake. Libraries are packed with danger."

I heard a familiar squeaking sound and folded it into my speech. "And our janitors have it worst of all. Think of what they inhale: mold, dust, sloughed-off skin cells, soot, red rot—not to mention all the chemicals. A lot of these guys have microscopic leechlike things living off the secretions of their tear ducts. Speak of the devil . . ."

A cleaning cart with a noisy wheel approached my now-captive audience.

"Mr. Paradis. May I introduce the South Bend Cougars."

"Sabertooths!" they corrected.

"Excuse me. Sabertooths. Mr. Paradis is the most senior member of our maintenance staff. No one knows this place better."

He shook his head. "Stop the soft soapin', Alexander."

"It's true, Mr. P. You're here when the rest of the staff arrives and you're still here when we all go home. I was hoping you might demonstrate your knowledge of the library holdings."

"Can't," he said, wheeling his trolley to a water fountain and removing a screwdriver from his tool belt. "Don't want to chance it—not after the Carborundum business."

The janitor's caution was the result of a run-in with Dinty over the maintenance of the great staircase, or more precisely the staircase's treads. Mr. Paradis had recommended treating the marble with Carborundum, but Dinty argued that nothing needed tending. Three weeks later, a researcher took a tumble and filed suit almost before hitting the ground. Dinty, being Dinty, denied he'd been properly alerted to the severity of the situation and redirected blame straight back to Mr. P. If the custodians union hadn't intervened, my friend would have lost his job.

I turned to Teenager with Attitude. "Name something you're interested in."

"Why?"

"Don't ask why. Just do it."

The kid thought for a moment. "Heavy metal."

Without missing a beat Mr. Paradis said, "Mineralogical or musical?"

The kid played an air guitar.

"That'd be under 'Rock music' and rock music's 781.66."

"What Mr. Paradis has just done," I explained, "is provide the Dewey decimal classification for the requested subject."

"The Super Bowl!" one of the Sabertooths shouted.

"You'll find that at 796.332," said the janitor.

"Suicide!"

"That'd be 362.28."

A hefty student punched Teenager with Attitude in the arm and said, "Pimples!"

"Check under 'Acne,' which is part of 'Medicine.' 616.53."

"How about the sabertooth?" someone asked.

Mr. Paradis thought for a moment. "Stumped me there. But tigers get classed as 569.75." He went back to fixing the fountain.

I moved the team along to the Reading Room and assembled them on the catwalk of the loge, within earshot of Norton. "My colleague here is scanning for what the head of our department calls the three Ls: loitering, lewdness, and larceny. Any action today?"

"We had a voyeur near the *Britannicas*. Mr. Singh caught the guy using one of those videocameras that got discontinued, the kind that sees through clothes."

I girdled the information and told the group how I maintained a list of Reading Room researchers, arranged by where they sat. Two or three Sabertooths wanted a summary of my observations, which I was only too happy to provide.

"See that ladder-back? That's where a Vietnam vet sat for

almost a decade investigating a carcinogenic defoliant he'd been forced to handle. He filed a successful action against the manufacturer based on work done right down there. And that chair against the wall? Rosalita Vasquez sits in it every Saturday and looks up case law for tenants fighting eviction. And the seat in the corner . . ." All eyes followed my finger. "That's where one of the most poignant poems of this century was composed."

Teenager with Attitude interrupted. "Jeez. Look at that guy!"

Focus shifted to a scruffy-looking man surrounded by dozens of books.

"He's been coming every Tuesday, Thursday, and Saturday ever since I've been here. Hasn't missed a day. Requests the same edition of the same children's encyclopedia, all twenty-some volumes. Claims to be memorizing the whole set, cover to cover."

Norton aimed his binoculars at the man. "He's up to *M*."

As I guided the group across the catwalk, I overheard two of the larger members wondering why anyone would do my job.

I turned and said, "Can any of you tell me the reason librarians get such a bad rap? I once had to give a brown-bag presentation about our profession and dipped into *Bartlett's* for a quotation. What do you suppose I found? I'll tell you. Nothing. Not one damn cite. There were quotes about libertines and quotes about lice, but librarians didn't make the cut. And that, my friends, is what *I* would call bogus. Mao Zedong, Casanova, Ralph Ellison, Stephen King—at some point each one of those guys worked in the stacks. Each one of them was an invisible man in a universe of printed words."

"So why do *you* do it?" one of the linebackers asked.

I was about to give them the old chestnut about my role as a merchant of thought and middleman of knowledge, when a butter-yellow vest caught my eye. "Why? Because of readers like that one down there." I pointed at Jesson, who was bending over an unabridged *Webster's*.

"The old guy with the funny clothes?"

"That's right. The other day I helped that old guy with the funny clothes investigate secret compartments in antique furniture."

"Awesome."

"I agree. I learned as much from him as he did from me, probably more. That's what keeps me going. That's what gives me the energy to talk to alienated high school kids."

The Sabertooths seemed to enjoy my little rant; they gave me a team roar.

Dinthofer, who had a gift for sensing dereliction, emerged out of nowhere and joined the group just as the growls were dying down. As quickly as I could, I reverted to the official script: "Notice if you will the quotation chiseled above the portals of the Reading Room. It is one of twelve Latin mottoes located on this floor. '*Habent sua fata libelli*.' Does anyone here know what that means?"

Teenager with Attitude cleared his throat. "Um, like . . ."

I prepared for the worst. "Yes?"

"All books have their fates?"

"Y-yes," I stammered. "That's right."

"We had to do Horace in Latin Club," he confessed sheepishly, over the approving hoots of his classmates.

Dinty cornered me after the group dispersed. "All books do

have their fates, Mr. Short. And so do their keepers—especially those who flout policy by personalizing tours."

"And what's my fate, Mr. Dinthofer?"

"I told you earlier. A bookmobile in Amish country if you insist on breaking the rules."

11

DINTY'S THREAT WAS, in its own way, oddly appropriate, for less than an hour after he had threatened banishment to an anachronistic world of beards and buggies, I returned to Festinalente.

This time Andrews guided me through the salon and into the library, a dark room composed of ten double-sided bookcases. Apart from the occasional engraving, hung from a fat purple ribbon like the one on Jesson's vest, the alcoves were devoted solely to books. Labels slotted into japanned sleeves of tinplate confirmed what I would have guessed: Jesson arranged his library alphabetically by subject. A brass rail running along the top of the shelves led me to a handsome mahogany library ladder with padded green leather steps.

Reviving my earlier rationale for nosiness (that Jesson

wanted me to poke about while he wasn't around), I rolled the ladder to the first alcove and parked in front of a shelf marked AMPUTATION. I pulled down a slender volume and determined instantly it was a little too technical for my tastes—though if I ever need to learn about the surgical techniques used to remove the index finger of Descartes, I'll know where to go. The amputation materials were followed by works on anamorphosis, Arcimboldo (the Italian artist famous, in my profession anyway, for his fanciful painting of a librarian made of books), and automats.

The last subject brought me up short. Was it possible Jesson and I shared yet another passion? Could restaurants that served iffy food out of tiny glass-fronted cubbies interest him too? Closer inspection revealed the answer to be no. Jesson used the word *automat* as an organizational term for his books on mechanical songbirds, antique windup toys, and other old-fashioned gadgets.

I dragged the ladder out of the As, pausing briefly at BES-TIARIES (to check the cockatrice reference Fin had provided during my visit to Genealogy), before proceeding through CHESS, DITTIES & DOGGEREL, and ECCENTRICS. The last label summed up not only the library's content and arrangement but its shelving methods as well.

When books get classed by subject, without regard to size, a common problem arises: wasted space. Collectors usually respond in one of three ways. They accept the displeasing sight of a jagged skyline, they include a catchall "oversize" shelf, or they cut down and rebind to impose uniformity—the last option being the organizational equivalent of eugenics.

Jesson had an altogether different solution. To maintain level rows, he placed blocks of lacquered wood, cut to measure, under the shorter volumes. On top of the plateaus created by these shims, he stacked more books horizontally.

"So what's the public librarian's opinion of my private collection?" Jesson had crept up while I was still taking notes.

"Pure magic. Though I worry that . . . Well, my library's conservator would raise a fuss about these." I tapped one of the blocks. "The varnish risks discoloring the bindings."

"You might tell your conservator that I borrowed the idea from Pepys. Can you think of a better way to avoid unsightly crenellation?" Before I had a chance to answer, Jesson dragged the ladder, with me on it, to the far end of the track and announced, "Last stop."

At a bookcase that included three intriguing shelf labels— SECRETS & SOLANDERS, UNFINISHED WORKS, and VOYAGES OF DISCOVERY—I climbed down and immediately found my eye drawn to the *Gulliver* with the fore-edge painting and the multivolume Hakluyt Jesson had mentioned in passing.

"Reconnoiter later," he said sternly. "Focus for the moment on these." He pointed to a pair of mahogany shutters hinged against the bookcase.

I pulled open the shutters and discovered they were hiding two remarkable Hogarth engravings of a randy young English couple. The prints hung on a second set of shutters.

"Keep going?" I asked.

Jesson gave a nod.

The inner shutters revealed two more Hogarths, which, like the rest of the pictures in Festinalente, were suspended from purple ribbons. The frames slapped against the wood when I pulled on the knobs.

"Careful," Jesson cautioned.

The third set of shutters hid yet another pair of prints.

The scenes turned increasingly somber the farther in I went, whereas Jesson radiated ever-growing whimsy. By my fourth yank his mood was almost elfin.

"Fine, just fine," he said giddily. "I can take over from here." He closed his eyes to gather his thoughts. "Get ready," he chirped. As he opened the final set of shutters, he pivoted to catch my reaction.

And what was my reaction?

Bewilderment. Instead of more Hogarths, I was looking at a room not much larger than my cage, only the flooring had been raised some eighteen inches off the ground. The platform was dominated by two curious chairs.

I mounted the stage and discovered that the chairs obscured a delicate ivory table on which a cardboard toy theater the size of a doll's house had been placed. The toy theater was fitted with a bright green curtain no bigger than a handkerchief. The curtain was lowered.

Jesson joined me on the platform and started adjusting the wicks on a row of thimble-sized footlights.

"Let me guess. There's another stage behind the curtain."

Jesson silently withdrew a silver matchbox from his vest pocket.

"At least tell me what's playing."

"Patience, Alexander." He struck a match and lit the footlights, which gave the air a nutty smell. "Colza oil," he said. "Aroma always enhances spectacle." He motioned at the tasseled cord on the side of a proscenium arch the size of a croquet wicket. "Care to do the final honors?"

I tugged the cord, and as the curtain rose, Jesson said, "Ta-dah!"

"Is *that* what you meant by a 'case'?"

The curtain had been hiding a mundane glass-fronted wooden cabinet subdivided into ten compartments. The contents of the case included a chipped nautilus shell, a grimy jar filled with a murky fluid, some withered vegetable matter hanging from a string, and an antique wooden doll.

"Startling, no?"

I shrugged, irritated that the word *case* had fooled me into fantasies of Conan Doyle.

"What do the objects say to you, Alexander?"

"Frankly, not much."

"Surely they evoke *some*thing."

"If pushed I'd say Minus McCarkle's discovery boxes."

Jesson gave a perplexed look. "The reference eludes me."

"I'm not surprised. Mr. McCarkle wasn't anyone important in the larger scheme of things. He ran the storefront library where I grew up."

"And his 'discovery boxes'?"

"Study aids that he kept on an old book cart near the catalog drawers. There was one carton called 'Colors' filled with pigments and fabric swatches. Another, 'Mineral Marvels,' contained pyrites, geodes, and other pretty stones. My favorite was 'What Am I Made Of?' Inside, Mr. McCarkle had put a fragment of bone, a test tube of water, a fingernail, and a six-inch braid of hair he later told me he'd picked up at a local beauty parlor."

"'What Am I Made Of?' How gorgeous—and how utterly apposite, for that's precisely the question this case poses."

At last, we were getting somewhere. "Do you mean what *you're* made of, Mr. Jesson?"

"Not me, heavens no. These objects register the life of a

man who died nearly two hundred years ago." He pressed a floor buzzer.

"The palanquin and the porter's chair, Andrews. We require them turned, like so." Jesson touched the insides of his wrists together to form a V with his hands, and while the butler rearranged the furniture, he guided me offstage.

"I need something from the library before we start," he said, taking us to the alcove nearest the shutters. "Would you kindly pull that volume down?" He aimed a finger at the top shelf of "Unfinished Works." I climbed the ladder and stretched toward an *Edwin Drood*.

"No, three to the left. The quarto bound in calf."

I read the spine title. "*Chronicle of an Engineer*, by Sebastian Plumeaux?"

"That's the one."

As I reached for the book, I lost my balance and almost clunked Jesson on the head with a lacquered block.

"Steady."

I regained my footing and grabbed the book, peeking inside before passing it down. The *Chronicle* was written in French and printed, to judge from the typeface and rag paper, sometime in the eighteenth century. I say "sometime" because it lacked a publication date. In fact, there was no front matter at all. The only distinguishing bibliographic feature was a bookplate that adapted the Jesson coat of arms.

"Hand it over, Alexander. There will be plenty of time later for proper study."

I lowered the *Chronicle*, which Jesson carried directly to the small room behind the shutters. He mounted the platform and stepped inside the palanquin, a kind of walled-in sedan chair I'd known only from movies. Through the window, he motioned for me to sit in the other seat, an equally unusual piece that resembled a wing chair with a tufted leather hood. And there we sat, he in his enclosure, I in mine.

Jesson placed the tape recorder on the ivory table, just below the footlights. "Could you start it when you're ready?"

I leaned forward, pressed RECORD, and sat back.

He drew the side blinds on his chair to obscure his face, then extended a hand toward the case, opening the glass door and grabbing an object.

I was expecting Jesson to remove the old wooden doll, in order to act out a play, but he clamped his fingers around the jar with the cloudy liquid. By shifting my weight, I got a glimpse of him through the reflection of the angled glass door. He sat motionless inside his chair, transfixed for a very long minute, before he positioned the jar next to the recorder and launched into a narrative that began, "The case of curiosities came into my possession at a Paris auction in the spring of 1983."

Over the next two hours Jesson transformed his humble wooden box into a treasure chest of picaresque adventure. It turned out that each item preserved in the case marked a singular moment in the life of an anonymous eighteenth-century inventor. The jar, to give just one example, contained the hero's severed finger, the gruesome harvest of a Calvinist surgeon who collected anomalous body parts. The medical details Jesson injected into the story brought to mind the books on amputation and reconfirmed the pragmatism of his reading habits. And yet despite this reliance on historical sources, his storytelling never suffered the clumsiness of the published essays. Jesson made the nine objects in the ten compartments breathe, speak, and clash, belch, bleed, and cry.

Once he was done, it was my turn to sit transfixed. And when at last I hopped over to the palanquin, I found Jesson slumped inside.

"Buzz Andrews," he croaked through the window. "Tell him to bring a bottle of the Barsac and the *rosquillas* that just arrived."

I relayed the message, then pressed about the origins of the extraordinary tale. "What exactly did I just hear, Mr. Jesson? Was it fact or fiction? Are we inhabiting the 800s, what Dewey called 'the realm of imagination,' or the 900s, the 'realm of recorded memory'?"

Jesson deflected my question. "Check that the taping contraption operated properly," he said, pulling down the front shade and disappearing from view.

I quickly tested the recorder and, finding it worked just fine, returned to the sedan chair. Hooking a finger on the edge of the shade, I peered in and observed Jesson hunched over the note roll I'd first seen him use near the municipal tax codes.

"Seems I'm not the only scribbler," I said.

He flinched and shoved the roll behind a velvet bolster. "Just taking down a few observations. You'd find them tedious, if not depressing."

"You said the same thing about paradise."

"Did I?" He allowed himself to smirk as he raised the shade, but said nothing to clarify his remark.

Andrews entered, per instructions, with a bottle, two glasses, and a large red tin, which he passed through the window.

Jesson wrestled open the container and attacked the cookies. "Are you familiar with these?" he asked, sugar outlining his lips. When I told him I wasn't, he said, "You must try one then. I consider them even better than the *baci di dama* one finds in Italy. A French friend sends me a tin every month from a border town near Spain."

The small talk became too much. "Mr. Jesson, could you *please* tell me what I'm doing here? Why exactly do you need me? It's not to transcribe your stories or eat your cookies. And you've clearly done a brilliant job researching the case."

"I'm happy you think so, but there are still gaps that need filling."

"What gaps?"

"Have a cookie."

"I don't want a cookie. I want—"

Jesson cut me off with a jabbing gesture.

"Why are you pointing at the doll?"

"I'm not pointing at the doll, which might better be described as a lay figure or manikin. Look below it."

"There *is* nothing below. Just an empty compartment. Oh, do you think it was once filled?"

"I do."

"With what?"

"Ah," said Jesson. "That's what I want you to discover. But before we revive the interrogation, allow me a glass of wine."

Andrews approached with the cork, which Jesson sniffed approvingly. Goblet in hand, he said, "Now, let me try to guess what you wish to know." He took a sip of the Barsac. "First, you are wondering how I learned so much about the case and its links to historical fact. Second, you want to know why I need your help. Third, you are curious about the empty compartment. Does that cover the basics?"

"More or less."

"Well, this should address the first question." Jesson passed the *Chronicle of an Engineer* through the window. "Most of what you just heard comes from this account. When you were looking at the book earlier, did you notice the missing title page?"

"The rest of the front matter is absent, too."

"The printing history of the *Chronicle* is a complete mystery to me. Of course, if a certain reference librarian could suss out those details, we might be better equipped to undertake our search."

I glanced at the spine. "What do you know about this Sebastian Plumeaux?"

"I presume it's a nom de plume. Common practice back then."

"Back when?"

"My amateurish analysis suggests the book was printed toward the end of the eighteenth century."

"And you base that on . . ."

"Punctuation, paper, typeface. The ligatured double *ss* and *f*s are pretty clear markers, and there's a wealth of internal textual reference."

"Was this helpful?" I held the book open to a tipped-in engraving I hadn't noticed during my cursory inspection on the ladder. The image was an exact representation of the case, right down to the empty compartment.

"Only insofar as it drew my attention back to the actual object."

"I don't follow."

"That engraving is what encouraged me to look more closely at the box."

"Everything in the picture matches the case—including the empty compartment. I can't see anything that suggests the tenth compartment was ever filled, Mr. Jesson."

"Look more carefully."

"Jar, *picture* of jar. Shell, *picture* of shell. Manikin, *picture* of manikin."

Jesson rolled his eyes. "For heaven's sake. You'll have to do better than that if you hope to hit the nail on the head."

As I Ping-Ponged my gaze between box and engraving, I was reminded of those restaurant place mats given to kids. Two seemingly identical agricultural scenes captioned "What's Different on Mr. Bundy's Farm?" It wasn't the nail I wanted to hit on the head, it was—

Suddenly I felt very silly. Jesson had chosen the cliché for a reason. The distinction between the two- and three-dimensional cases had nothing to do with the objects. The difference was in the cabinets. The actual case included something the engraving didn't show.

"That nail?" I said.

Jesson tipped his glass. "Bravo. Our task is to find out what once hung from it."

"Maybe the nail was added recently."

"Added, yes. Recently? Unlikely. That particular example of metalwork predates the oliver."

"And an oliver is what exactly?"

"A treadle-powered hammer used in the mass production of

nails. Look at the head. See its four-stroked rose pattern? Such hand forging is rare after the mid-1850s, when high-tensile steel wire started flooding the market."

"How do you know all this?"

"Let's limit the questions to the case, shall we?"

"Fine. Tell me what's so important about finding the last object, if indeed there was one?"

"An incomplete case makes for an incomplete story and that's something I detest. It's bad enough if one's *horror vacui* stems from simple deficiency. But when it arises from loss or disappearance, that is much, much worse. My case was once filled, Alexander, and with any luck it will be filled again. *That* is why I need you: to locate the fugitive object and return it to its rightful resting place. I want you to take the *Chronicle* and the taping device home with you. Consult the book as you transcribe the cassette, then integrate the two accounts however you deem appropriate. When that is done, our real work begins."

"Do you have any notes I should look at?"

"My missteps would only poison the purity of your investigations. That, by the way, is the only reason I am occasionally less than forthcoming."

"But—"

"Please, Alexander. No more questions. Do what you can with your catalogs and computers, and come back next Saturday. Let's plan on spending the whole day together. And don't worry. I'm not expecting miracles. A faithful record of your efforts will be more than enough to animate my cloistered world."

"About the tape. I assume you want only your words transcribed."

"Absolutely not! Include yours as well."

"Why?"

"It's always a good idea to throw one's net wide. There's a Grub Street ditty I unearthed years ago that makes the point succinctly." Jesson took a sip of wine and sang:

> *The viewer paints the picture,*
> *The reader writes the book,*
> *The glutton gives the tart its taste,*
> *And not the pastry cook.*

"So who's the glutton and who's the cook? I'm still confused."

"Let's continue this next Saturday."

"That doesn't allow much time for research. It's pretty crazy at the library these days and there's talk of a stack shift, which could throw my whole schedule off."

"I'm confident you will find the time, Alexander."

And with that, Jesson lowered the shade of his sedan chair and ended our exchange.

12

WHEN JESSON SAID he lived in a cloistered world, he wasn't speaking figuratively. As I discovered the following Saturday, the French doors at the far end of the salon opened onto a small courtyard that refuted, by the simplicity of its design, the densely furnished interior.

Paved in unpolished black and white stone, the courtyard exuded a monastic tranquility that begged to be girdled. I drew up a brief inventory while sitting on a plain stone bench: "glass + iron canopy, 12 Corinthian columns, 4 dwarf palms, pr. of cooing doves, 8 gargoyles, 1 marble fountain."

Jesson emerged from behind a column and waved me over. "Shall we stroll?" he said, latching onto my arm.

We walked the perimeter twice before he broke the churchlike silence.

"Now then, tell me what you have to report." But before I could respond, the mourning doves started pecking at the transcript, which I'd left behind on the bench.

"That's my only copy, Mr. Jesson. Maybe we should rescue it." He allowed me to reclaim the envelope but resisted my efforts to place it in his hands.

"I'd prefer we just talk. I hope you don't mind. Any difficulties with the tape?"

"A garbled word here and there—nothing major. The real problem came when I was comparing your account with the one in the book. The antiquated French and the obsolete verb forms were tough to work out."

"You did say you have a French wife."

I had no recollection of mentioning Nic's nationality. "We can't really count on her to help. She's kept pretty busy."

"Pity. Did you make any progress on the empty compartment?"

"I checked the online catalogs and our black books. I couldn't find a single cite for the *Chronicle*."

"That's curious."

"It's the lack of front matter that's causing the problems. Anglo-American Cataloguing Rules don't recognize spine titles. What got stamped on the binding is either incorrect or incomplete. Plus it's been rendered in English."

"Couldn't you trace the book through its author?"

"There's no Sebastian Plumeaux writing in the eighteenth century, at least not that I could find. As far as my library is concerned, your book doesn't exist."

"Forgive me if I beg to differ. What about the engraving?"

"The best resource for that kind of inquiry is probably the French National Library. Only that would require a trip to

Paris since the early volumes of their published catalog are dismally incomplete."

"As it happens, I have already paid a visit to the Biblio-thèque Nationale. Except for its proximity to a café that makes a devastating *tarte au citron*, the library was of little use." We walked maybe five or six steps before Jesson said, "Talk of dessert has activated my sweet tooth. Would you summon Andrews? You'll find a buzzer hidden in the claws of that cockatrice."

After asking the butler to fetch some cookies, Jesson guided us back to the stone bench. "The transcript. May I please have it now?" I assumed he wanted, at last, to look through my work, but that wasn't what he had in mind. "The chill of stone is so punishing on old bones," he said as he slipped the envelope under his rump.

I hid my annoyance. "I've been meaning to ask how you got the *Chronicle* in the first place."

"Purchased it at the auction house where I bought the case. An overweight Mediterranean of suspect character sold it to me in the lobby of the Hôtel Drouot. A bus strike had caused him to miss the sale."

"What made him suspect?"

"His general demeanor, and the fact that he told me to avoid showing the *Chronicle* in public."

"That would explain the missing front matter. It was prob-ably cut out because of some traceable stamp or seal."

"Plausible," said Jesson.

"You'd be amazed how many stolen books get mutilated to hide ownership."

Jesson's stomach gurgled. "Where are those biscuits? Would you mind ringing Andrews again?"

On my second trip to the buzzer, I looked at the cockatrice more closely. "It's *you*," I shouted. "Right down to the nose!"

"My features aren't so chiseled, alas."

I cited Finster Dapples. "I've been told only the weasel can do it in."

"That's not entirely accurate. The cockatrice is also vulnerable to its own reflection. It protects itself by the stench of its breath."

"That's a pretty common weapon. Believe me, after working on the reference desk, I know."

Jesson smiled. "The sculpture is modeled on a sixteenth-century satire housed among the bestiaries in alcove 1."

Andrews arrived with the biscuits, which he placed between us on the bench. While Jesson indulged his craving, I gave in to mine.

"What are you writing now?" he asked.

"Notes on how to proceed."

A sugary finger touched my girdle book. "May I?"

"You wouldn't get much out of it. I use a quirky form of shorthand."

Jesson extended his hand, palm up. "You might be surprised." He thumbed through my encoded notes. "A form of Pitman, if I'm not mistaken."

"A related method," I said, startled by his learning.

"The consonantal marks are difficult to make out, and the vowel clusters aren't like any I've seen before. I can't decipher much beyond a couple of the headings. This one right here. 'Chairs of Extinction' is it?"

"'*Distinction*,'" I corrected. "A compendium of researchers, arranged by seating."

"How charming." Jesson leafed ahead. "What's this? Have you granted *me* the letter *J*?"

I nodded. "As you can see, there's still plenty of blank space."

He ignored the nudge. Flipping back a few pages, he said, "Why all the observations under 'Enclosure'?"

"It's not important."

"I know avoidance when I hear it."

"The *E*s are where I register a lot of personal stuff."

Jesson scrutinized my notes more closely. "I believe I can decode a phrase or two. 'Neotherm 2300' . . . 'casket-casket' . . . Mind elaborating?"

"I'd prefer not to."

"You sound like Bartleby when you say that."

"Well, I am just the scrivener."

"Nonsense. I'm sure your notes are highly original. In fact, I tell you what—since my bones are feeling achy and this bench is hell on my back, let's go inside and do this right."

"Do *what* right?"

"Isn't it obvious? Since you seem exceedingly interested in me and I wish to know about you, I propose the following: tell me about your life and I'll tell you about mine. My sixty-odd years for your thirty."

"And the case?"

"One set of enclosures at a time, Alexander."

13

JESSON HOBBLED THROUGH the salon and into the library, where he opened the shutters that led to the room with the raised floor. Both the cardboard toy theater and the case of curiosities had been removed, as had the ivory table. Only the two ornate chairs remained.

"Now then," Jesson said, settling in his palanquin as if it were a confessional booth, "let's start with 'Neotherm 2300.'"

"You don't waste time, do you?"

"'Neotherm 2300,'" he repeated.

"That's the model number of an incubator. I was born premature."

"And 'casket-casket'?"

"My parents died while I was still in the preemie ward.

My mother from toxic shock, my father in an accident on the Cross Bronx Expressway as he was racing to the hospital."

Jesson sighed. "Poor thing . . . And your adoptive parents?"

I shrugged. "They're okay."

"That's a rather terse opinion."

"We've never been close. For years I questioned whether my real parents were actually dead. I even insisted on being taken to their grave site. I was six at the time. The story goes that when we got to the cemetery I raised a fuss about walking on their plot. I was terrified they'd get hurt if stepped on. I still remember sitting beside the headstone. It was shaped like an open book. I must have spent an hour just tracing the chiseled letters with my finger."

"Is that your first memory of books?"

The question threw me. "I suppose."

"Poignant. Though I must say, Alexander, you seem oddly unemotional about all this."

"It is possible to have feelings without showing them, Mr. Jesson. Did you know that for the longest time Dewey didn't even include emotion in his classification system?"

"And you consider that omission wise?"

"No, I'm only saying that librarians often don't *do* feelings all that well. It's no accident that Dewey avoided categories of sorrow and despair. You've probably figured out that I tend to focus my notes on concrete matters. Like the next girdled *E*—the one I mentioned when you showed me your case."

"Remind me again what you said."

"It's about the discovery boxes. The brainchild of Mr. McCarkle, my first mentor. He ran a branch library not much bigger than your alcoved collection."

"I suspect his holdings differed."

"Somewhat. I'm pretty sure Mr. McCarkle never purchased a run of Johnson's *Idler* bound in scented midbrown Russia."

"Smelled that, did you? The Burlington at Chiswick has a similar set. But go on about McCarkle."

"He's the one who drew me into the world of books."

"When was that?"

"Fourth grade. The first time I walked into his library, he came right over, knelt down on one knee, and said, his eyes level with mine, 'You're a 597.8 if ever I've seen one.' Naturally, I didn't have a clue what he meant. But by the time he'd plucked a field guide to amphibians from the shelf, he had caught me in his grip like . . ." I fumbled for an analogy.

"Like a frog catches a fly?"

"Close enough. Actually, he was a lot like the books he stocked: sturdy, entertaining, educational, but never preachy. Not that McCarkle pandered. He believed in shaping desire rather than obliging it. He'd say in his Highland accent, 'Och, there you are, Alexander. I've been meaning to show ya something *trooly* special.' Then he'd walk me over to his kneehole desk and dig through the due-date stickers and book pockets until he found a volume he'd set aside. One time he handed me a package wrapped in kraft paper and tied with twine, and he said: 'Now listen to me. I'll let you be the first, the very first, to paw this, but only if you take it right away.' I tore off the brown paper and found myself holding a nifty Guild Classics edition of *Gulliver's Travels*."

"So it was McCarkle who first sent you to Lilliput?"

"And who nurtured my love of libraries. He taught me how to empty the returns box, presort the reshelves, tape broken spines, arrange the catalogs. I filed above the rod for two years before Mr. McCarkle let me drop the cards. By the time I left for college, I was fluent in Dewey."

"Book lovers beget book lovers," said Jesson.

"For better or worse. If I hadn't met Mr. McCarkle, I'd never have ended up in library school. And if I hadn't gone to library school, I wouldn't have worked for Professor Sharansky."

"A replacement copy for the Scotsman?"

"A deluxe edition is more like it. Witold Sharansky wasn't one to get his fingers sticky glueing book pockets into new arrivals. He preferred eighteenth-century broadsides to *Make Way for Ducklings*. His scholarly reputation rested on his paleographic work, but he had wide-ranging interests and even took time from his research to give the first lecture in Introductory Reference. That was one hell of a talk. He told us to forget about query quotas and mindless memorization. He said that if we felt compelled to commit something to memory, we should remember Brecht's exhortation. I can still recite part of it:

> *You with the intentness of your studies*
> *And the elation of your knowledge*
> *Can make the experience of struggle*
> *The property of all*
> *And transform justice*
> *Into a passion.*

Jesson gave an appreciative nod. "It had that effect on me, too," I said. "Those words served as a kind of wake-up call— made me aware just how radical libraries can be. That entreaty was one reason I ended up studying the work of Melvil Dewey."

"It's John, isn't it?"

"You're thinking of the educational reformer. *Melvil* Dewey was also guided by moral imperatives, but made his mark more broadly. He invented the loose-leaf binder and vertical filing, and of course a system of classification that's used all over the world. Did you know it was Melvil who developed the idea of the traveling library? He probably did more to spread knowledge than Bill Gates."

"Another name I don't know."

"Doesn't matter. The point is, Dewey created a method by which the whole universe could be enclosed in ten distinct classes. It's a lot like your case of curiosities, come to think of it. Anyway, Dewey got me interested in shorthand. He advocated a modified version of Lindsley, which itself is a modified Pitman."

"Fascinating."

"Coming from anyone else, I'd suspect you were pulling my leg."

"You've seen the care I give my handwriting."

"Then you might also want to know about the simplified spelling system Dewey promoted. For instance, he rendered his own name D-U-I. Minus McCarkle, who was a Dewey disciple, signed all his personal correspondence with a single horizontal line."

"Sorry?"

"He used a minus sign in lieu of his Christian name. I never got *that* carried away, though I did write a paper on the system while working as a page."

Jesson grinned. "You were a *page* in a library?"

"That's what entry-level hires are called."

"How does it work? You start out a page, then get promoted to chapter?" Jesson sensed that his joke fell flat. "Forgive me. Continue."

"My paper was about Dewey's appropriation of Lindsley's shorthand method. Professor Sharansky liked the analysis enough to submit it for a prize. And believe it or not, I won. That got me a small travel grant to attend a library conference where I received a pair of cuff links just like the ones Dewey wore. They had these big bold sans serif *R*s on them, which stood for Reform."

Jesson glanced at my wrists.

"I don't wear them. Never did."

"Why?"

"Because of a conference lecture that revealed some pretty unsavory things about my hero. Of course, I already knew of his chauvinism. Everyone in library school learns how Dewey dedicated more space in his classification schedules to local YMCAs than to all of Oriental Buddhism. But I didn't know he was a bigot. It turns out he founded a private country club and dictated the membership rules himself: 'No Jews or strangers or consumptives or other people who can be fairly annoying to cultivated people are received under any circumstances.'"

Jesson said, "It would appear your Mr. Dewey applied his class guidelines to more than books."

"The lecturer called it DUI: Discriminating under the Influence. Dewey, when he wasn't going after Jews and blacks, apparently found the time to abuse his female colleagues. He even got sued for his unwanted advances, which must have taken some doing back in 1906. The conference talk included copies of the court papers and a picture of the damaged whalebone corset one of Dewey's victims entered into evidence."

"Your idol certainly kept himself busy."

"Ex-idol. The lecture woke me to the fact that the *R* on the cuff links stood for Racist and Rapist. Needless to say, I was devastated. I'd built Dewey into something he wasn't—a mistake my wife tells me I often make. She thinks my biggest flaws involve judgment."

"Do you still have them?"

"The flaws?"

"The cuff links."

"No, I tossed them. Flaws are harder to shed."

"You've tried?"

"If you mean have I seen a therapist, yes, briefly. Nic insisted I consult a shrimp—that's what she calls them."

"And did the fellow help?"

"Not at all. Mostly he used me to test out his half-baked theories."

"Half-baked shrimp doesn't sound terribly safe."

"Believe me, it isn't. Have you ever heard of bibliotherapy?"

"The cognates are transparent enough. Treatment through books?"

"It's mostly used in prisons. The Shrimp wanted to broaden the application, so he prescribed a special reading list tailored to the needs of a graphomaniacal, emotionally stunted librarian."

"And this list . . ."

"Self-help drivel. You wouldn't recognize the titles."

"Sounds ghastly."

"It was. The therapy was short-lived. We had our final dustup when I asked about an unexplained diagnostic code on an insurance form. The Shrimp told me I shouldn't worry about it. Well, obviously, I did worry. Worry was one of the things that had brought me to his office in the first place. I became indignant, demanded that he tell me what he was telling my insurance carrier. The Shrimp's reply? 'Very well, Alexander. Since you insist. I am indicating a concurrence of symptoms that fall under the rubrics of obsessive compulsive disorder and depressive neurosis.'"

"Did that surprise you?"

"There's a world of difference between sensing something's wrong and being told *clinically* what that something is. So, yes, it did. His diagnosis so upset me I left the office without getting a signature on the damn form that caused the argument in the first place. Which meant trudging back for further humiliation. The double doors were open when I returned to his office. The Shrimp was on the phone—or so I thought at first. But the uninterrupted stream of jargon soon made it clear he was talking into a tape recorder."

"Damnable devices," Jesson snarled.

"He was saying, 'Employment of books as a therapeutic adjuvant has produced only marginal improvement in patient, who shows pathological attachment to notebook he calls his scribble-scribble . . . Contents of journal manifest displaced psychosexual ambivalence, need for father figures, plus possible neurosis of destiny.'"

"I'm impressed you remember all that."

"Graphomaniacs take good notes, Mr. Jesson."

"Indeed. And the business about neurosis of destiny?"

"Had to look that up myself. It's a kind of moral masochism in which the patient arranges his life to guarantee setbacks."

The door of the sedan chair opened and Jesson emerged. "Perhaps we should take a break," he said as he stretched his legs. "How does lunch sound? Some foie gras and fresh greens to take your mind off the Shrimp?"

"I'd like that."

"And maybe your wife would wish to join us. She could amplify your account."

"Nic's under a lot of stress these days."

"Then she might welcome a break. I have a Sauternes that would go well with the goose liver. I place great stock in the mollifying effects of extravagance."

Jesson buzzed for a telephone. Andrews came in moments later with an ancient handset, which he plugged into a funny-looking jack.

The call didn't last long.

"Nic? Mr. Jesson was wondering if you'd like to come over for lunch. Might be nice for the two of you to meet."

She sighed. "Dive for the master's coins if you want, but don't ask me to join you."

I cupped the mouthpiece. "Says she's drowning in work."

"Try harder, Alexander."

"No way you can make it, Nic? Mr. Jesson's preparing a wonderful meal."

"*Pas pour moi!*" She hung up.

"Well?" Jesson asked.

I shook my head.

"Pity. I'll tell Andrews two, then. I must say, your wife's refusal only reinforces a long-held suspicion of matrimony."

"Have you ever been married, Mr. Jesson?"

"That's rather a personal question."

"I've just told you some very intimate things. Doesn't that earn me a bit of latitude?"

"Fair enough. No, I have never been married. I tend to put my faith in friendship. Plato had it right. All of us are born partly for our native land, partly for our parents, and partly for our friends. He makes no mention of wives and husbands."

"What *about* your native land and parents? You've said nothing about either. In fact, your whole life still feels like an empty compartment."

"Perhaps it's best it remain so."

"We made a deal." I held up my girdle book as if brandishing a summons.

"All in good time," Jesson replied, refusing to say anything more.

14

IN THE VOCABULARY of the library cataloger, Jesson was still as infuriatingly N.E.C. (Not Elsewhere Classified) as he had been before I opened up. Each time I tried to push him to keep to his part of the bargain, he'd shift the conversation. I'd ask about schooling, he'd talk about foie gras. I'd mention his overtly literary name, he'd discuss the lettuces he'd grown on his Long Island farm from seeds purchased in Aix.

"Seeds, soil, and sun," he said. "The gardener's sacred trinity. I have a hothouse that you, as a student of enclosure, would adore."

I kept up the pressure. "Has the farm been in your family long?"

"How do you find the beans?"

"Mr. Jesson, please."

"If you're so keen to know who I am, take a look around. My life is best narrated in the objects I collect. I'm a lot like the anonymous composer of the case—defined by the whence-abouts of things kept close at hand."

"*Whenceabouts*?"

"The stories behind the objects. What more typically is called provenance."

Andrews entered with a fresh tin of cookies before I could work up a response.

"The *rosquillas*, at last!"

"Can we get back to your past, Mr. Jesson?"

"If only that were possible," he quipped as he foraged through the tin.

"At least tell me how you acquired all this." I waved my hand around the salon.

"Very well." He pointed at a massive bureau. "You see that *Knorpelwerk* with the lovely writing window? I found it in a shop off the Ringstrasse."

"I meant, where did the money come from?"

"If you must know, I was privy from an early age to what Mother called 'an ample sufficiency.' "

"A trust fund?"

"You could call it that, though it was, predictably enough, established because of an absence of trust. Mother insisted on irrevocable financial support for us both when she realized she had married a brute and a bore."

"When was that?"

"Do dates matter? All you need to know is that Mother finagled the arrangement because she and my father were al-ways fighting. They even bickered about my name, I've been told. Mother wanted to call me Bartholomew, to honor a beloved ornithologist uncle known for some pioneering work on the marsh birds of Nantucket. My father refused, insisting I be named Henry, after himself.''

"And his father before him.''

"No, the 'III' only came later. I was christened Henry Ford Jesson Jr., which should tell you where I was born. Tributes of that kind are quite common, or were, in Dearborn, Michigan. Henry Ford So-and-Sos rolled out of the local maternity wards like Model Ts off the assembly line.''

"I take it Henry Senior was in the automobile business.''

"Only tangentially. He mostly worked in iron and steel.''

"As in Jesson Secondary Metals? *That's* why you were able to identify the iron nail in the empty compartment.''

Jesson nodded. "My father took an active interest in teaching me the family business. One of his tools was a special tin rod called the Motivator. He carried it everywhere he went.''

"Are you saying he *hit* you?''

"Whenever he could. I spent much of my childhood hiding under an oak side table, playing with my collections of marbles and stones. Believe me, you're not alone in appreciating the virtues of protected spaces.''

"Couldn't your mother do something?''

"She did—often. But that only made matters worse. My father may have been a violent, foul-mouthed vulgarian, but Mother was no walk in the park. Dance instruction, sailor suits, French lessons, classes in elocution, riding lessons at the farm. I'll avoid enumerating the dietary fetishes to which I was subjected, except to say that the woman banned absolutely anything that had taste, especially sweets.''

Jesson walked over to a tortoiseshell dish and lifted the lid. "See this? Mother insisted I place a nickel in here each time

I made a grammatical mistake. Every wrong *who* or *whom*, every grunt, every mumble, meant a trip to this bonbonnière, which I assure you *never* contained candy."

"Your father still sounds worse."

"Don't be so sure." Jesson popped a mint into his mouth. "I'll tell you a story. I was eight at the time, the year my father moved us, and the business, from Michigan to New York. On the day in question, he returned home early, furious about some scrap metal contract that had slipped through his fingers. Mother must have sensed the imminent appearance of the Motivator, because she rushed us out of the house."

Jesson released a rueful sigh. "I still see the scene vividly. We're in a boutique off Madison called Chez Christine. I'm standing outside the dressing room. Bored, I bend down and peek under the saloon-style swinging doors. And what do my eight-year-old eyes observe? Stockings, garters, socks. Four exposed calves, pant legs bunched over a pair of hideously scuffed wing tips. There are muffled sounds and an odor I shall never forget. If Mother had been obliged to pay into the bonbonnière, those grunts and groans would have cost her a small fortune.

"From Chez Christine we headed over to Abercrombie and Fitch, where I was supposed to get fitted for a blazer. But I'd become so agitated that I refused to stand still while the tailor tried marking my sleeves with soap.

"'Henry Jesson Jr.,' Mother scolded. 'Stop squirming! Those pockets are stitched shut for a reason. Sticking your hands inside will absolutely ruin the line.' Apparently, I failed to heed her warning, because the next thing I knew she had boxed my ear."

"What did you do?"

"I jumped from the tailor's block and took refuge behind a stuffed rhinoceros. Mother eventually hunted me down and discharged another thwack. And another, and another. For many years, I never went near the pockets of my jackets, which for an aspiring collector took a terrible toll."

15

TWO DAYS AFTER Jesson told me about his father's business, I called up the articles index of a serials list devoted to the scrap metal industry. On the flyleaf of a bound set of the *Daily Metal Reporter*, I came across a neatly penciled note indicating that the whole run had come to the library as part of a donation from the now-defunct Scrap Iron and Steel Institute. The online collection-level description indicated the gift was housed in Manuscripts, a division of the library exempt from most electronic cataloging protocols. The relevant portions of the screen read:

DESCRIPT   Originals: 46 linear feet (72 boxes, 41 letter books, 3 v., 6 scrapbooks).

NOTE   Apply in Special Collections Office.

NOTE	The Scrap Iron and Steel Institute papers (SISI) consist mainly of correspondence, with typed documents, printed matter, photographs, and scrapbooks documenting the organization's activities between 1901 and 1964. Correspondence is with key leaders in the field.
NOTE	Finding aid available in repository.
SUBJECT	Junk Trade—American.
SUBJECT	Metal Castings.
SUBJECT	Metal Industry.
SUBJECT	Metal Wastes.
SUBJECT	Scrap Metal—American.
SUBJECT	Waste Products.

I would never have taken the search further if it hadn't been for the note about the finding aid. Anyone who's worked in Manuscripts knows such guides are the best (and sometimes the only) way to get a sense of what a particular collection contains. Because manuscript holdings receive no individual class marks (that is, call numbers), a lot can be missed by researchers who rely on computers alone.

Diligence paid off. The SISI finding aid, a thirty-five-page typescript cobbled together from accession records generated long before the library went online, included a solid-gold listing: "Box 59, Jesson Secondary Metals—Misc."

And "Misc." it was! More a wastebasket than a document box. There were loose sales receipts, order slips, a matchbook from the Stork Club, a bill from a seed importer, as well as three bound volumes: a journal, an album, and a letter book.

The journal contained sketches of junkyard layouts and page after page of metal inventory, composed in an illegible hand.

The album, which had the words A SCRAP MAN'S SCRAPBOOK embossed on the cover, gathered together newspaper cuttings, press releases, and photographs celebrating the entrepreneurial successes of Henry Jesson Sr.

Direct proof of my employer's link to the company surfaced only once, in a glossy publicity shot of a decommissioned battleship purchased for scrap at the end of World War II. The photo showed Henry Senior standing near a massive anchor, son and wife shunted to the side. Closer inspection revealed the patriarch gripping a metal rod, an object I might have mistaken for a walking stick if I'd been ignorant of its sinister use. Facing the photo was a mimeographed history of Jesson Secondary Metals written by its founder.

According to the self-congratulatory account, Jesson Senior got his start collecting tin cans for a Dearborn junkman. By fourteen, he was subcontracting with neighborhood children and leasing a horse-drawn wagon for "a dollar a day, plus fifty cents for feed." He took over the junkman's operation at the age of twenty and purchased his first steel mill by the time he was twenty-seven. JSM (the company's acronym seemed unfortunate) bought up closed copper mines, outdated coast guard cutters, and fleets of German warships. It was the first scrap metal concern to locate profit in the advent of diesel locomotion. By cornering the market in old iron rails and turning them into reinforcing bars for the burgeoning interstate highway system, JSM became one of the three biggest scrap operations in the country.

The history concluded with a quotation from the founder that disparaged the man for whom I worked: "I suspect my bussiness [sic] will die with me. No sign 'Jesson & Son' will ever hang over the gates of my yards and mills."

I closed the album and turned to the letter book, which was crammed with telegrams, invoices, even Jesson Senior's last will and testament. But what I found of particular interest was a draft sketch of the family coat of arms. I say "draft" because it differed in small but significant ways from the bookplate and the coat that Norton had downloaded. And intriguingly, two elements of the archived design bore annotations in the distinctive handwriting of "my" Henry Jesson. The first note, linked by an arrow to a four-fingered fist gripping a mace (retained in the coats I had seen), said, "Father = Wrecking Ball/Destruction." The second notation, connected to an imaginary beast replaced in the bookplate by the cockatrice, read, "Harpy: a fabulous monster, rapacious and filthy, having a woman's face and body and a bird's wings and claws. A minister of divine vengeance." Here, too, there was a dark equation: "Mother = Harpy, i.e., woman + vulture (or leech?)."

Clipped to the annotated sketch was a letter from a Dutch genealogist named Andries Van Wesel addressed to Jesson Senior. The letter detailed a failed attempt to trace the family name to noble antecedents in Ireland. Van Wesel tempered the bad news by mentioning that as a founding member of the Society of Genealogical Inquiry, he could, for a fee, register a coat of arms designed by the client himself.

The sketch I held in my hands, as well as its substitute, was obviously the result of Van Wesel's proposal. That explained, among other things, why the coat had failed to surface in the registries Finster Dapples had consulted. Uncovering this fabrication provided a small sense of triumph. I only wished that the element I found most compelling—the book within the book—had received a clarifying note.

16

BACK AT FESTINALENTE, I wasted little time presenting Jesson with copies of the shipyard photograph, the will, Van Wesel's letter, and the draft coat of arms.

He was understandably taken aback. "All these documents were in your archives?"

"I was surprised myself."

Jesson waved the copy of his father's will in the air. "Did you read through this?"

"Skimmed it."

"Did you notice that the bastard added a codicil with an in terrorem clause? For an entire year following his death I was required to work at company headquarters."

"And if you'd refused?"

"I would have received the princely sum of one dollar. The executor told me my father borrowed the idea from Groucho Marx, who apparently used the same ploy to keep his exes in line."

"So you worked for the family business?"

"I did. And by so doing brought myself within a hairs-breadth of a complete breakdown."

"What saved you?"

"Not what, Alexander. Who."

"Okay then, who?"

"I was saved by a shrimp, as your elusive wife might say. An émigré Jungian named Edvard Stümpf. It was Stümpf who pulled me from despair. Who helped me resurrect, and over-come, the memories of childhood misery. Now, I'm not sug-gesting Stümpf just snapped his fingers and put everything right. There were many sessions, especially in the beginning, filled more with angry silence than with comforting words. Over time, however, Stümpf helped me tremendously. He was the one who teased out the recollection of Mother fornicating in the dressing room. Without Stümpf I never would have connected my refusal to unstitch jacket pockets to that trau-matic shopping trip. Do you know that within hours of re-viving that memory, I was cutting open every blazer, tweed, and tux in my wardrobe!"

"Your shrimp did a lot more for you than mine did for me."

"So it seems, though they did share one trait. Both believed in the therapeutic effect of books. Once, when I was feeling particularly slothful and self-pitying, Stümpf tossed a copy of *Oblomov* in my lap. This was around the time Penguin

brought out the Magarshack translation. He told me that resistance to the family business had been done before, and with
a good deal more finesse."

"He didn't exactly pull his punches, did he?"

"Never, though he praised as often as he chided." Jesson
laughed. "Do you know that he'd even toot a pre-Columbian
ocarina whenever I said or did something germane."

Jesson flipped through the photocopies and pulled the Van
Wesel letter. "This whole episode is linked to one of the more
toot-worthy moments in my therapy. I'm amazed it ended up
in your library. My father wrote to this Dutch fellow thinking a coat of arms would mask his working-class roots. He
didn't count on dying before Van Wesel could respond."

"So you designed the crest for him?"

"Certainly not. I designed it for myself. When I told
Stümpf about the letter, he asked me what graphic emblems
I'd select to represent my past."

"Neat question. Again, a bit like the engineer's case."

"I hadn't considered that, but I suppose. Anyway, Stümpf
suggested I take up the Dutchman's offer and compose a personal shield. At the next session, I brought along a copy of
the Jourdan family emblem. Jourdan, Jesson. The names were
similar and I liked that the Jourdans hailed from Limerick,
punster that I am. Their family motto also seemed apt. *Per-
cussus resurgo*. 'Struck down, I rise again.' Perfect for someone
intent on rebuilding his life."

"What did Stümpf say?"

"He told me I should leave the recycling to Jesson Secondary Metals. My job, he said, was to devise an *original* shield
that addressed not only who I was but who I wished to be."

Jesson traced the scalloped edge of the crest with his finger.

"Heralds call this a bordure wavy. I chose it to invoke my father's bastard past. As for the mangled hand holding the mace-cum-wrecking ball . . . that was a nod to his work in metal and destruction."

"And the missing finger?"

"My father had a mishap with an alligator shear when he was first starting out. You may have noticed the door knocker and the books on amputation. Those, too, are paternal tributes."

"And your mother? Where is she represented?"

"Mother was more of a challenge. I initially wanted to include her as a harpy, a leech woman, but I abandoned that idea when I learned of the beast's solitary nature. Mother, as you know, was decidedly more social. In the end, I depicted her with an escutcheon of pretense, a mark of marriage below one's station."

"How did Stümpf respond?"

"Not as I expected. He took one glance at the drawing and said, 'Where are *you* in all these unsavory emblems?'"

"He had a point."

"Of course he did. Stümpf told me Van Wesel's challenge harbored a potent truth I had failed to recognize: namely that the past is not inherited so much as made. He said the son must create the parent in order to invent his past. He read me the riot act—insisted I represent myself without pettiness or equivocation. So after brooding over a heraldry text, a bestiary, and two dictionaries of symbols, I selected something fittingly first person—to wit, the cockatrice."

"A creature that recoils at its own reflection?"

"I was awfully low at the time."

"And the book within the book?"

"Plucked from a recurring dream that had me stranded in a desert, naked and dazed, doing what the abandoned often do in such situations—walking and walking and eventually passing out. When I would come to—this is still in the dream—I'd find myself stretched out next to a book half buried in the sand."

"What book?"

Jesson chuckled. "That was Stümpf's first question. It never had a title, nor did the book I'd invariably discover inside. I tried to convince myself that the specific book was unimportant, much the way the *kind* of water given to a man dying of thirst doesn't matter."

"Stümpf didn't buy that, did he?"

"Not for a second. He considered the book within the book an instance of regression that betrayed an infantile desire to make things last forever. Also, he challenged my casual disregard for the untitled nature of the volumes."

"You've said yourself that you dislike the unknown and incomplete."

"Stümpf was the one who helped me identify that trait, who, if you will, led me out of the desert."

"One last question. Why the name change? How did you go from being Henry Ford Jesson Jr. to Henry James Jesson III?"

"That was my special homage to a writer Stümpf suggested I read. He thought I'd find reassurance in the way James transcended the lethargy of early adulthood."

"And did you?"

Jesson gave a nod. "For the longest time, I wanted nothing more than to wed knowledge and liberty à la Isabel Archer.

It seemed the only way to save myself from the corrosive world of scrap. I so admired James that I changed my middle name."

I resisted the impulse to mention the novelist's famously ambiguous sexuality. "I still don't get the 'III.' Did you add the numeral for aristocratic effect?"

"Actually, it was more for the meter."

"How did Stümpf respond to the revised shield?"

"Favorably. In fact, he published an account of our exchange in the *Proceedings* of the Burghölzli. 'Therapeutic Benefits of Heraldic Self-Invention.' He concluded that my 'armorial autobiography' led to a classic expression of individuation. Which it did. By the time I had my bookplates printed up I was a new man with a new name, protected and rendered whole by a new coat of arms. Many of the passions I now pursue—from scholarship to collecting first editions such as the *Chronicle*—can be traced to Stümpf's seemingly whimsical challenge and the reflection it prompted."

Jesson's pronouncement startled me. "How do you know the *Chronicle* is a first?"

"The fellow at the auction house must have said something. Why? Is it important?"

"Did he mention subsequent printings?"

"Not that I can recall. Would it matter if he did?"

"Don't you see!"

"I am sorry, no."

"I've got to go," I announced. "And don't worry, I won't phone unless I find something earthshaking."

As I was grabbing my things, Jesson said, "Did you bring rain gear?"

"No."

"Then we had better buzz Andrews. Take a look outside."

Through the French doors, I could see rain streaming off the cloister canopy.

After a brief exchange with his employer, Andrews presented me with an exquisite English umbrella that had a burled walnut handle.

"I can't borrow this," I told Jesson. "It's obviously precious."

He made a face and said, "Consider it a gift."

"For what?"

"For whatever it is that is making you so eager to run off on my behalf."

17

I *WAS* EAGER. I wanted to squeeze in an hour at the library before it shut down for the night. Unfortunately, subway delays made that impossible, so I tramped back up the station steps and caught a bus home.

I was in the cage, girdling a few notes about the *Chronicle*, when I started to hear a scraping sound. I turned and discovered Nic's hand hanging over the edge of the loft. She was rubbing something back and forth across the former teller's window. I took a closer look.

The blood started rushing to my head. "Jesus, Nic. Where did you get that?"

"*Dans ton pantalon*," she said, pressing the image of a naked woman against the lattice. I'd forgotten all about leaving the strip joint with the bull's-eye coaster in my pocket.

"*Vilain,*" she said coyly.

"I took it for Speaight," I stammered.

"*Bien sûr.*"

"Seriously. He said he wanted the thing for the center."

Peeking over the edge of the mattress, she gave me a come-hither wink. "*Le loft, mon chéri. Tout de suite.*"

The full scope of her response to the target declared itself only when I climbed up the ladder.

Nic had slipped into a cat suit and had chalked a series of concentric rings onto the black spandex. The rings, needless to say, zeroed in with the same specificity as the cardboard original.

"*Pan-pan,*" she teased, her French sound effects beckoning me to take aim.

Despite her efforts, I felt a near-physical tug downward, to my research.

Nic was no fool. She sensed the resistance. "*Très bien,*" she said, turning toward the wall. "Go back to your scribble-scribble!"

It seemed pointless to argue or apologize, and any update would have been read as an act of aggression. Without a word, I retreated to the cage.

A few minutes later, Nic climbed out of the loft, walked to the kitchen (I heard the thud of the fridge door), and returned to her perch. The sounds that followed told me she'd retrieved the tarot cards from the meat compartment to chart our respective futures.

Generally speaking, I'm pretty accepting of Nic's superstitions. If umbrellas aren't to be opened indoors or if the number 19 is to be avoided when choosing a travel date or the volume level on the radio, I try not to make a fuss. I even tolerate the potions she boils up, though the steam is bad for our books. But tarot cards affected me differently. Nic's unquestioning embrace of their prognostic powers seemed to poison our life with an absurd sense of the inevitable.

For a few minutes there was silence overhead, a prelude, I knew, to more conflict. And sure enough, Nic climbed down the ladder and pressed a card against the cage.

"*Regarde!*"

The image showed a hobbled old man holding up a lantern. A bilingual motto printed at the bottom of the card read, "*Trahison*—Betrayal."

"Don't tell me. It's a sign."

"Yes," she hissed.

"Can we try talking this through rationally?"

Nic shook her head. "I'm sick from words."

"Well, that's a shame. You're married to a librarian."

"Maybe I shouldn't be." She smacked the card against the bars of the cage. "The Hermit, he *always* makes trouble. Don't work for him. *Don't.*"

"It's a good job, Nic. It pays well, and it's a lot more exciting than the crappy stuff Dinty has me doing. I can't see why Jesson bothers you so much. We'll have plenty of time for our projects when this is over."

But Nic wasn't interested in my explanations or pledges. She jammed the card between the brass bars of the teller's window and disappeared into the loft.

18

JESSON'S CASUAL MENTION of first editions triggered an embarrassing realization. My bibliographic queries about the *Chronicle* and Plumeaux had been worse than sloppy. I should never have limited the search parameters to the eighteenth century since that risked excluding editions dated after 1800. I also had to face the fact that I'd been too accepting of the suspect information on the spine. (An English title for a French text?) And without proper front matter, who's to say the book hadn't been written by someone else altogether?

My amateur assumptions and oversights recalled an exam question on Sharansky's Introductory Reference final: "Supply the full citation for Manteuffel, J. *Les papyrus et les ostraca poecs*, 1937."

At first I had thought, *Piece of cake*. But the question soon threw me into a panic. I thumbed my way through card catalogs, serial lists, finding aids and indexes, the black books, and a vast network of obstinate databases.

Les papyrus was nowhere to be found.

Sharansky explained why when he passed back the tests. Manteuffel's essay constituted the fifth chapter of a composite work that, though written in French, appeared in a German serial edited by a Polish scholar for an archeological society based in Cairo. On top of which, "*poecs*" was actually a misspelling of the word *grecs*.

"Remember," Sharansky bellowed. "Library work is not a science, whatever claims our profession might make. Never forget that luck and error are the handmaidens of all research."

With that warning buzzing through my head, I renewed the hunt for the (putative) *Chronicle of an Engineer* by the (probably pseudonymous) Sebastian Plumeaux. I drew up a checklist of variant spellings, in French and in English, for both title and author before revisiting the Library of Congress Name Authority File, the National Union Catalog, and OCLC. No citation. I then called up Barbier's *Dictionnaire des ouvrages anonymes et pseudonymes* and a lesser-known English relative, *A Dictionary of Revealed Authorship*.

While waiting for the bibliographies to emerge from the stacks, I sought out Norton, who agreed to post a message about my "nonexistent" work on a couple of the better electronic bulletin boards. By the time that was done my references were waiting at Delivery. They brought the first comforting news of the day. *A Dictionary of Revealed Authorship* cross-referenced Sebastian Plumeaux to someone named Houdin, who received the following entry:

Houdin, Pierre. (?−†1844) Writer, editor, printer, tutor, lawyer (expelled from the Paris bar). Author of novels, doggerel, and juridical *mémoires* published anonymously and under various pen names, including Henri Delacroix and Sebastian Plumeaux. His works include: *The Deck of Fate* (1786), a tale told through the progress of a card game; *The King's Pawn* (1787), employing a chess match for similarly contrived effect; *A Utopian Trilogue* (1790), in which three oil portraits argue with one another from the walls of an Arctic palace; and *The Book of Hours* (n.d.), narrating the life of a mechanical engineer through a collection of objects housed in a glass-fronted cabinet. Houdin is also credited with writing *The Wandering Whore* and an unauthorized translation of Walpole's *Hieroglyphic Tales*.

I ran over to a terminal and typed, "ti: Book of Hours," which was clearly a variant edition of the *Chronicle*. The title request produced more than a thousand bibliographic records. When I added the author's name, however, the screen declared:

NO ITEMS FOUND FOR: TI:("BOOK OF HOURS") AND AU:HOUDIN.

I dropped "Houdin" and fiddled with the date parameters. Listed among works attributed to the Catholic Church and Rainer Maria Rilke was the *Book of Hours* I sought. The holdings screen identified two suppliers. The first was a Chicago research library with a lending policy stingier than Stanford's. The second turned out to be my very own institution.

I started fantasizing. Could the renamed, *revised* version of *Chronicle of an Engineer* contain text describing the contents of the now-empty compartment in Jesson's case of curiosities? I printed the citation, filled out a call slip, and made a beeline for the tube clerk.

"Left the author box blank," the clerk mumbled.

"It's anonymous."

"Well, then . . ."

I emended the slip and slid it back, flicking my staff badge for good measure. The clerk gave the slip a perfunctory glance before turning his attention to a magazine.

"Sorry to be a pain, but could we speed things along?"

"Not unless you're a mechanic. The zip tubes are down." He tapped the mouthpiece of the ancient apparatus to confirm malfunction.

Pneumatic dispatch transmits its paper cargo at a mile a minute when working properly—when it isn't, book retrieval slows to a crawl. Forty minutes after I submitted my call slip, the dumbwaiter spat it back with a check mark filling the N.O.S. box.

I approached a page at the delivery window. "This came back 'not-on-shelf.' Can you get someone to check again?"

"No way. The tubes are on the fritz. Nothing I can do."

19

THOUGH I HAD told the South Bend Sabertooths that the reference staff was barred from the stacks, I hadn't told them why. The reason was Dinty.

After he had learned, at an ALA security study group, that librarians fit the profile of the modern-day book thief, he initiated a campaign to curtail employee stack access. Armed with trumped-up "lossage" statistics, he hoodwinked the director into revising the "Procedures and Policy for Library Use." Memos got circulated, forms got printed, locks got changed, and all of us were handed new badges, color-coded picture IDs that banned everyone but the stack crew and senior administrators from searching shelves without written authorization. Since looking for *The Book of Hours* legitimately would have required Dinty's okay, I chose to pursue less formal channels of inquiry.

"Boning up, Mr. Paradis?" I found the janitor sequestered in a broom closet, poring over a sheet of call numbers.

"Less than a month to Class Struggle," he said, referring to a competition similar to *Jeopardy!* that tested the staff's knowledge of the Dewey decimal system. Given Mr. P.'s decades in the stacks and his extraordinary memory, he always proved a serious contender. "I ain't interested in lettin' that Irving Grote beat me two years runnin'."

"I hear you. The guy's a royal pain in the—"

The janitor cut me off. "Neck pain gets classed under 617.53. You'll find most of the medical texts down on level 4."

"And where do you think I'd dig this up?" I showed him my call slip.

He made a face when he saw the mark in the N.O.S. box. "Ain't on the shelf, eh? You sure the stack crew even looked? Can't tell you how often I catch those fellas clackin' dominoes or pawin' Speaight's girlie magazines."

"I wouldn't know," I said abjectly. "The stacks are off-limits to my kind."

"Want me to poke around, is that it?"

"No one knows this place better than you."

"Thing is, as soon as my break's over, I have to tend to the zips. Compressor's misbehavin'. But I tell ya what I *can* do." Mr. Paradis folded up his crib sheet and tucked it into his overalls. "Come on."

He wheeled his cleaning cart to the main stack entrance

and unlocked the door, ushering me past the bas-relief of Dante and its well-known warning about hell.

"Nose around on level 3. That's probably where your book is."

The connection between the stacks and the *Inferno* was in actuality more elaborate than I'd let on to the Sabertooths. Both Dante's netherworld and ours were composed of nine levels; both claimed to enclose the mythical and historical personages of all times. Both contained vast expressions of villainy, abandonment, and malice, and both were built on words. Yet there was at least one significant difference: the library stacks failed to adhere to the strict order of Dante's universe, which in a way made our hell more infernal since we did Chaos better.

Descent proved oppressive. The stairwells were narrow, the ceilings were low, the air was hot and thick with the musty microbial odor of old books. The wheezing of the failing zip tubes and the clang of the radiators made me feel as if I'd entered a giant mechanical lung. On level 3, the pulmonary rasps were drowned out by laughter and the click of dominoes.

The dereliction of the stack crew had a calming effect; it meant I could prowl about as freely as I had before Dinty's restrictions. From those earlier, legal expeditions, I knew to treat location markers skeptically; stack shifts and periodic weeding made the original shelf numbers useless. Even the more recent locators, scrawled on strips of masking tape, only hinted at actual placement; they served as zip codes more than specific street addresses.

Mr. P.'s indictment of the stack crew turned out to be unfair. The "missing" work was, indeed, missing. Where *The Book of Hours* should have been, I found a block of wood that had a relocation tag rubber-banded around it. The tag said, HAND-CARRIED TO CONSERVATION.

20

"SO, SHORT, WHAT brings you to my bailiwick?"

Irving Grote was scowling over a parchment scroll at the back of his lab when he noticed me enter. "If it's to discuss your assault on that hymnal, you can save your breath. I said what I had to at the staff meeting. The regulations stand, full stop. Next time I catch you abusing unopened gatherings, I'll haul you in front of the Executive Committee."

"Actually, I'm here on another matter." I showed him the returned call slip for *The Book of Hours*. "Seems this got sent down for treatment."

"And how do you know that?" Grote demanded.

I avoided mentioning my unauthorized stack search. "Delivery had somebody double-check the shelves."

Clutching the slip in his cotton-gloved hands, Grote walked

over to his desk and consulted a ledger. "Your information is correct—this time. It is one of mine." He unlocked a fenced-off storage area and located a gray phase box, which he carried to a workbench as if transporting unstable explosives.

Stay cool, I told myself. *Hide your interest.* "Mind if I take a gander inside?" I asked timidly.

"Not a chance. Treatment's undetermined. And come to think of it"—Grote fiddled with the string that kept the box closed—"so are your motives."

"It's for a reader," I explained.

"You'll have to do better than that."

"Just tell me what I have to do to get a peek, *please*."

"Hmm, let me think," said Grote. "Oh, I have an idea. Let's make this a *learning* experience. Why don't you read through the memo on how to slice open the gatherings of books? Maybe then we can have a look inside."

Grote tightened the string around the box's plastic washers in a slow figure eight and ordered me to bring him a three-ring binder constituting *The Collected Wisdom of Irving Grote*. Highlights included "Notes on the Proper Employment of Pencil," "Procedures for the Avoidance of Water Damage," "Findings on the Liabilities of Post-its," and "Regulations Addressing the Photoreproduction of Books." Only after I'd thoroughly digested the regulations set forth in "The Unopened Gathering: Standard Guidelines and Restrictions," did Grote untie the string and ease *The Book of Hours* from its protective cardboard case.

"What's the prognosis?" I asked, trying hard to suck up.

Grote fingered the edges, bands, and spine of the book, then gave it a gentle shake. "Erasure crumbs," he muttered with disgust. When he finally allowed himself to open the book, he did so only long enough to sniff the gutter and press a page to his cheek, like a mother checking her baby's temperature.

"Short, make yourself useful. Fetch my treatment log and the Aqua Boy."

I did as told and watched Grote slip the tongs of the humidity tester between two pages of the book.

"Just as I thought. Moisture level's off the charts."

I've been around Aqua Boys enough to know how easy it is to manipulate a reading by applying too much pressure. But there was nothing to be gained by challenging Grote. "Maybe we should flip through the book to see if it needs immediate attention."

"I do not 'flip,' Short. I move from the outside of the book in. It saves wear on the spine."

Several minutes into his prolonged inspection, Grote arrived at a tipped-in engraving. I was standing to the side, so it was hard to get a good view, but what I could see made it impossible to stay calm.

"Mr. Grote! Turn back!"

That was all he needed to hear. He closed the book and placed it on a wedge of foam. "You may take the rest of your *gander* after I've completed treatment."

"But—"

Grote held up his hands to display the rust-colored powder on his gloves. "This, Short, is red rot. Red rot means your reader won't be getting his book for quite some time."

He opened the treatment log and jotted down some notes: "Reinforce hinges. Check for marginalia. Address sporing and leather rot. Clean gutters."

Trying to compose myself, I said, "Sounds like you're restoring a house."

"Hardly. Tending to quarter-bound goat is a lot tougher."

"I'm sure you're up to the challenge, Mr. Grote."

He gave me a long, hard look. "You must really want this, Short. Are you going to explain your uncharacteristic, though entirely justified, deference?"

"You know what readers are like."

"Alas, I do. You'll have to do better than that."

"It's simple. I'd be a hero in an old man's eyes if you let me show him the engraving in that book. Even a copy could clear up a mystery he's worked on for years."

"If he's been at it that long, he won't mind waiting."

"Do I have to beg, Mr. Grote?"

"Don't bother. I doubt the book would pass the three-fold test needed to approve photocopying." That Grote would rely on so discredited a procedure indicated just what a Neanderthal he was in matters of book repair.

"Can we double-check?"

The conservator grabbed a microspatula from a jar on the workbench, opened the book, and used the flat-edged tool to fold down the corner of page 49, pressing along the crease. To my relief, the "ear" didn't break off.

"That's one," I said.

"I can count," snapped Grote. He lifted the corner and repeated the procedure, this time applying greater pressure. The tiny triangle again survived. I kept quiet, watching nervously as Grote turned down the corner a third and final time. The action caused no damage—until Grote bent the ear back up.

"Oh, isn't that a shame," he said, smugly presenting the broken-off tab for inspection.

I had a powerful urge to perform the three-fold test on Grote himself.

"Don't look so defeated, Short. Once I finish prepping the *sefirot* broadsides for the cabala show and encapsulate some award certificates for the donors dinner—there aren't more than forty of those—I can turn my attention to backlog." He placed *The Book of Hours* inside the phase box.

"Note the order. The bottom flap goes up first and *then* the top comes down. You and your colleagues are always getting it wrong. You ought to reread that memo, too."

He carried the box to the storage area and clanged the gate shut. "Try back in a few months," he said, testing the padlock. "If I make your request a priority, it could be ready by spring." He walked over to his desk and scribbled some more notes in the treatment log, then weighted it with a large bronze casting of a book louse.

As soon as I left the lab, I rang Festinalente.

"Mr. Jesson, your case used to contain an oracle, an animal, an engine, and a god."

There was a pause. "Are you telling me the empty compartment held a watch?"

"I am. And it's a real stunner! I've just seen another edition of your book—a *later* edition. It has an engraving that shows the empty compartment filled by a pocket watch. The timepiece probably wasn't added until after the first edition got published."

"Is that what this new edition says?"

"No, that's me hypothesizing. I haven't had a chance to read the thing yet."

"Why not?"

"It's complicated. The book has been sent to Conservation,

which means I can't have access until after treatment is complete."

"How long will that take?"

"A few months, at least."

"Ridiculous. Bring the matter before your superior."

"That wouldn't do us a bit of good. My boss would never bend policy for me."

"To hell with policy!"

"Look, Mr. Jesson, I'll beg, borrow, or steal to help a reader in need, but—"

"Fine. Here's your chance."

21

THERE WAS A time, at the start of my career, when librarians could sneak something out of the building without much worry. Dinthofer's manipulation of the employee theft stats changed all that. Electronic alarms and security guards wielding parcel probes without fear or favor made surreptitious loan unthinkable. My friend Mr. Singh had distinguished himself only a month before by catching a nun in flagrante delicto. (She had a rare edition of *The Story of O* duct-taped to her thigh.)

And so contemplating the relative risks and rewards of unauthorized removal of library property, I quickly came to an incontrovertible conclusion: There was no way I could swipe a book on my own.

"Norton, do you really believe what you said at the staff meeting?"

As usual, he was tapping away on a keyboard. "Maybe. What'd I say?"

"About taking books from the building."

"Natch." He typed for a few seconds. Then his fingers froze and he shot me a look. "Whoa there. Backspace."

"You know that cite I've been investigating?"

"*Chronicle* of something or other. I posted the query, but the server's down. Some sort of connectivity disruption."

"Forget it. I managed to rustle up a later edition, published under a different title. The problem now is, it's with Grote."

"I take it he's making things nonoptimal."

"That's being generous. I need to compare Jesson's edition with the one in Conservation."

"Let's be clear about this. You want me to help you steal a book?"

"I see it more as a temporary loan of an unauthorized nature."

Norton grinned and leaned back, his conspiratorial mind clamping on to the challenge. "How big is it?"

"The book? What difference does that make?"

"I'll have to buy a lead-lined film pouch. I've read they do a dandy job deflecting exit sensors. Best to play it safe."

"Octavo."

"Can you provide *precise* dimensions?"

I handed Norton the catalog record for *The Book of Hours*. He ran his finger down to the format line.

"Eighteen centimeters. Should be a snap." His confidence diluted my fears. "I'll go to the photo shop," he said. "You track down Mr. Paradis and see if he'll unlock the lab after Grote leaves for the day."

Norton had assumed our biggest problem would be slipping the book past the exit desk. He'd overlooked (because I had failed to mention) a more immediate obstacle: the lab's padlocked storage area, for which Mr. Paradis had no key.

We first tried to reach the phase box by sticking our arms through the wire fencing. But when it became clear neither one of us could get within two feet of the shelf, I climbed onto the workbench where Grote had tortured me only hours earlier and surveyed the room. "Norton, near the fume hood . . . grab that roll of leather."

He lugged the leather to the lockup and gamely used it to extend his reach, though with little practical benefit. "Too bad we don't have extension grippers," he said, flexing his hand robotically.

"Bingo! Be right back." I raced up to Periodicals and retrieved a wooden newspaper stick. The stick, roughly a yard long, was equipped with a rubber gasket that locked around flexible tines. Minutes later, I was measuring the rod against my arm.

"This might actually work," Norton said.

It did. A couple of well-aimed taps knocked the phase box to the floor. A few more got it over to the fence, which had a gap that allowed us access. We carried the box back to the workbench, unwound the string, and removed *The Book of Hours*.

"You might find this handy," said Norton. From his plastic grocery sack he produced a substitute volume of identical size. "Wouldn't want Grote getting suspicious because the box felt empty."

"Jeez, Norton. *Bibliokleptomania: An Anatomy of Book Theft*? Not the safest choice. We'd better hope he doesn't look inside."

"Just check if the heft seems right."

I placed the monograph in the box, closing the flaps—bottom up, *then* top down—and wrapped the string counterclockwise around the plastic washers.

"Well?"

I balanced the box in my hand. "Can't feel the difference," I said admiringly.

The next step—returning the box to the shelf—proved trickier. We had to slide the dummy volume through the gap on the floor, jigger it up to the right height, reinsert the newspaper stick through the mesh, pry open the wooden tines, and secure the tines around the box. Only then could we attempt the transfer. I say "attempt" because the box kept dropping, which meant starting all over. The whole procedure had the feel of one of those arcade games that require the transport of a plush toy in the greased pincers of a miniature crane. Eventually Norton succeeded in repositioning the box on the shelf.

"Okay, let's get out of here," I said.

"Slow down. We still have to check the treatment log."

I knew better than to ask why. Norton had shown enough foresight to be spared my second-guessing. I took him to Grote's desk, removed the insect paperweight, and read through the notes. To the earlier directives about hinges and gutters, the conservator had added: "Replace Tattle-Tape. Consider rebind. Status: Nonpriority."

"Bastard! He knew I needed this done fast."

"Don't sweat the small stuff. The delay buys us time. My concern is the Tattle-Tape." Norton gently fingered the boards of the book and peered down the channel of its spine. "With Tattle-Tape you've got to be supercareful. The folks in binding prep sometimes used to insert *two* strips, one obvious and one hidden." He rubbed his finger over a sensor tag affixed to the pastedown. "I'm pretty sure this is the only one."

"*Pretty sure?*"

Norton reached into his wallet and pulled out a credit card. "We won't know for certain until you've passed the alarm gate."

"Wonderful. And what's that for? You think Singh can be bought?"

Norton began pressing the edge of the plastic card against the borders of the Tattle-Tape. After he'd lifted each of the corners he moved in on the center.

"There we go," he cooed, as if he'd just peeled a Band-Aid from a child's knee. "All better." Where the tape had been, there was now only a ghost mark. Norton slipped the credit card back in his wallet, along with the magnetic strip.

"What are you planning to do with that?"

"Who knows? Could come in handy." Norton again reached into his trusty grocery sack.

"Let's see. One smelly T-shirt—check. Four soiled sweat socks—check. One pair of sneakers—check. One rancid jock-strap . . . Where is it? . . . Ah, there you are, my lovely. *Check*. And, finally, the pièce de résistance: one lead-lined film protector from Forty-first Street Camera. By the way, you owe me six bucks."

He placed *The Book of Hours* inside the pouch and folded the top down.

"Perfect fit," I said.

"That's a relief. I was a little worried. Format lines in catalog records aren't exactly reliable." Norton shoved the pouch deep into the grocery sack and piled on the smelly athletic gear, granting the unwashed jockstrap pride of place at the top.

"Now tell me honestly, do you really think Singh is going to risk poking around in *there*?"

That night, the guards were more diligent than usual, prodding each of the bags and parcels that passed the exit desk. The closer I got, the brighter the neon signs seemed to flash over my head: UNAUTHORIZED LOAN! UNAUTHORIZED LOAN! UNAUTHORIZED LOAN!

My anxiety wasn't exactly diminished when I noticed Emil Dinthofer step in line behind me. Could he be on to us already? Unlikely, since no dragnet would have been complete without Grote on hand to revel in my public disgrace.

Mr. Singh offered his usual cheery salutation. "Greetings, Alexander."

I managed a smile but said nothing. While he inserted his dowel deep into the plastic bag, I stared off at the donor plaques, as if searching out a particular benefactor from among the names carved in stone.

All seemed fine until Mr. Singh mumbled a Punjabi oath. I

turned to face him and watched as he made jabbing motions in and out of the grocery sack. "Alexander? Would it be possible for this situation to be remedied?"

"S-s-something wrong?"

I followed his gaze to the pungent jockstrap; it was skewered on his dowel.

"Oops. Let me get that." I held on to the athletic supporter while Mr. Singh extracted the probe. Once it was free, he waved me on, as eager as I to conclude inspection.

Only the sensor screens remained. I braced myself. What if Norton had been wrong? Suppose there *was* a second strip of Tattle-Tape?

I took a deep breath and marched through the electronic gate.

And then . . . And then nothing, beyond the usual hubbub of the exit desk at closing time.

As I waited for Norton on the far side of the checkpoint, I started thinking through how to present the book to Jesson. Was it better to hand it over casually or to wrap the thing in fancy paper? The sudden blare of alarm bells cut short my self-congratulatory musings.

In the commotion that followed, I readied to get dragged away by a security guard. After all, nothing would explain a purloined library book stashed in a plastic bag. And nothing would stop Dinty from having me fired. He might even press criminal charges; he already knew the pertinent passages of the penal code by heart.

I looked for Norton, but he hadn't yet reached the sensor gate.

Someone started shouting. "This is outrageous! I have done

nothing untoward. Do you *hear* me? Nothing! Take your hands off me at once."

Rubberneckers at the exit desk made it tough to see, but I knew the voice.

"This is insanity! Search my briefcase. It contains no library property whatsoever!"

I craned my head and got a brief glimpse of Mr. Singh's turban and a clipboard. Norton passed through the sensor screens grinning from ear to ear.

"You see who just got nailed?" I said.

"Hard not to. I told you that Tattle-Tape might be useful."

"You mean . . ."

"I'm just wondering how long it'll take Dinty to check the cuff of his pants."

22

JESSON JUMPED UP with surprising agility and lunged for *The Book of Hours*. (I had decided against gift wrap.) "You prevailed! You obtained authorization."

"Not exactly."

"I thought library books can't leave the building without someone's signature."

"That's right."

He began leafing through the volume but stopped himself. "No, first I want to hear how you procured this little beauty."

Jesson was ecstatic by the time I'd finished describing the unsanctioned loan. "Let me see if I'm following this. The book was in a box that was in a cage that was in a lab that was in the library?"

"Correct."

"If *that* doesn't play to your love of enclosure, I don't know what does!"

"To say nothing of my contempt for Irving Grote."

"What happens if he discovers what you've done?"

"The risk is minimal. Unless he unties the phase box and looks inside, I'm fine. I inserted a replacement volume of identical weight and size."

"Very smart. Now suppose we find out if all this larceny was worth the effort." Jesson rose from his lounging chair and pushed through the salon like a man on a mission. He entered the library and went straight to the end of the first alcove, where he placed the *Chronicle of an Engineer* on a lectern.

"Put your book beside mine," he said.

A curious collaboration ensued—a mix of translation and textual comparison that required moving back and forth between the two books, Jesson's and the one from the lab. Sadly, there was nothing of real consequence to distinguish the English and French editions. Once we'd navigated the inevitable differences of language and registered the variations of typeface and design, we were forced to conclude that the novelty of *The Book of Hours* resided primarily in the altered engraving.

As I had already explained on the phone, the second picture implied something neither book mentioned in print, that the case of curiosities had once contained a pocket watch. But nowhere did the books identify the type of watch or the name of its maker, and nowhere was it explained where the watch had gone.

None of this dampened Jesson's mood. "Don't you see? We have all we need to continue our *recherche du temps perdu*."

I tried to reclaim *The Book of Hours*, assuming it served

no further purpose, but Jesson stopped me. "If you don't mind, I'd like to have photographs made."

"But—"

"You yourself said its absence would go unnoticed for a while." Over my objections, Jesson stowed the book under the lectern.

As soon as I'd left Festinalente, I started to worry about Nic. The less she knew about the borrowed book the better for all concerned. She'd have boiled me alive in some of her mother's herbal brews if she'd learned what I'd done.

I also kept quiet about my growing commitment to Jesson and about the comfort his support provided. Still, Nic felt the shift. Ever since our tarot card standoff, we had been keeping separate schedules, sleeping in separate beds. Nic took the loft and the studio; I claimed the futon and the cage. Her existence was reduced to a collection of sounds: the whine of the pencil sharpener, the *kathunnk!* of the board shearer, the thud of the fridge door, the hum of the airbrush compressor, the laments of her favorite chanteuse. And selfishly I accepted partition because it gave me time to pursue the anonymous watch.

The next chance to investigate came three days later, during a typically stop-and-go shift of phones. Tel-Ref (the ugly hyphenate is the library's, not mine) is an unpredictable assignment. One minute things are quiet, the next you've got seven callers on hold: "How can I open a car wash in Istanbul?" "Which weighs more: an elephant or the tongue of a blue whale?" "What's a good recipe for pancakes?" "How do you divide fractions?" "Is there a difference between a cockroach and a water bug?" "Are oral and genital herpes the same?" "Can you find me a history of wishes?"

Once I finished up with the callers, I focused on my query. There's an unwritten rule of research that says big guns rarely hit small targets. Since the target fit snugly into a four-inch-by-six-inch compartment, I had to think long and hard about my choice of ammo before approaching the tower-shaped lazy Susan of reference works that dominates the center of Tel-Ref.

I spun the wheel and placed my bets on the *Encyclopedia of Associations*, a multivolume resource that does a sensational job identifying the professional and recreational pluralism that makes America America. Ufologists, urologists, eugenicists, Euclideans, Unitarians, and enthusiasts of Uri Geller all have individual listings.

So, too, watch experts.

On a page registering the Etch A Sketch Club of Bryan, Ohio, and the G.I. Joe Special Forces of Schaumburg, Illinois, I found the National Association of Watch and Clock Collectors. I called and got an interminable recording stating that the offices were closed and inviting me to leave my name "after the tintinnabulation of the Westminster clock, affectionately known as Big Ben, built in—"

I hung up, feeling anything but affection, before the start of the gongs. Norton came in as I was slipping off my headset. I told him what was up.

"How about checking with that arcade Frederick Stolz is constructing in New Jersey?"

"The guy who bought the Automat?"

"If I were looking into outmoded technology, that's where I'd start."

I gave the lazy Susan another spin and plucked the *Directory of Museums* from the buckram blur.

"*Of course* the arcade has watches," said the eager-sounding curator at the other end of the line. "We count the Thatcher Keogh Horology Collection among our recent acquisitions. Mr. Stolz purchased the entire library and related timekeepers en bloc. Had to end-run the auction houses to get it. I don't think I'm betraying confidences if I tell you that Mr. Stolz is a real pit bull. An insatiable completionist."

"You think I might be able to consult the collection?"

"Depends," the curator said. "The timekeepers are in the arcade proper and the arcade hasn't opened."

"What about the library?"

"The library's fine, as long as you can deal with lots of musty old books."

23

"YOU'LL DEFINITELY BE needing an overview," said the curator, whose name was Cavanaugh.

"That's not necessary. Don't want to be a burden."

"You're hardly that. We're opening soon so I'm always looking for guinea pigs."

Cavanaugh walked us past a fleet of dump trucks and back-hoes, onto a dirt road encircling the compound. As we advanced toward the library, he said, "Welcome to the Frederick R. Stolz Arcade of Obsolescence. Three hundred thousand square feet of exhibition space and research facilities devoted to industrial archeology. When it opens next year, this complex will be, quite simply, the largest private arcade of technological history anywhere in the world.

"Why 'arcade,' you may ask. Because what you see before

you will not function as a museum in the classic sense. Quite the contrary. There will be no dusty displays, no cases of any kind. Our venue will *animate* the march of innovation. And why is that? Because Frederick R. Stolz, founder and chief executive officer of Stolz Industries, realized long ago that he could only grow his companies if he embraced the principle of movement—in capital markets, in digital imaging, in exhibits of things mechanical. Hence the complex you see before you, a tribute to technology—past, present, and future." Here Cavanaugh clarified the arcade's organizational structure by pointing at three massive hangars, which resembled huge soda cans buried on their sides. He took a breath and continued.

"Note the curves. Curves can be found throughout the compound. The ring road we are walking on, the arcuate skylights, the doors and the windows . . . all make use of the semicircle." Cavanaugh tapped his lapel pin—two hologram crescents forming a jazzy *S*—to reinforce the observation and then guided me through the library doors.

"Good luck," the curator said as he brought me to a metal table that looked like an oversized pie pan. Thoughtfully, he'd prepared for my visit by pulling the original catalog drawers of the Thatcher Keogh Horology Collection.

When I tried to thank him he said, "Don't thank me yet. I better warn you, you're on your own with those things. I can't make head or tail of them."

I sat down and flipped through the cards. It instantly became obvious why the records caused him trouble; they required a thorough knowledge of pre-ALA size scales: "F" for folio, "Q" for quarto, "Fe" and "Sf" for . . . for *what*?

There were other headaches. The disorder of the cards and the absence of subject headings rendered the drawers unusable. I abandoned the catalog and headed for the book-shelves, which radiated spokelike from the table.

By contrast to the chaos of the cards, the books made a hand-some sight: massive elephants and royal folios on the lower shelves; folios, quartos, octavos up above. The smallest works were hard to reach, but their inaccessibility didn't worry me since it seemed unlikely that teensy duodecimos and sextodeci-mos would contain images, and it was images I was after.

I spent several hours pulling large leather tomes off brushed-metal shelves, searching for a photo of a watch that would match the one in my engraving. Split-second chrono-graphs, half hunters, minute repeaters, Continental complicat-eds . . . After a while, they all started to look alike. With dozens of unhelpful books heaped about, I suddenly felt I was living proof of Norton's first law of research, which argues that the more you look up the less you learn.

Norton supported this observation by invoking a Reading Room regular, a mathematician who rarely submitted a call slip. The man carried his work materials—a thin packet of index cards and two stubby golf pencils—in the breast pocket of his button-down. It was this restraint, Norton contended, that won the fellow a Nobel Prize.

Cavanaugh sensed my mounting frustration and proposed a diversionary tour of the compound. I declined.

"May I?" He picked up a copy of the engraving. After a brief inspection, Cavanaugh said, "Never have liked his work. Can't understand why everyone makes such a fuss. I won't deny the designs are stylish. But as an innovator reggae doesn't hold a candle to some of his British counterparts."

"What's reggae have to do with anything?"

Cavanaugh looked puzzled, then chuckled. "Not reggae. Breguet. With a *B*. B–R–E–G–U–E–T. It *is* one of his, isn't it? Or an imitator? He had so many."

"How can you possibly tell who made this watch? There are no identifying marks."

"Don't be silly. I know a Breguet hand when I see one. The way the needle extends beyond the circle." Cavanaugh traced the shape in the air.

My pulse started racing.

"What does the Keogh have on Breguet? Never mind. I'll check myself." I ran over to the card catalog and pulled the A–E drawer. There were two cites under "Breguet, Abraham-Louis (1747–1823)": a board-bound octavo written by a descendant of the watchmaker and a quarto privately printed in 1921 by a London watch collector listed as "Sir David Lionel Goldsmid-Stern Salomons, Bt., M.A., F.R.A.S., M.Inst.E.E., A.Inst.C.E., &c."

Since my primary interest was pictures, the octavo, which had none, could be set aside. Cavanaugh approached and cleared his throat as I was about to dive into the quarto.

"Closing time," he said.

"Last book," I replied. "Scout's honor."

I suppressed the jolt of recognition when I first saw her face through the glassine sheet. Twice before I'd come across plates that showed watches I was sure matched the one in my engraving. Both times closer inspection had revealed some minor difference. Only after confirming that the hands and internal dials were identically positioned did I succumb to that rare feeling of joy that imbues, with almost electromagnetic force, the phrase *conducting research.*

Imagine, then, my disappointment when, supercharged by archival triumph, I reached Festinalente only to discover that Jesson couldn't see me.

"He's napping," Andrews announced through the judas hole.

"He won't be for long," I said.

The butler, shocked by my boldness, allowed me into the vestibule of the residence, where I grabbed a sheet of Jesson's personal stationery from a stack on the table near the door. I scribbled a hasty note:

> *Dear Mr. Jesson,*
> *Please wake up! I went to a private library in New Jersey and managed to ID our engraving. The timepiece we're looking for has one hell of a pedigree.*
>   *It was made for Marie Antoinette!*
>   *Let me know how to proceed.*
>   *Yours,*
>   *A.*
> *P.S. I've got great documentation.*

The moment I'd tucked the note in an envelope, Andrews tried to show me the door, but I insisted on waiting for a reply.

Pigheadedness paid off. I couldn't have been alone more than a minute before the butler rushed back in. "Mr. Jesson wishes to see you," he said.

By the standards of the downstairs rooms and cloister, the second floor of Festinalente—at least that portion of it that led to Jesson's bedroom—was unnoteworthy except for a series of Piranesi prints hanging from the requisite purple ribbons.

Bleary-eyed, Jesson lay buried to the neck under a snow-drift of comforters. He coughed and beckoned me forward. But when I attempted to hand him a copy of the photo that identified the watch in the engraving, he turned on his side and said, "I'm in no condition to analyze pictures."

He had me sit at the foot of his bed and tell him what I'd discovered.

"As I said in the note, the watch was made for Marie Antoinette. It was commissioned by her Swiss Guard, who attached only one condition to manufacture—that the maker spare no expense."

"I assume that condition was deemed acceptable."

"Apparently. Gold and platinum replaced more common metals wherever possible. Sapphires were used for pallets."

"How could such a masterpiece go unsigned?"

"It *was* signed, Mr. Jesson. Just not on the dial, which was made of transparent rock crystal to show off the complex movement. The watch includes a thermometer scale, a perpetual calendar—that means it corrects for leap years—and a bunch of other gizmos I couldn't begin to describe. Hence its name—the Grand Complication, though I should mention some experts consider that a misnomer."

"What do they prefer?"

"The *Perpétuelle*, the Everlasting, the Marie Antoinette, the Queen. Take your pick. Sir David Salomons, the man who owned her for a while, tended to refer to his Breguets by the serial numbers in the company logbooks."

There was a sudden rustling. "The watch we want is a Breguet?"

"You've heard of him?"

"Better than that."

Jesson tossed off his comforter and sat up. Swinging his legs to the floor, he insisted that I help him on with his dressing gown. "We must continue this downstairs." He pushed through the salon to the three-paneled screen.

"You have yet to . . . to see . . ." He stopped to catch his breath. "To see my gallery of mechanical wonders."

The room behind the screen was as long and narrow as a railway car, only instead of seats there were baize-covered tables lining the sides and far wall. The tables accommodated a staggering assembly of fanciful contraptions: automata, music boxes, . . . clocks.

As Jesson threaded his way down the aisle, his gait became so unsteady that I half expected I'd have to step in and wind him up like one of the toys on display. But when he reached the opposite end of the gallery he regained his energy and equilibrium. "What's the verdict?" he chirped. "How do you like my *pendule sympathique*?"

We were standing in front of an Empire-style clock that cradled a stunning silver pocket watch. Unlike the Breguet I had identified, these two timepieces bore the maker's name.

"My Breguets may not have the Queen's lineage," said Jesson, "but they are special nonetheless. When that pocket watch is returned to its holster, the master clock adjusts and resets it. Do you see how the watch is a little slower than its stationary protector? Observe what's about to happen."

Jesson fiddled with the hands of both mechanisms.

"The cannon pinion of the clock, that needle-sized steel

tube right there, will insert itself into the pocket watch like so." He made a slightly lewd gesture with his finger.

"Now, see how the clock is winding and adjusting the pocket watch? The one provides motive force to the other."

A series of dull chimes announced the hour and, sure enough, the hands began realigning themselves.

"The master clock charges, recalibrates, and fixes all manner of irregularity by sympathetic control," said Jesson. He removed the pocket watch and casually presented it for inspection.

"Except for when I once touched a *Bay Psalm Book*, I don't think I've ever held anything so valuable, Mr. Jesson. It's giving me goose bumps."

"Excellent."

"I can't wait to hit the library."

"I'm pleased you're charged up," said Jesson, returning the watch to its perch. "But I doubt very much the library will help us trace the Queen's current whereabouts. If you don't mind minor recalibration, might I suggest that we now venture beyond books?"

24

JESSON'S ADVICE WASN'T easy to accept. Abandoning the library meant no subject catalogs, no citation indexes, and no guides to electronic databases; it meant disregarding the comforts of print and pixels in favor of a resource my profession sometimes neglects: people.

The face-to-face inquiries began at an Upper East Side auction house, where an expert from the clocks and watches department patiently inspected my photos. With consummate courtesy he said, "And might this inquiry involve the potential for consignment?"

"Afraid not."

"In that case, I believe you'd be better served taking this matter up with the reference staff of your local library."

Ignoring the irony of his suggestion, I made my way to the

second stop of an itinerary I'd constructed (pace Mr. Jesson) from the Manhattan Yellow Pages. Each of the watch dealers I visited replicated, with minor variation, the auction house two-step: kindly attention followed by a brisk heave-ho. Because Dinty had me scheduled for desk duty at one o'clock, I suspended investigation a little before noon. On my way into work, at Forty-eighth Street and Fifth, I fell in step with a Hasidic man carrying a large battered briefcase and wearing an overcoat straight out of Gogol. He turned west one block south. Until that moment, I hadn't thought to poke around the Diamond District, which is less known for watches than for gems.

The first establishment I entered sold Breguets, but they were modern and, while handsome, did nothing to advance the search. Dealers two and three pushed less elegant stock and, like the fellow at the first place, knew nothing about historical timepieces. My luck changed, however, near a display of "used" wedding bands (presumably yanked from the fingers of the divorced or deceased). I was drawn to a triangular wooden sign:

TIME-

PIECES

OLD & NEW

BOUGHT & SOLD

E. ORNSTEIN, PROP.

A gold arrow pointed to a shop not much larger than a newsstand. I tapped on the door. Two old men, each one disfigured by a jeweler's loupe screwed tight against an eye, interrupted their negotiations to stare at me. Unimpressed, they returned to their business, forcing me to knock again. This time I countered their scowls with an idiotic smile and got buzzed in. I was made to wait as the men passed a clunky wristwatch back and forth while arguing in Yiddish. Their talk heated up, cooled down, heated up again, then stopped. The shop owner broke off the exchange and repositioned his jeweler's loupe to a spot in the middle of his forehead, where it stayed thanks to a thin band of wire. He then reached under his yarmulke to extract a key that he used to unlock an ancient floor safe. But no sooner was the wristwatch nesting inside a felted tray than the customer tried to revive the haggling. The shop owner rebuffed him by slamming the safe door shut. As the customer stomped out, the dealer turned to me.

"And how can Emmanuel Ornstein help you?"

"I need to find a watch."

"Votches is vot Emmanuel Ornstein is here for," he said, slipping the safe key back under his skullcap. He motioned toward the sign.

I plunked my satchel on the counter and, as I had a half dozen times that day, presented a copy of the photograph from the Salomons book.

Ornstein lowered his loupe and scanned the image. "So?" he said, letting it fall on the counter.

"Do you know anything about it?"

"Listen, mister. I buy votches, I sell votches. Even sometimes I repair votches. I don't teach. You need a teacher, go find a rebbe."

"It's a Breguet."

Ornstein stared straight at me, his right eye monstrously

distorted by the loupe. "It's not *a* Breguet!" he shouted. "It's *the* Breguet, the Marie Antoinette. You know maybe her location?"

"Actually, that's what I'm trying to find out."

He shrugged. "So who isn't?"

"I don't follow. You're telling me you know about the case of curiosities?"

"The vot?"

I pulled a copy of the engraving from *The Book of Hours*, which depicted the watch in its snug, dovecoted home. "As you can see, Mr. Ornstein, the Queen used to hang in this case. Where she is now I have no idea."

"Case-schmase. All I'm saying is the votch got stolen."

"*Stolen*? From where?"

"Look, mister. Can't you see I'm busy?"

I surveyed the sad little shop.

"Okay," he admitted. "Maybe I'm not so busy. Vot's the votch to you?"

"The wooden case in this picture, the *actual* case, is owned by the man I work for. It's absolutely complete—except for the Marie Antoinette. I'm supposed to find her."

"And this man, he pays you?"

It was obvious where we were headed. After I shelled out a small "commission" (which I knew Jesson would reimburse), Ornstein disappeared behind a curtain. When he returned, following a few noisy minutes of rummaging, he had in hand a sheaf of papers clamped together by a rusty spring clip.

"Still they send me these bulletins," he said proudly. "They know Emmanuel Ornstein has his votch business since almost fifty years."

"And the bulletins come from where, Mr. Ornstein?"

"The Art Theft Archive," he said. "That fancy-schmancy outfit on the East Side."

I girdled a note to make contact and asked if I could help him read through the circulars. Ornstein refused, insisting on earning his fee. That meant watching him drag his loupe over each line of each sheet of paper, as if he were inspecting for a flaw in the table of a five-carat diamond.

"Here," he announced. "Just like I said. The votch got stolen."

"From?"

"From the Mayer Institute for Islamic Art. It's in Jerusalem."

"How does a watch that was made in Paris and sold to a Jewish collector from London end up at an Islamic museum in Jerusalem?"

"Details they don't give."

"When did the theft take place?"

Ornstein squinted. "April of '83. It's never been seen since."

"When was the report issued?"

More squinting. "In '84."

"Maybe the watch has been recovered in the meantime."

"Listen. Emmanuel Ornstein may not do business so much like before, but he knows vot goes on. Take last year. A man I know says he knows someone who knows someone. Says he can maybe have the Marie Antoinette found. So I tell him, 'Go ahead. Have it found.' But does he?" Ornstein shook his head.

"Could you contact him?"

"Depends."

After I provided additional financial incentive, Ornstein agreed to ask around and phone me if anything came up.

When I left the shop, I felt buoyed by my progress. News of the theft legitimated, retroactively, the Conservation break-in. After all, without the unauthorized loan I'd never have learned that the watch we sought was famous and hot.

I should have alerted Jesson to the theft straight away. Instead I held off, reasoning that the archive report, as rendered by Ornstein, raised more questions than it answered. I wanted to pull together a fuller account of the heist before providing an update.

The following day, I got to work early and, breaking Jesson's embargo on library prowling, burrowed into a newspaper database that stretched back to 1982, one year before the crime. Fearing electronic overkill, I kept the date qualifiers narrow and typed K=BREGUET. That got me bombarded by Falcon 90s and Mirage 4Ps, jet planes built by a French aviation company of the same name as the watchmaker. I quickly abandoned BREGUET in favor of MARIE ANTOINETTE but that proved to be a washout too. I tested various Boolean combinations drawn from a growing list of keywords—JERUSALEM, HEIST, SALOMONS, THEFT, STEAL, STOLEN, WATCH—until I finally typed K=SCREW IT and quit. An electronic corollary to Norton's first law popped into my head as I turned away from the computer: the greater the number of search terms the feebler the results of the search.

I retreated to real books printed on real paper, but stumbled there, too. Someone had walked off with the *New York Times* index for 1983. While a page hunted it down, I checked the *Reader's Guide to Periodical Literature*, plus a couple of suspect governmental products—the *Foreign Broadcast Infor-*

mation Service and the *Joint Publications Research Service.* None of the references made any mention of the crime. British sources proved similarly useless. Under "Theft" there were plenty of dog and cat snatchings but nary a stolen watch. When at last the rogue newspaper index resurfaced, I discovered to my great satisfaction a worthwhile citation. The gods of reference continued to smile on me in the microform department, where I located the needed spool. A wire report amplified the information Ornstein had provided:

JERUSALEM, April 16 (Reuters)—Thieves broke into the L. A. Mayer Memorial Institute for Islamic Art Friday night and stole watches and clocks, rare books and paintings valued at more than $4 million in what the Israeli police today described as the city's biggest theft.

A police spokesman said the thieves smashed through a window of the museum building, which is near the official residence of Israel's president in the western part of the city.

"They must have known what they were doing. They picked only the most valuable items," the spokesman said.

He said the thieves would have difficulty disposing of the objects because of their rarity and value.

"They will find it hard to leave the country. All exits are sealed," the spokesman said. "We are investigating the possible involvement of an unscrupulous collector."

The museum opened about 10 years ago and contains a wide variety of timepieces and Islamic cultural objects.

The dispatch made obvious that researching the whereabouts of the watch demanded some basic skills I lacked. I didn't read Hebrew and I didn't know my way around Israeli resource materials. Fortunately, there was someone on staff who did.

Mr. Abromowitz, curator of Judaica, welcomed my underworld distractions. Within the hour he was running his silver Torah pointer down the margin of a Hebrew-language news magazine.

"Very colorful woman, this Vera," he said as he tapped a grainy picture with his yad.

"Who's Vera?"

"Sir David's daughter. Guiding force behind the construction of the Islamic institute. Did you know she tried to *buy* the Western Wall?" Abromowitz gave the weekly another tap. "It's all in here."

"Great." I pulled out my girdle book. "Now, if you can tell me what it says"—I made a tapping motion of my own—"we'll be all set."

My version of Mr. Abromowitz's translation will never win a prize for style, but it did record how Breguet's timekeeper made it from a Paris workshop to London to Jerusalem. It also clarified the circumstances of the watch's disappearance:

Sir David Salomons d. 1925. Leaves bulk of estate to daughter Vera. Stocks, leaseholds, liquid assets +imp. watch coll. After funeral V. goes abroad. Falls in love w/ Palestine, then under Brit rule. V.'s Zionism ↑. Swaps comfort of London for "vitality" of J'lem.

Tries to buy Western Wall after viewing donkey urinate against stones near rabbi bent in prayer. Fails. Brits nix offer of £100,000 to Muslim trust that owns the property.

V.'s subsequent campaigns (on behalf of orphans, handicapped, the dispossessed) get better results. Supports Leon Mayer, distinguished scholar of Arabic art. Leon and V. become "companions." V. builds research institute in his honor but 50% of the exhibition space is devoted to Sir D.'s clocks and watches. At ribbon-cutting, local architecture critic praises institute's fortresslike appearance. The break-in (Apr. '83) reveals looks can deceive. Police discover burglar alarms never connected, guards badly trained, doors unlocked.

Crime gets major journalistic play. Suspects (none named) include: Arab terrorists, local criminals, local criminals posing as Arab terrorists, and the "unscrupulous collector" mentioned in wire story. Last possibility ridiculed by watch collection's caretaker, Ohannes Tashjian. He says, "The Queen was one of my children—my dearest child. And now that child is gone."

25

THE JERUSALEM MATERIAL, and in particular the grief of the caretaker, enthralled Jesson. "Anyone who likens a watch to a child is someone I need to meet."

"We could call him. I did pull the number."

Jesson grimaced.

"What did you have in mind?"

"A tête-à-tête," he said. "Perhaps even a private tour of the crime scene."

"But you told me you don't fly."

"There are other ways to travel, Alexander, quite pleasant ones, in fact. Or perhaps you could serve as my emissary. You certainly know the particulars of the case better than I do."

The proposal floored me. "I'm flattered, Mr. Johnson. But there's no way I can go to Jerusalem. If my boss didn't kill me, my wife . . . Why are you smiling?"

"You just called me *Johnson*."

"Really?"

"What would your shrimp say to that, I wonder. Actually, the slip isn't terribly surprising. The age span between us does correspond to theirs."

"Did Boswell get a reprimand because his query quotas were below the department mean?"

"I'd have to check, but offhand I don't recall reading about that in the *Life*."

"And did his wife accuse him of all-consuming friendships?"

"That certainly. There was the instance of a liaison with—" Jesson stopped himself. "Is that what your wife thinks of *our* association?"

"More or less. Nic's a bit jealous about the time we spend together working on the case. One thing I can tell you, she'd be furious if she knew I'd swiped a book for you."

"Don't worry about that. What should concern you is this unreasonable picture she has of our collaboration."

"Better not call it that if the two of you do ever meet. The word *collaboration* reminds Nic of Vichy informants."

Jesson's face reddened. "This is absurd. Go home and talk to her. Persuade her to join us next Saturday."

"You heard what happened last time I tried. She hung up on me."

"Try again. To entertain uncertainty is to invite failure, and failure is something I reject. As do you, I suspect. After all, consider what you have accomplished. When you started helping me, did you expect to identify the object missing from my case?"

"No."

"Yet you managed to do so. And when that object was nothing more than an image in an anonymous engraving, did you anticipate uncovering its royal origins?"

"Well, no."

"But you did."

"Yes, but—"

"Given what you've already achieved, don't you think that convincing a headstrong wife to come for drinks should be a relatively simple task?"

"You want an honest answer? No, I don't."

Nic was particularly unapproachable that week, a hellacious deadline having thrown her into a creative frenzy. My first real opening only came the very afternoon we were expected at Festinalente. Nic burst into my cage asking for help getting the final mock-ups of her project, a life-sized pop-up leg splint, to an ad agency in Midtown.

We'd already performed the rituals of departure, the police lock wedged into place on one side of the front door, the sneakers of menace on the other, when Nic realized she'd forgotten her string bag. Scavenger that she was, she never went anywhere without it.

I waited for her on the corner, where Mr. Lopez stood barking orders at a deliveryman while his son, back inside the abandoned TV set, took aim with his paint roller at the woman who ran the travel agency next door. The woman was posting weekly specials on a felt board in the window:

```
SANTO DOMINGO. . . . $149
CARACAS. . . . . . . . . $139
MIAMI  . . . . . . . . . $129
DIVORCE. . . . . . . . $250
```

Closing my eyes, I tried to take refuge in thoughts of Festinalente, with its globe of paradise, burbling fountain, cooing doves, and protective calm. But by the time Nic reemerged clutching her bag, a nasty little samba was running through my head: *Santo Domingo, Caracas, Miami, Divorce . . . Santo Domingo, Caracas, Miami, Divorce.*

I did my best to ignore the tune by talking to Nic about her birthday, which was only two weeks away. "What if, after we drop this leg off, I get you that cordless glue gun you've been talking about?"

"I thought we were broken," she said.

"Not since I started working for Jesson."

"Buy me nothing with *his* money."

"Why are you so tough on the guy? You've never even met him."

"I don't have to. I see what he does to you."

"Is it that you're scared you might actually find him appealing? Spend some time together and I'm sure you'll change your mind."

"Are you daring me?"

I looked Nic straight in the eye and said, "*Oui.*"

26

OUR HOST GREETED us in his usual house garb: embroidered slippers, cashmere sweater, baggy cords.

"Henry James Jesson III," he said. "*Très heureux de faire votre connaissance.*" His French did little to ease the tension.

"Hello," said Nic, silently surveying the salon, with its profusion of antiques.

"As you can see, I've never been one for restraint," Jesson said as he guided us to a drinks trolley. Next to it he had placed the ivory table from the theater. The case of curiosities was resting on top.

"That's what all this is about? That box of *bricolage*?"

"It's more than the sum of its parts," I said.

"I'm pleased to hear you say so, Alexander." Jesson turned

to Nic. "Your husband has discovered what once hung from that little nail right there. The story's really quite incredible. As it turns out, we're looking for a timepiece made by one of your compatriots."

"Actually, Breguet was born in Switzerland, Mr. Jesson."

"Don't nitpick, Alexander. I'm trying to charm your wife."

Nic remained aloof. "Why not leave the compartment empty? I prefer it incomplete."

"And why is that, my dear?"

Nic shrugged.

I jumped in to temper the growing awkwardness. "You know what I was told by a curator I once helped? That paintings stimulate more interest when they *can't* be seen. He said his museum did a time study in its Old Masters wing. A little tag that read "Temporarily on loan" got 75 percent more attention per viewer than the Rembrandt hanging ten feet away."

"Your point?" said Jesson.

"Only that some folks seem to go for empty spaces."

"To my mind, the visitors were staring at the tag out of a sense of loss and betrayal. Longing is what made them linger." Jesson said to Nic, "As your husband will attest, I abhor vacancy and the uncertainty it creates. Empty walls and empty cases run counter to my aesthetic. My motto has always been, I collect, therefore I am."

"But what if—"

Jesson cut Nic off. "But what if . . . I cannot have what I need to have, to *be* who it is that I am? I don't ask myself such questions. I told your husband just last week that to do so invites doubt, which in turn invites failure. Alexander never thought you'd come, but here you are, in my house, though clearly not all that happily. Perhaps a drink might help."

Jesson walked over to the trolley and reached for a crystal pitcher. "I've had Andrews prepare a Pimm's Cup—a summertime drink that I hope will brighten your mood." He swirled a silver spoon and raised slices of cucumber to the surface of the punch.

Nic declined, so Jesson filled only two tankards. Handing one to me, he took the other to a lounging chair. "Now, where were we?" he said as he sat down.

"Why am I here?" Nic demanded.

Jesson took a sip of his drink. "I asked you over to discuss a collab—" He caught himself. "To discuss a commission." He flipped the hinged armrest on his chair and extracted a tattered volume from the secret hollow. "Would you mind taking a look at this?"

The minute Nic registered what she was holding, her attitude underwent a major revision. "A Meggendorfer!" she said gleefully.

I peered over, as surprised as she was. "The boards are in incredible shape."

Jesson smiled into his tankard.

After the initial shock wore off, Nic said, "How did you know I love his pop-ups?"

"Forgive me, but I prefer the term *eccentrics*."

"Did Alexander tell you?" she pressed.

"I suppose," he replied.

"Did I?" I wondered aloud. I couldn't recall mentioning my wife's interests with that kind of specificity.

"How else *could* I have known?" Jesson pulled three or

four more books from the chair's cavity. As he displayed their whimsy, Nic displayed hers. A pull-tab ziggurat prompted a giggle, a miniature Venetian blind that "blinked" scenes of explicit sexual engagement produced a whoop.

Nic was peering through the peephole of a German tunnel book when Jesson began his pitch. "I imagine you could produce this kind of work."

"Perhaps," she answered modestly.

"Would you be willing to try making me an eccentric?"

"I thought you were looking for a watch," she said.

"Indeed. But the written account of its retrieval also concerns me."

"You've already hired a scribbler."

"Alexander can handle the content, of course. But I was hoping you might give our project *depth*." Jesson reached over and expanded the tunnel book to reinforce his point. "Come with me, both of you. I have something further I wish you to see."

We followed Jesson to a baroque cabinet at the far end of the salon. He directed our attention to a mirrored inset about the size of a cigar box. Two small wooden columns bracketed the niche. He pivoted toward Nic. "Would you mind nudging the column on the right?"

She complied.

"Perfect. Now stick your hand inside the opening and try to find the release. The trick, my dear, is knowing how far to push and knowing not to push farther." Jesson gave me a sly wink.

There was a click.

"That's fine. Now press the hidden button, which you should reach a few inches in."

Nic must have hit it, because the column suddenly popped forward to expose a vertical drawer.

"Please remove the contents."

Nic opened the secret compartment and pulled out an old cardboard Advent calendar that still had its numbered windows sealed shut. From a design standpoint, it wasn't nearly so engaging as the armrest books. The calendar depicted a banal sleigh-driving Santa Claus urging his reindeer toward a generic alpine village.

"My interest in the card is purely structural," Jesson said. "Would either of you be kind enough to open Day 1?"

Nic perforated the window with her fingernail and folded over the flap. The image underneath was as trite as the one on the surface: a lamb sleeping in a hay pile behind a scrim of isinglass.

"My idea is simple," said Jesson. "I would like the written account of our search to incorporate windows like these. With your assistance, my dear, we could hide representations of each of the case's objects under paper flaps. Ten chapters, ten windows—"

"Ten objects under glass," I interjected.

"Exactly."

I turned to Nic. "Think about it. *Your* images, *my* words."

"I do have a roulette knife that can make the perforations," she admitted.

"Why not place the windows at the beginning of each chapter?" I proposed. "Like the initial letters of an illuminated manuscript."

"Glorious," said Jesson. "Our very own *Très Riches Heures*."

"I need to know what the watch looks like," said Nic.

"Fine. I'll show you the book your husband very kindly spirited out of his library."

Nic whipped around. "What do you mean? He took a book without permission?"

Flummoxed by Jesson's indiscretion, I admitted to the break-in. Nic wasn't pleased. She shut the window on the Advent calendar, and with it all hope of assistance.

"I am going," she said. "It doesn't interest me to be a *collabo*."

"Perhaps you should both leave," Jesson said, calmly fishing a cucumber slice from his tankard. "I need to be rested for my little trip."

This was news. "Where are you off to?"

"We can talk about that later. Right now I think it's best you take your wife home."

"How could you have stolen for him?" Nic demanded on the bus.

"I only borrowed the book."

"Borrowed, stolen. You could lose your job."

"Are you angry about what I did or that I did it for Jesson?"

"Stop working for him."

"Why? Because your tarot cards say to?"

"I don't need the cards for that. And stop talking about me with him."

"I don't."

"Then how did he know I like pop-ups?"

"Probably the same way he knows I love enclosures. He's got uncanny instincts."

Nic started counting off names. "McCarkle, Dewey, Sharansky, the Shrimp . . . Jesson. It's always the same with these old men of yours, always." She punched her palm. "*Chtock! Dans les dents.*"

We rode the rest of the way home in angry silence and, as I had earlier in the day, I tried to distract myself by focusing my thoughts on the beautiful objects in Festinalente. I couldn't. The nagging samba soon returned: *Santo Domingo, Caracas, Miami, Divorce . . . Santo Domingo, Caracas, Miami, Divorce.*

27

WHITE SHEETS COVERED the salon chairs, globe, and harpsichord, and the apples that normally lined the mantel were gone, their fragrance replaced by the heavy scent of lemon oil. A monogrammed set of luggage, assembled where the drinks trolley had stood only a few days before, made me wonder about the scale of Jesson's "little" trip. (The banded steamer trunk alone could have accommodated all twenty-nine volumes of his 11th edition *Britannica*.) Scanning the faded French Line labels plastered onto the suitcases, I suddenly felt a touch of envy. The stickers conjured up exotic locales I knew I'd never visit.

"He's in the cloister," Andrews said, nodding toward the French doors.

The fountain had been drained, the doves caged, and absent

the usual burbling and birdsong, the noise of the city traffic pierced the courtyard canopy. But the biggest change was Jesson himself. Gone were the slippers and roomy corduroys, exchanged for bench-made walking boots polished to deep luster and a woolen suit of trim, ageless cut.

"Where are you going?" I blurted out.

He beckoned me to his side. "Let's speak of travel plans in a moment. First a little stroll."

As his old-fashioned footwear clicked against the walkway stones, I sensed that the counterclockwise movement around the perimeter was the tactic of a man determined to propel himself, and me, backward in time.

"I need you, Alexander."

"I'm touched, Mr. Jesson."

"What I mean is, I need you unencumbered by the burdens you suffer at home. Without absolute, unpoisoned focus, we will never complete the case."

"Don't worry about Nic, Mr. Jesson. Jealousy is what the French do. It's like perfume and champagne—practically an export product."

"Then it's time to impose a few trade restrictions."

"Trust me, they're already in place. Now, can you *please* tell me where you're going?"

"To the scene of the crime, of course."

"*Jerusalem*? That's hardly a *little* trip."

"Let's not quibble over adjectives. I did ask if you wanted to go."

"And I told you I can't take off."

"Which is why the task falls to me."

"How long will you be gone?"

"Longer than I'd like." Jesson produced a copy of his itinerary. An ocean liner and a series of express trains would take him as far as Istanbul, where he'd catch a chartered boat to Tel Aviv. From there, a driver would shuttle him to the King David Hotel in Jerusalem.

"The whole continental leg is a disaster," he complained. "My agent had to reserve a standard wagon-lit in lieu of the Orient Express, which has abbreviated its service unconscionably."

"While you're gumshoeing around the Middle East, what do you expect *me* to do?"

"Don't get tetchy, Alexander. I count on you to continue your investigations. Do you know whom Prince William of Hesse considered his most important adviser while he was traveling abroad? I'll tell you. His director general of the Delights of the Eye. That's how I think of you."

"And what did this director general do exactly?"

"What do you think? He helped fill cases."

28

BOOKS, ANY CONSERVATOR can tell you, suffer when subjected to sudden change; the same is true for their keepers.

Jesson's departure demoralized me terribly. I missed the pontifications and the obscure references, the queries about my queries, the laughter and the challenges and the childish love of sweets. I even missed the moments when he shooed me away from the sedan chair while he tended to his roll of notes.

The practical result of our separation was that the watch inquiries, at my end anyway, came to an abrupt halt. After confirming an appointment with the Art Theft Archive for the afternoon of Nic's birthday (the only time they'd see me), I procrastinated shamelessly by tracking Jesson's itinerary.

This shift from task to taskmaster eventually brought me

to the map room, where I pulled a chart of Atlantic shipping lanes. Using it in conjunction with a Hammond *Atlas* and a Cook's *European Timetable*, I plotted Jesson's movements day by day, hour by hour. Girdling Dep.'s and Arr.'s put me in his stateroom cabin and in the first-class train compartments that would take him as far as Turkey.

I was just starting a shift of phones, contentedly extending the pencil line on my map to Vienna, when a call came in.

"Telephone Reference," I announced.

"Might I steal a moment of your time?"

"Mr. Jesson?"

"They told me you'd pick up."

"Is everything okay? You hate phones."

"Indeed I do, but I'm occasionally compelled to acknowledge their utility."

"How's Vienna?"

The question prompted a chuckle. "Keeping tabs, are you? How endearing. Vienna is *wunderschön*. I am happy to report that the Hotel Sacher's eponymous torte is as delectable as ever. Now, tell me, will the last compartment be filled by the time I get home?"

"Don't count on it. Truth is, all I've managed is an appointment with the Art Theft Archive, which naturally falls on Nic's birthday."

"Cancel," Jesson said. "It would be better for all concerned if you were to patch things up with your wife."

This newfound concern surprised me, but before I could ask about his change of heart, the door flew open and Dinty strode in. I plucked a book off the lazy Susan and tried to appear as though I were answering a genuine query.

"Here we go, sir. The dodo. From the Portuguese *dóudo* for simpleton. Became extinct in 1681. Do you need the exact citation?"

"Can't talk anymore?"

Dinty was now so close I could smell the Bag Balm moisturizer he used on his hands.

"That is correct, sir."

"Then we'll catch up when I return. Until then, I insist that you cancel the archive appointment and celebrate your wife's birthday."

29

JESSON'S TOUCHING CALL left me with an uneasy feeling. It didn't seem right skipping the single legitimate appointment I'd made during his absence, which is why I decided to satisfy my obligations both to the watch and my wife.

The Art Theft Archive rented space on the top floor of a private men's club that had a dress code I trumped handsomely by arriving with the English umbrella Jesson had given me. A file-cabinet-gray sky was threatening rain, and I didn't want to put my notes at risk.

"Excuse me, son. You didn't register." A *Racing Form* lowered to reveal a seasoned, diligent guard of the Singh school. "Take yourself back to the foyer and check in."

I did as I was told and signed a cheap four-column ledger

that didn't open flat. By the time I returned, the guard had swapped his tip sheet for a clipboard.

"Name?"

"Alexander Short."

The guard moved his eyes down the page. "You're not here."

"I believe I am."

"On the list, son. On the list. Have you come on club business or archive business?"

"Archive."

Without rising from his castered desk chair, the guard rolled himself to an ancient switchboard some twenty feet away and inserted a wire into a numbered hole. He flipped a switch and brought a disk-shaped receiver to his ear.

"There's a Mr. Short down here," the guard shouted at the mounted mouthpiece. "Not on the list . . . Nope . . . Yes . . . Okay."

He scuttled back. "Ain't expected. Not by Miss Barton anyhow."

"I made this appointment over a week ago."

"Must have talked to Vivien. Vivien's out sick."

"Look, I'm under lots of pressure. Could I see the person you just spoke with?"

The guard rolled back to the switchboard and rang again. "Wants to see you, Miss B. *Says* he's under pressure." He turned to me. "Miss B. is asking what kind of pressure."

The truth was too complicated. "I'm writing an article for the *Horologist*," I said.

The guard gave me a funny look.

"That's horologist with an *H*. As in the study of clocks and watches." I tapped my wrist. "I have to research the whereabouts of a timepiece that the archive registered as stolen in 1983. I was hoping to see the files. You can assure who-ever's upstairs that I'll be in and out. It's my wife's birthday."

This last detail seemed to soften the guard. When he re-peated my plea into the mouthpiece, his voice sounded more gentle.

"Elevator to five," he said, pulling the wire. "Might have to jiggle the gate. Left at the top of the stairs. And the um-brella stays down here." He pointed at a hollowed-out ele-phant's foot.

"I'll keep it with me, if it's all the same."

"It's not," he said. "If it don't stay, you don't go."

I deposited the umbrella in the stand but snatched it back as soon as the guard had refocused his attention on the ponies.

The elevator stalled on two. Only after I'd jerked the scissor gate back and forth a few times did I get the motor to jolt back to life.

I threaded my way through a labyrinth of dented file draw-ers to a primly dressed woman typing away at furious speed.

"Ms. Barton?"

"It's *Miss*," she corrected without lifting her gaze from the computer dominating her desk. "And you're Mr. Short, I presume?"

"That's right." My outstretched hand went unshaken.

"Must finish up this theft in Brno. Still have a Torah breastplate to input, so take a seat over there." Miss Barton pointed to a stool placed below a dormer.

A mousy woman sorting photographs at a nearby desk smiled as I propped my umbrella against the wall.

"Meredith, make sure Mr. Short is comfortable and that he touches nothing. Inform him that archive files are proprietary and as such cannot be consulted by anyone other than staff."

I called out, "I'm sorry to be so pushy, but I did make this appointment a while back."

"Not with me you didn't," Miss Barton snapped. "You must have scheduled with Vivien. Vivien's out sick for a change."

It was another ten minutes before Miss Barton completed her data entry and summoned me back. "Suppose we start at the beginning. You work for . . ."

"The *Horologist.*"

"Your article's about what precisely? And if you say 'clocks' you can consider this meeting over."

"I'm interested in a pocket watch made for Marie Antoinette."

"Not my favorite period," said Miss Barton, fondling a Victorian cameo clasped at her throat. "Vivien's the person you should be seeing. Are you sure you can't come back?"

"Positive."

"I suppose we could consult Virginia—especially now that she's been equipped with a video visualizer."

It took a moment to distinguish Vivien, the colleague out sick, from Virginia, the massive computer Miss Barton was now fondly patting. I adjusted my response accordingly.

"A video visualizer? That definitely warrants a mention in my piece, especially if Virginia can help with the stolen watch."

Miss Barton seemed to soften. "When was the theft?"

"April of 1983."

"That's too bad. Virginia only joined us in '87. The records you need are in one of our cabinets." The way Miss Barton said "cabinets" didn't sound promising.

"Could we look?"

"I suppose. What's the registry number?"

I consulted my notes. "Eighty-three point ninety-five point zero seven."

"Follow me." We snaked through the maze of file drawers until we reached the bathroom. "As you can see," Miss Barton said, "we've got a slight space issue."

In addition to the usual fixtures, the bathroom housed a fax machine, photocopier (the latter placed on a carton inside the bathtub), and still more records.

"Here we go," said Miss Barton, pulling a manila folder from a cabinet in the shower stall. "Eighty-three point ninety-five point zero seven." She scanned the contents. "There isn't much besides a standard alert from Interpol." She fluttered a faded sheet of thermal paper under my nose. "Plus the registry report Vivien generated before writing up the public bulletin you saw."

"Could I—"

"Sorry. All files are proprietary. You wouldn't want me getting into hot water."

The shower tap was temptingly close. "At least tell me who's used the records."

Miss Barton shook her head. "We can only do that for the objects in Virginia's database. The archive has no documentation regarding how, or even if, the older files get used. Like I said, it's Vivien you need to speak with."

The mousy woman stuck her head in.

"Sorry to interrupt, Martha. Call for you from Tulsa. A collection of Hester Bates spoons just got reported."

"Oh no, not the spoons!" Miss Barton clutched her cameo theatrically. "Let's just hope the Hummel figurines and the commemorative plates were spared."

"They want to fax us the details," said the Mouse.

"Tell them we don't do collectibles."

"I tried."

"Would you excuse me?" Miss Barton stepped out of the shower stall, placed the file folder on the toilet tank, and left.

The proximity of the photocopier in the tub and the file on the toilet made my next move obvious. While Miss Barton took some poor Tulsan to task, I surreptitiously copied the file. Emerging before she'd gotten off the phone, I gestured that I'd call if I had any more questions. Then I hurried downstairs, keen to get home.

"Don't forget to check out," the guard barked from behind his tip sheet.

"Sure thing."

But to spite him, and the poorly bound sign-in book, I didn't, adding unregistered departure to my growing list of misdemeanors.

Sadly, Miss Barton had accurately represented the meager contents of the file. The Interpol fax proved especially irritating. How could anyone place faith in a document that transformed Abraham-Louis Breguet into someone called "Lewis Brequet"? The registry report turned out to be more detailed but was set in type so small it made me wish I had Ornstein's loupe:

Registry Number: 83.95.07.
Object: Watch. Perpétuelle Marie Antoinette. [1783–1827].
Artist: BREGUET, Abraham-Louis.
Locus of creation: Paris.
Locus of theft: Jerusalem, Israel. L. A. Mayer Memorial Institute for Islamic Art.
Date of crime: 4/83.
Reward: N/A.
Contact organizations: Interpol, L. A. Mayer Memorial Institute for Islamic Art, A.T.A.
Description of object: Gold with rock crystal covers back and front.
Dial: rock crystal with Roman numerals, alternative dial enamel with Arabic numerals. Diam. 6 cm. Dial signed Breguet et Fils. No. 160. Subsidiary dial for seconds containing day of the week, blued steel hands with jumping hour hand, sectors at left for equation of time and state of winding, sectors at right for date of the month and thermometer scale, signed Breguet. Movement: plates, bridges, and wheels of gold, equal lift and locking lever escapement with sapphire pallets and roller, compensation balance with recessed screws and parachute suspension, gold helical spring with terminal curves free-sprung, minute repeating on a gong, hours and quarters à toc, perpetual calendar corrected for leap year, equation of time, seconds hand marking whole seconds, bi-metallic thermometer, two going barrels with provision for locking the platinum winding weight when fully wound, levers at the edge of the dial for arresting the balance, arresting the seconds, setting the month and date, regulating the speed of the repeating train, and locking the winding weight, all friction surfaces jeweled in sapphire, winding weight and buffer spring rollers of sapphire, platinum winding weight supported in sapphire bearings with a parachute suspension.
Circumstances of theft: Weekend penetration. Security system disengaged. Vandalism in conjunction with crime.

Was it too much to expect the name of a suspect? Or maybe a clearer sense of motive? Or a hint about where the watch had ended up? The only noteworthy detail appeared at the very end of the report: "Vandalism in conjunction with crime."

30

IN THE MATTER of Nic's birthday, the logic I applied was this: since nothing purchased would go over well—Jesson being the source of my newfound revenue—I'd *make* a gift. To that end, I decided to cook a special dinner.

The menu came together as I was standing in front of the fish counter and recalled Nic's regular references to the Shrimp. The association inspired me to buy two pounds of giant peeled prawns, which I made the centerpiece of a birthday banquet composed entirely of my wife's most delectable idioms. I was sure she'd get a kick out of a meal featuring smashed potatoes, Islamic vinegar, and a type of smoked salmon she had rechristened (if that's the right word) Nova's Kosher.

When I got home and told Nic I was cooking, she was so pleased she decided to get dressed up. For the first time in months, an amorous feeling started to pass between us.

"Zander?" she called out friskily. "*Je suis prête.*"

"Restaurant opens in five minutes," I yelled back, dashing about lighting the candles and positioning the menus I'd decorated with a vignette of open books.

"*Le dîner est servi,*" I finally announced.

Nic came in wearing pixieish tights (one leg red, one green), a skirt stitched from squares of raw silk, and a stunning Japanese schoolgirl's smock. As she approached the card table, Nic smiled and wiggled her rump, drawing attention to the shiny satin bow that completed her ensemble.

"It's *your* birthday," I said.

"I know." She gave a wink and reached for the menu. Her face hardened.

I tweaked the bow. "What's the verdict?"

She flinched.

"You okay?" I asked, knowing she wasn't.

"You serve me my errors?"

"C'mon, Nic. Where's your sense of humor?"

She stabbed the menu with a fork. "What's *wrong* with my saying Nova's Kosher?"

"Actually, it's Nova, *space*, Scotia. As in the place the salmon comes from."

"Was this his idea?"

The pronoun needed no clarification. "*He* isn't even in the country."

"Which is why you have time for me?"

"Look, Nic. I know you want me to stop working for the

guy. That you resent my commitment to something that doesn't involve you. Well, I'm sorry about that. Jesson *wanted* you to join in. You refused."

Nic grabbed a fistful of prawns. "Here! You need these fucking shrimps more than I do."

Within minutes, I was fleeing the apartment, dodging a fusillade of seafood and smashed potatoes.

31

"WHAT THE HELL'S THAT?" Norton demanded when he noticed me jotting down a list of keywords.

"Prelims for some online work," I said.

Norton shook his head. "I'm seeing some major redundancy in your search terms, my friend. Plus, you're not thinking about the proximity operators and vector-space queries." He took a mechanical pencil from his shirt pocket and started scratching words off my list. "You've got to be supercareful with date parameters."

"I know all about date parameters, but if you'd like to do the honors, be my guest."

Seconds later Norton was at the keyboard on my behalf. He typed:

MARIE W/2 ANTOINETTE

The screen flashed:

> YOUR SEARCH HAS BEEN INTERRUPTED BECAUSE IT
> PROBABLY WILL RETRIEVE MORE THAN 1,000 DOCU-
> MENTS. YOU HAVE NOT BEEN CHARGED FOR THIS
> STOPPED SEARCH.

"What about including 'watch' as a wild card?" I proposed.

"Don't think that's a good idea, but you're the boss." Norton added:

> AND WATCH!

That got us:

> YOUR SEARCH REQUEST HAS FOUND 404 STORIES
> THROUGH LEVEL 1. TO DISPLAY THESE STORIES PRESS
> EITHER THE KWIC, FULL, CITE OR SEGMTS KEY. TO
> MODIFY YOUR SEARCH REQUEST, PRESS THE M KEY
> (MODFY) AND THEN THE ENTER KEY.

"Not bad," I said.

Norton rolled his eyes. "I told you wild carding 'watch' would be *highly* nonoptimal. You've pulled in references to 'watchful' and a lot of other static besides."

"Point taken."

Norton changed the terms and inserted a date qualifier, which winnowed things down significantly:

> YOUR SEARCH REQUEST HAS FOUND 27 STORIES
> THROUGH LEVEL 2.

"Bravo," I said, pressing the KWIC command to get the "key word in context" for all twenty-seven articles.

The first piece, titled "Off with Her Head . . . and Shoulders," reported the commercial failure of a dandruff shampoo sold under the name Marie Antoinette. The second and third articles were no better. In fact, the Jerusalem break-in received a mention in only one of the stories, a profile headlined "Man of Many Faces: A Wily Wizard and His Time Machines, Abraham-Louis Breguet."

Smithsonian, May 1985

Radical in appearance and conservative in accuracy, Breguet **watches** changed the face of timepieces while their owners did the same to Europe. Whoever clung to power between 1785 and 1824—years that the novelist Stendhal considered more monumental than the previous 2,000—also clung to a Breguet pocket **watch**. Stendhal did. So, too, most of the Continent's aristocracy. The mightiest nobles timed battles, hunts, and amorous rendezvous to the muted chimes of a . . .

Of the 5,000 **watches** logged in the Breguet books, no fewer than 1,000 survive, treasured by museum curators and private collectors . . .

The horological heist of the decade offers exasperating homage to the revolutionary **watchmaker** . . .

Among other items, the thieves selected the finest Breguets, including his chef d'oeuvre known as the "**Marie Antoinette.**" It has never been recovered. The previous owner, Sir David Salomons, captured the passion of all collectors when he observed: "To carry a fine Breguet

watch is to feel that you have the brains of a genius in your pocket."

"Let's go full-text," I said.

"You sure we couldn't use our connect time more robustly?"

"Please, Norton."

He gave a nod and brought up the article. Like the others, it proved useless. He pushed QUIT and leaned back in his chair. "Before taking this any further, let's review what we have."

A few minutes spent matching documents to keywords raised a red flag. "What a cretin!" I exclaimed.

"You or me?" said Norton.

"Me! Take a look." I showed him the Reuters dispatch. "There's no mention of the Marie Antoinette by name. The stuff we know *now* isn't necessarily what they knew *then*. She should never have been part of the search string."

"So off with her head—and mine," Norton said, relinquishing his place at the terminal.

I drew a line through MARIE ANTOINETTE, cracked my knuckles, and substituted the royal reference with the word JERUSALEM. The screen responded promisingly:

YOUR SEARCH REQUEST HAS FOUND 6 STORIES THROUGH LEVEL 1.

Norton reached over and hit the CITE key. The first two stories bore no connection to the crime; the third was a rewrite of the wire report. Cite 4, however, was entirely new and relevant:

Dateline: London, April 17

Headline: Watch Theft a Zionist Crime

Body: The Islamic Arts Foundation called today for an international inquiry into the **theft** of four million dollar's worth of art objects from a **Jerusalem** museum on Friday . . .

The London-based foundation, set up to promote Arabic art, also appeeled to dealers and auction houses throughout the world to help recover anceint **watches** and clocks, stolen from the museum . . .

"This is nothing less then a systematic campaign to destroy Islamic heritage and holy places since the Israeli usurpation and occupation of Palestine," a spokesman said.

"It is ominous that the **theft** comes in the wake of the wanton destruction of the Institute of Palestinian Studies in Beirut last year," he added.

Police in **Jerusalem** say that the thieves could have trouble deposing of the items because of there rarity and value.

"Someone should learn to spell," said Norton.

"The typos bother me less than the tone."

"Finger-pointing's an art form in Israel. I wouldn't give it much credence."

Cites 5 and 6 corrected the spelling mistakes but provided no additional information.

"Turn your head, Norton. What I'm about to do is super-nonoptimal." I typed:

(THEFT OR THIEF OR STEAL OR STOLE OR BREAK W/2
IN AND DATE AFT 1/2/86 AND MARIE W/2 ANTOINETTE
OR SUSPECT OR BREGUET)

"You can look now," I said, astonished by what the search proffered. "Seems we've got a suspect—our very first goddamn one."

The screen read:

Dateline: Newport, Rhode Island, March 18
Headline: Queen's Fan Club Prez Charged in Burglary
Body: Mr. Christopher Lyons, a Manhattan resident, was detained yesterday afternoon at The Breakers, the famed Newport, Rhode Island estate, and was later charged with attempted burglary.

Lyons was stopped while allegedly attempting to **steal** a pillow that had once belonged to **Marie Antoinette,** the ill-fated queen of France. The pillow came from a carriage used by the decapitated queen when she fled from revolutionaries with her husband, Louis XVI.

Lyons, president of the Antoinettes, a fan club devoted to honoring the memory of the famous French queen, characterized the incident as a mistake.

"I am absolutely not a **thief,**" he said. "I just wanted to touch her pillow to my cheek."

A spokesman from the police department refused comment pending an investigation.

32

"YOU DO KNOW she was a *major* fan of *show-co-lah*. That's what the French call hot cocoa. So have a seat on the divan and I'll whip us up some."

Christopher Lyons made the offer while gliding down the corridor of his gun-barrel Chelsea apartment, raising his arms as if picking something up and shifting his weight oddly each time he passed through a doorway. After directing me to a couch blooming with needlepoint roses, he disappeared behind the louvers of an adjacent kitchenette.

"So, anyway," he called out, "what's this all about?"

Hospitality is not generally the hallmark of the thief. Still, I had to follow through; Jesson would expect nothing less.

"I'm a reporter," I said, reviving the archive ploy.

"Who for?" Lyons asked, over the sound of clinking tea-cups.

I was about to say the *Horologist*, the affiliation that had more or less thawed Miss Barton. But then I realized that if my suspect *did* possess the watch or had illicit knowledge about its disappearance—remote though the possibilities might be—mentioning a journal devoted to timekeepers risked tipping my hand. "Ever hear of *Art & Antiques*?"

"Sure. I've got a friend in their production department."

I backpedaled. "Well, it's not for *Art & Antiques* per se. It's for a magazine like *Art & Antiques*."

"Does this magazine have a name?"

A whistling kettle granted momentary reprieve.

"*Art & Industry*," I said when Lyons reemerged.

"Well, whoever you're writing for, if it's about *her* you've come to the right place." He deposited a crowded tray on a gilded table and lowered himself into a chair upholstered with cherubs and clouds. "I know her like I know my own mom, so get me going and you'd better cancel your day."

"Consider it canceled, Mr. Lyons."

"Christopher."

"Christopher."

He smiled. "I can become pretty evangelical, if that's the right word."

"Let's find out." I withdrew my girdle book and gripped it as a reporter might. "How did this interest of yours begin?"

"Hmm." Lyons considered the question while pouring the hot chocolate. "I'm nine, maybe ten. My mom's reading to me from a book about famous monarchs. Anyway, most of the stuff's totally boring. Cleopatra wore this, Henry VIII liked to do that." He waved his teaspoon dismissively. "As if I cared. Then my mom gets to the Marie Antoinette chapter, and I see this *amazing* portrait, a Vigée-LeBrun, and I'm . . . well, entranced is what I am."

He turned and gazed lovingly at a reproduction of the painting, framed in gold and flanked by candles.

"So my mom reads to me about her entire life, and when we reach the part where she's killed and her head gets shoved onto the end of some stupid pole, I pretty much freak. I have my mom find another bio and make her read it to me, and another, and another. I figure if we read enough, it might change the destiny of her life. And you want to know something? It did. The more we read, the more I began to see that Marie Antoinette was actually a very strong woman, especially in her final days.

"Have you ever seen that famous David drawing? The one where she's being carted off to the guillotine? That's the real Marie Antoinette. Strong, proud, defiant, with those incredible boobs.

"When I read that they'd restored her private rooms at Versailles, I went straight to Air France. Paid full fare, and this was way before frequent-flyer miles. But do you want to know what I felt when I got inside the palace? Disappointment. Her bedspread was the only thing that really felt real. I know, because I snuck up and touched it. The rest of the stuff left me cold. Her apartment was worthless compared to the goodies in the Met show. Did you see the Met show?"

"Missed it, I'm afraid."

"Now *that* was incredible. They had this stunning lace collar she wore. They mounted it on a really thin wire you couldn't even see. Just the collar. Nothing else." Lyons gripped his neck. "Drop-dead gorgeous is what it was."

He gazed over at the poster once more. "Look at her. Just the slightest whisper of suffering. Like she *knows* how it's all going to end. I read someplace—we can find the article in my scrapbooks if you want—that she was menstruating heavily on the day of her execution. Did you know that?"

"Actually, I didn't."

Lyons nodded. "She wanted to wear white, but . . . Well, you don't need me connecting the dots. Anyway, after she was beheaded the guards searched her cell and found this bloodstained rag she'd used to clean herself. She'd hidden it in a crack in the wall. Now that's dignity."

Lyons caught me looking at a photo resting near the tea tray. "Halloween, three years ago," he said.

"It's a beautiful robe."

He set down his cup. "And a bitch to make. Guess how much silk I needed for the train."

"I wouldn't have a clue."

"Try sixteen yards. I have a video of the whole ball, if you're interested. I came in third."

"I'd love to see it sometime but right now I really need to discuss her actual possessions."

"Fire away. Just *please* don't tell me you're writing about that silly diamond necklace affair."

"Not to worry."

Lyons poured some more cocoa in my cup and excused himself. He returned clutching a videotape.

"Halloween?"

"Better," he said. "A copy of the 1938 biopic starring Norma Shearer. Some of the Antoinettes prefer the Michèle Morgan vehicle, but for my money this one's tops. Norma's so much more opulent, so much more MGM."

Lyons popped the cassette into his VCR, joined me on the couch, and fast-forwarded over the trademark lion, the opening credits, and a two-paragraph summary of life in pre-Revolutionary France. As soon as he hit PLAY he began reproducing the gestures and dialogue of the actors.

At the library I see this kind of behavior all the time. The Reading Room is packed with people mimicking the books they call up, but none of our would-be Emmas, Gatsbys, or Garps could hold a candle to Lyons.

"You're nice to share this with me," I said. "But I don't want to take advantage."

"Oops, I've gone overboard, haven't I? Better just zip to the highlights." As the tape advanced, a ballroom scene woke me to the fact that the swiveling motions of the panniered ladies were the source of the curious hallway pirouette Lyons had performed earlier. He twisted this way and that to imitate the physical constraints of a ball gown.

"You see that old dowager on the four-poster? That's Marie Antoinette's mother, Maria Theresa. The cow spends most of her time brokering marriages like some Hollywood agent. That's how she snags Robert Morley for Norma. Did you know Marie Antoinette was stripped naked at the border crossing on her first trip to France? She had to exchange all her Austrian clothes for French ones. Can you imagine?" Lyons sighed.

"The girl knew suffering. Like this scene here, where Du Barry sends her a teeny-weeny cradle to needle her about being infertile, which, of course, she wasn't. Louis had a weird foreskin problem. Finally had to have surgery, not that that's in the film. Just like they don't show her bratty kids testifying against her at the trial . . . Oh, this is the scene where she tries to warn Louis about a big-time palace scandal. Only he's more interested in his locks and clocks. Louis loved to tinker."

At last, an opening. "That's good to know," I said. "It's watches I'm focusing on. One in particular."

Lyons grimaced and pushed up his shirtsleeves to expose his bare wrists. "The only thing watches tell you is that life is ticking away. I can do without the reminder, thank you very much." He shook his sleeves back down. "I've never gone for those fake Marie Antoinette timepieces they sell at the Hameau. They're even worse than the Sèvres milking jugs." He reached for a scrapbook. "This facsimile note is as close as I've gotten to owning something of hers." He removed a piece of paper from a transparent sheet protector.

"It's blank," I said.

"Hold it up to the light and you'll see that the words shine through the tiny holes. The story goes that Marie Antoinette wrote a note just like it in jail, after all her pens got confiscated. Pretty clever, to think of using a pin. I came so close to touching the original. That's the only time I get to experience *real* Antoinettiana, in museums. You know the magnificent carriage she escaped in—the one Tyrone Power gives her?—I felt the actual pillow from the actual carriage. It's at The Breakers, in Newport. Boy, did that cause trouble. All I wanted to do was touch the silk against my face, but this macho security guard—the guy was built like the Conciergerie—saw me reaching over the rope." Lyons shuddered. "I *told* him I'd put it right back. He wasn't interested. The whole situation got *way* out of control."

"You were arrested?"

Lyons cocked his head. "You saw the papers, didn't you?"

There seemed little reason to say I hadn't. "To be honest, it's how I found your name."

My admission threw him, but only for a moment. "You do know they ended up dropping the charges?"

It was time to put my cards on the table. "Mr. Lyons."

"Christopher."

"Christopher. I'm here because I'm trying to track down a watch commissioned for the queen, a Breguet made of gold and platinum about yea big." I formed a circle with my thumbs and index fingers.

"Never heard of it."

"It was stolen from a Jerusalem museum."

Lyons stiffened. "I get it. Because of the business at The Breakers, you think I'm involved. Sorry, you've got the wrong man. If I ever did decide to swipe something of hers, it'd be that lace collar I was telling you about, not some stupid watch. Or, better yet, a silk camisole I saw once in Paris. It had tiny fleurs-de-lys stitched around the bust."

"I wasn't accusing you. I just thought, with your network, you might know someone who could point me in the right direction."

"Not offhand. But I can call Mr. Thomas."

"Mr. Thomas being?"

"A big collector and acting secretary of our society. The man has no standards whatsoever. I bet you *he* has a Sèvres milking jug. Still, he maintains incredible files. I'm seeing him in a few days. I'll let you know if he knows anything."

"That would be great." I wrote down my phone number and address.

Lyons said, "Now, what's this *really* about? You're not a

journalist, are you? I've never heard of *Art* and whatever it's called."

Given his obvious innocence, to say nothing of the potential help his friend Mr. Thomas might provide, I came clean.

Lyons responded sympathetically. "This old guy you're working for—sounds like you're pretty devoted to him."

"I am."

"The queen has a way of doing that, bringing people to-gether." And to prove the point, Lyons walked over to the VCR, ejected the tape, wrapped it in some tissue paper on the counter of the kitchenette, and placed the cassette in my hand.

"Here, I want you to have this," he said. "I feel a teensy bond too."

33

THE MINGLED SCENT of the mantelpiece apples and a cedar fire welcomed me back to Festinalente even before Jesson said hello.

"How was the trip?" I asked as I crossed the salon and took my place in the vacant lounging chair facing the glowing hearth.

"Exhausting. Boat travel can be so punishing to one's insides." He patted his belly, then motioned toward a plate of salad rimmed by a circle of beets.

I again asked about the journey, but Jesson, up to his old tricks, deflected my questions by saying he couldn't both eat and talk. And so the conversation progressed as it so often seemed to, on *his* terms and in *my* words.

He listened calmly to the inventory of dead ends and false leads, occasionally asking for amplification, as he ate roughage grown, he told me unnecessarily, in the hothouse of his Long Island farm. He was slipping his napkin through a silver ring when I mentioned my visit to the Art Theft Archive.

"You went? After I specifically told you not to?" He slammed the ring down on the tray.

"It's a good thing I did go. Otherwise, I'd never have learned about the vandalism. And if I hadn't learned about the vandalism I'd never have done another online search. It's that search that got us our one potential lead."

"Slow down," said Jesson, "and leave nothing out."

By the time I'd finished explaining how the archive file had drawn me back to the computer and how the computer had led to Lyons, Jesson's odd agitation had died away.

"Apologies for the outburst," he said. "You've been brilliant in my absence."

"Let's not go overboard."

"As someone who's just spent the better part of a week crossing the Atlantic, I stand by the compliment."

"All I did was dig up a Marie Antoinette groupie who's promised to make inquiries."

"You're sure this Lyons is above suspicion?"

"The charges against him were dropped. Besides, there's a huge difference between reaching over a rope to bring a cushion to your cheek and jackhammering into a museum to steal a priceless watch. No, if he's helpful, it will be because of the people he knows."

"How true," said Jesson.

"Does that 'how true' mean you discovered something during your trip?"

"I'd prefer you decide for yourself."

And with that, Jesson popped open the armrest of his lounging chair, extracted the tape recorder, and tossed it in my lap.

34

I SETTLED INTO the cage and hit PLAY.

My dear Alexander. I trust you know how much I loathe these devices. The insidious way they record errors of speech resurrects the most unpleasant memories of Mother and her misused candy dish. So please, rectify my grammatical lapses and anything else that might offend. I apologize in advance for the rhetorical stiffness. Tape machines constrain me ter-ribly.

A crash, the sound of running water, heavy breathing, foot-steps.

Excuse the interruption. I just took a spill in the cloister. One moment, while I make a few adjustments.

More footsteps and heavy breathing, the creak of a door hinge, a long sigh.

*There we are. Now I can begin my chronicle of chronoklep-
tomania. I'll skip the guide-book minutiae. Suffice it to say,
the trip proved unremarkable. Boat, train, ferry, train, train,
train, sloop, car. The last vehicle was supposed to meet me
at customs in Tel Aviv. I include this detail because the driver
engaged by my travel agent never deigned to arrive. I'd still
be on the docks had it not been for an entrepreneurial fellow
named Uri, who offered to take me to Jerusalem.*

*"Vuz beeg story. In all papers," Uri declared, happy to
present a conspiratorial analysis of the crime, one that attached criminal guilt to unnamed Arab terrorists. By the time
we reached the hotel, Uri had broadened his indictment, blam-
ing Palestinians for, among other things, water shortages in
the Negev, violence on the West Bank, and the paucity of a
recent orange crop. When I asked for proof of Arab involvement, Uri shot back, "Proof? Who needs proof?"*

*Once inside my suite at the King David, which I must
report hasn't aged very well, I placed a few phone calls, an
activity, as you know, I detest. Mercifully, I encountered pass-
able English everywhere.*

*The Mayer Institute was at the top of my list. I first asked
to speak to Mr. Tashjian, the caretaker so poignantly quoted
in that article you found. Alas, I was told he had resigned.
This, it turned out, was only partially true, though more on
that later. I then asked for the director, but as soon as I uttered
the words* **Marie Antoinette** *the receptionist informed me he was
not, and would not be, available. Without a trace of irony,
she stated that he didn't have the time.*

*I next phoned the police and spoke with an assistant to the
commissioner who replaced the commissioner who had investigated the crime. The assistant informed me that her supe-*

rior's predecessor now worked as an attorney in private practice. So I called the commissioner turned lawyer, who surprisingly answered his own phone. He agreed, after a not inconsiderable amount of wheedling, to see me. The following morning Uri—have I mentioned I ended up hiring him per diem?—drove me to the office of Arie Kimmelman, advocate.

He was not what I expected. None of the lawyers I have known wear their shirts open to exhibit a maximum of chest hair. When I asked about the theft, Kimmelman said, "Verst burglary I investigated. Too many rumors and bad informations." Before I could get him to elaborate, the damn phone rang, leaving me to twiddle my thumbs while he dealt with the exigencies of a divorce, a fact made clear by the words palimony and prenup, which kept creeping into his Hebrew counsel. To bide my time, I did what you would have done, Alexander. I took stock of the surroundings.

Book-lined law chambers these were not. Kimmelman decorated the office walls with black-and-white photographs of crime scenes he'd investigated in his former life. Since police work was clearly still a passion, I played to it when he finally got off the phone. I asked about his days on the force—triumphs, dissatisfactions—pointing to this photo and that, until I managed to steer him to our case.

Kimmelman said his investigators determined that no fewer than four thieves had burgled the institute and that a mattress, pushed through the window, cushioned the intruders' fall. Then, he explained, they either selected their booty judiciously or snatched things up pell-mell, he was not sure which. Besides the mattress, the thieves left behind various tools, two cans of carbonated beverage, and a partially eaten ham-and-cheese sandwich. I asked if there were any fingerprints or telltale bite marks on the sandwich. Kimmelman laughed and said I'd been watching too much television.

What else? The thieves disconnected the institute's burglar alarm even though the device wasn't operational. This raised an obvious question: did the criminals, aware the security system wasn't functioning, tamper with it to mask inside knowledge? Or did they "deactivate" the disarmed device unknowingly? Kimmelman couldn't say.

The abandoned ham-and-cheese sandwich posed a similar conundrum. Was it intentionally left behind to suggest indifference to Islamic and Jewish dietary laws? Or was the sandwich shrewdly planted to misguide the inspectors? And while we are itemizing ambiguities, there is the matter of the display-case signs. Why, as Kimmelman informed me, were the English-language labels taken and the Hebrew ones left behind? Again, he confessed to being stumped. He showed me a picture of his investigators standing behind a table piled high with watches. "Looks like a pickpocket's wake," I said. "Why the long faces?"

Kimmelman said, "Spend three months following bad rumors. Then ask." He told me about the cockamamy insurance-fraud hypothesis, discounted when it was confirmed that the institute had almost no coverage. He went through the ideological-heist theory, rejected since no ransom note or political screed ever came to light. And lest we forget, the ever-popular but wholly unproven rich-American scenario, suggesting that the crime had been commissioned.

I put it to Kimmelman directly: "You have no idea who did it, do you?" He said instinct told him it was petty criminals unaware of what they were taking. I told him that seemed improbable. My challenge angered him. "You really think pro-

fessionals would do what these people did?" I asked what he meant. "More I will not say."

I caught him inspecting a boxed watch hand cushioned by cotton. "Is that hers?"

He again stonewalled. "That I cannot discuss."

On the way back to the hotel, Uri indulged in another of his harangues. "It's them, I tell you. It was reported every-where." He held up his newspaper, and that gave me an idea. I asked Uri if he knew where the editorial offices of the Jeru-salem Post might be located. He drove me straight there.

Imagine, Alexander, a giant warehouse of broken furniture. Add to said warehouse journalists and editors of similarly derelict condition and banish the cleaning staff for a year. That's what greeted me. I've never seen such decreptitude, and remember this is coming from the son of a scrap man!

After pleading my case, I was taken to a grimy room and handed a thick file marked, "Crime, Local, 1983." Most of the clippings documented misdemeanors: "Stolen Carpet Passed through Customs," "Missing Cash Found in Airplane Passenger's Underpants," "Guard Arrested with 38 Sheep." Our burglary was far and away the most serious, but the only clipping worth copying was a follow-up that quoted Ohannes Tashjian. "I will carry her loss with me always," he said. A large photograph accompanied the piece. The caption read, "Ohannes Tashjian in front of his recently opened watch shop in the Old City."

So next stop: the Old City. Uri left me at the Jaffa Gate and said I'd have no trouble finding my way. His confidence was misplaced. It took all of five minutes for me to fall victim to the nodular chaos of the Christian Quarter. Outside the

Chapel of the Flagellation, I approached a priest and showed him a copy of the Post article. He said, "Ah, yes, the key man. He's well known around here." The cleric guided me directly to the doorway pictured in the article, so by way of thanks I made a donation to his church, the Armenian Patriarchate of St. James.

With that transaction completed, I knocked on the window of the shop and was received by a rotund man some ten years my senior. "Mr. Ohannes Tashjian?" He smiled appreciatively at my careful pronunciation. I introduced myself as a collector of pocket watches, Breguets in particular, and asked if we might have a chat.

"That depends," he said, rubbing his stomach, an action that drew attention to the innumerable winding keys chained around his waist.

An invitation to lunch was all the encouragement Tashjian needed to agree to close up shop. He took us to a superb neighborhood café run by Muslim twins. "I am sorry," he said as we sat down, "but no alcohol is served here." I was sorry, too. Given the morning's failures, I'd have welcomed a pitcher of Pimm's or whatever its Middle Eastern equivalent might be.

Tashjian more than compensated, thank goodness. Over a succulent meal of roasted goat, he regaled me with stories about his "children." Never, Alexander, have I heard such un-alloyed enthusiasm for watches. He even gave me a guided tour of the oversized charm bracelet circling his belly. And what a trip that was! Cranks, skeletons, chased Continentals. At a certain point he said, "Maybe we can't get drunk, but I can show you my Tipsy." Fortunately, I'd read enough to *know he was referring to a clever winding key invented by Monsieur Breguet. I asked if the Queen's key was also on his chain. He told me grimly it was not. "Stolen, I take it." He shook his head and said, "Locked away at the institute."*

This news triggered a thought, a plan, you might say. I pressed Tashjian to show me the crime scene, as one Breguet lover to another. He thought the request strange but agreed after I promised to post him a tin of Spanish biscuits and a case of my beloved Pimm's. He said he had to go there anyway, to treat the ropes of the institute's Dondi astrarium—Oh, damn it. . . . Andrews, I've spilled my punch. Could you lay out a fresh pair of trousers? . . . I'm sorry, Alexander. I must stop.

And then the tape went silent. I fast-forwarded and pressed PLAY. No sound, not even birdsong or burbling water. I flipped the cassette over and found the other side hadn't been used. It was there that Jesson ended his account—without a word about his visit to the institute or the "plan" hatched at the café run by the Muslim twins.

35

BACK AT THE apartment I called Norton and asked how we could have missed the articles in the *Jerusalem Post*.

"Give me a nano."

When he came back on the line, he said, "Wasn't our fault—at least not completely. The *Post* wasn't full-text until '88, five years after the crime."

"I thought the database goes back to the late seventies."

"The database does, just not all the sources on it."

"Damn. These mistakes are making me look pretty lame."

"Hey, I'm the one who's supposed to know computers." As Norton tried to lift my spirits by explaining the pitfalls of retrospective conversion vis-à-vis database management, I leafed through the mail on the kitchen counter and came across a letter with a wax seal the color of Burgundy. There was no return address but I knew from the loopy lettering that it hadn't come from Jesson. I sliced the envelope open and pulled out a card that appeared to be blank and made me think, *Great, another nonclue.* Until, that is, I felt the surface. Puncture marks, hundreds of them, prompted me to hang up on Norton and head straight for Nic's Luxo lamp.

An inkless message! Just like the one Christopher Lyons's royal heartthrob had "pinned" on the eve of her beheading.

The holes were too fine to read, even with the Luxo lamp, so I rubbed the back of the card with a pencil, a childhood trick that eventually raised the letters. The message said: IT WAS NEVER HERS. CHECK THE DATE. VIVE LA REINE!

Check the date? Check the date of *what*? The monarchy? The queen's execution? The crime?

I called Lyons but got his machine. I left a message, then tried calling Norton back. He had just gone home. Not wanting to contact Jesson before I had decoded the note, I pulled out all my documents and began circling, with bright red marker, every date I could find. It was only when I went back to the registry report photocopied in the bathtub of the Art Theft Archive that I began to make sense of my blunder. The key lines were:

> *Registry Number: 83.95.07*
> *Object: Watch. Perptuelle Marie Antoinette. [1783–1827].*
> *Artist: BREGUET, Abraham-Louis.*

I had assumed that the bracketed dates identified the years of Breguet's birth and death. But if he'd been born in 1783, how could he have made a watch for Marie Antoinette? She was decapitated in 1793. Ten-year-olds typically don't produce horological masterpieces. I did some more checking and confirmed, from a more scrupulous reading of my own notes, that Abraham-Louis Breguet was born in 1747, not 1783.

Which meant what? Which meant the dates on the registry report were the watch's, not the watchmaker's. And that meant the queen—the flesh-and-blood, let-them-eat-cake spendthrift—had been finished off by revolutionaries some thirty years before her namesake had left Breguet's shop.

This, perhaps, explained why Lyons was unaware of the timepiece. Because the Marie Antoinette had never belonged to Marie Antoinette, it had escaped the attention of her fans. The watch had as much to do with the queen of France as the Lincoln Tunnel has to do with the sixteenth president of the United States!

I began tallying up the mistakes I'd made since the start of the search and suddenly realized that a number of them—most in fact—concerned matters of time. The overly restrictive date parameters that almost had me miss *The Book of Hours*. The sloppy database consultation that allowed the *Jerusalem Post* to escape my attention. And now this, the misidentified completion date. How would I explain my gaffes to Jesson?

Maybe I could characterize the screw-ups as *re-clarifications*. Argue that the misinterpretation was actually a good thing since it enabled us to prune the Antoinettes from the list of potential suspects. If pressed, I might even quote a bit of Sharansky, who famously announced, in his legendary lecture on cataloging, that "essence emerges from exclusion." If so, we certainly were making progress.

It seemed unlikely Jesson would go for this kind of sophistry, but at that moment I didn't have much else to offer.

The phone rang. It was Lyons returning my call.

"Thought you might give me a ring," he said.

"How'd you do it?"

"Traced the message on a stencil, taped the stencil to a card, then went over both on my Singer—with no thread, naturally. I'm just mad at myself for using that boring old stationery instead of something with a fleur-de-lys motif. That would have been *much* more period."

"I meant how did you find out that the watch was completed *after* the queen got beheaded?"

"Can't take credit there. All I did was ask around if anyone had heard about this stolen watch of yours. No one had, which seemed *très* strange. Then someone said maybe it was just *named* after her. Anyway, there's a guy who keeps these incredible files. I think I told you about him. Rusty Thomas? It was Rusty who figured it out. Now that that's out of the way, tell me what you thought of the film."

"Haven't had a chance to watch it yet."

Lyons, hurt by my admission, spent a few minutes isolating favorite scenes, soliloquizing about the décor, Norma Shearer's costumes, the music, and the fact that the screenplay was based on a marvelous bio by Stefan Zweig.

I felt so sheepish after we hung up that I decided to bite the bullet and view the tape. It was in my hand when a key turned in the lock. Nic, back from teaching at House of Paper, saw the gift-wrapped package.

"*Pour moi?*" She must have assumed it was a belated birthday present, a gesture of remorse to compensate for the disastrous meal.

"Actually—"

She dropped her string bag, snatched the package out of my hand, and ripped through the tissue paper. "A video?" She headed for the VCR before I could stop her.

"This isn't for me!" she roared, pretty much in unison with the MGM lion. She stormed off to the sound of the "Marseillaise."

36

"WE CAN TAKE Lyons and Co. off the list once and for all."

"And why is that?" Jesson asked.

"Because the Marie Antoinette never belonged to Marie Antoinette. A watch she never touched holds zero appeal for Lyons and his associates."

We were sitting on the stone bench of the cloister, separated by the glass coffeemaker, porcelain cups, and a fresh tin of Catalan cookies.

"Could you elaborate?" said Jesson.

I propped the pinpricked note against the cookie tin. Jesson rubbed his fingertips on a linen napkin to remove the buildup of confectioners' sugar, then gingerly reached for the envelope. He glanced at the wax seal approvingly before extracting the "blank" card.

He turned the card over in his hands a few times and raised it toward the canopy. The light filtering through the roof proved inadequate, so he tried to read the message by the candle flame keeping the coffee warm. That didn't work either.

"No use," he said, returning the card to the tray. "My eyes aren't strong enough."

"It says, 'Check the date.'"

"What date?"

"The watch's. It seems Breguet didn't complete the thing until well into the nineteenth century."

"Preposterous. The Swiss Guard commissioned it for Marie Antoinette. You said so yourself."

"Commissioned, yes. But the piece never had a chance to reach her."

"You're telling me that the queen's ticker stopped before Breguet's even started?"

"I wouldn't have put it that way, but yes. And as I said, Lyons's passion extends only to items she used personally. That's why he's never heard about the watch."

Jesson treated himself to another cookie. "Nice work, Alexander. Knowing who *didn't* do the crime brings us that much closer to the individuals who did. Especially considering what Tashjian told me."

"What *did* Tashjian tell you? The tape ended before you detailed your plan."

"I must apologize for the abrupt suspension. I spilled some punch, and by the time I'd changed, well, I'd lost my momentum."

From the far side of the cloister a noise intruded. We turned to find Andrews tapping a wooden tennis racquet against the French doors. I pretended not to notice. "About the plan . . ."

"Again, I'm going to have to apologize," said Jesson. "Talk of Jerusalem will have to wait just a little longer. I'm off to the club to shed a few of these *rosquillas*. Wouldn't want my belly to start looking like the key man's."

"No risk there—especially if the two of us were to take a brisk walk around the courtyard. That would meet your needs and mine."

Jesson considered the proposal as he drained the sugary sediment from the bottom of his demitasse. He then raised a hand, fingers spread, toward his butler, who solemnly acknowledged the five-minute delay.

"Now, if I remember correctly," said Jesson as we began another of our counterclockwise strolls, "I left off at the café run by the Muslim twins."

"No, you covered that. You and Tashjian were already on your way to the institute."

"That's right." Jesson took a few contemplative steps. "Uri drove us there after lunch. Even though Tashjian had given up his full-time duties, he'd been kept on retainer to maintain the timepieces that hadn't been stolen. His most temperamental charge, a Dondi astrarium, required weekly care. After tending to the mechanism's ropes and winding weights, Tashjian showed me around what was left of Sir David's collection."

"Was it difficult to get him to open up about the theft?"

"Quite. I had to approach the topic gingerly. Tashjian loved to talk of watches, but I knew he'd tolerate only the gentlest application of pressure when it came to discussing the heist. The way his mood had soured back at the café when I mentioned the Queen's key suggested I should proceed with caution. I asked lots of mundane questions. How long had Tashjian worked at the Mayer before opening his shop? Which watchmaker did he most admire? What was the most challenging repair he had ever performed?

"At a certain point, I noticed him sidestep a display cabinet. I walked over to see why. Between an enameled pocket watch from Blois and a Nuremberg table clock, I picked out a faint outline, a kind of ghost mark in the velvet some three inches round. 'Her former throne?' I asked. 'Yes,' Tashjian said from across the room. 'The director wants the cloth replaced. I refuse. I tell him someday she will be returned.'"

"Did Tashjian justify his optimism?"

"On the contrary. And I wouldn't characterize his mood as optimistic. He described the crime in morose detail—detail Kimmelman had refused to provide. Apparently, the thieves ripped the hands from a number of the watches and clocks, scattering some, taking others. Tashjian told me that in the weeks immediately following the break-in the police were expecting the missing hands to arrive at the institute with a ransom demand, like the severed ear of that Getty boy."

"None did, I take it."

"No. Tashjian confirmed what Kimmelman had said. The thieves haven't made a peep."

"Why couldn't Kimmelman tell you about the destruction?"

"I asked Tashjian the same thing. Facts were withheld to vet rumors. Keeping the business of the removed hands out of the papers allowed investigators to evaluate the reliability of their informants. Not that the tactic helped. Tashjian considered the news blackout worse than absurd."

"He sounds a bit bitter."

"He is, thank goodness. That's what made him receptive

to my plan, which began simply enough. 'Mr. Tashjian,' I said. 'That key the thieves left behind must offer you *some* solace, knowing you still have a memento of your charge.' He scoffed. I said, 'Could I see it?' When he asked why, I produced a copy of the engraving from *The Book of Hours* and provided a potted history of the case."

"How'd he react?"

"Again, as I had hoped. His interest increased considerably. He hadn't known that an engineer had owned the Queen before Sir David. I confessed a strong urge to touch the key that 'gave life' to the object of our mutual passion. Tashjian agreed without a moment's hesitation. Reaching for his belt, he—"

"Wait a sec, Mr. Jesson. On the tape you said that her key was *not* on his belt."

"The key he reached for, Alexander, opened a supply closet."

"Oh," I said. "Sorry I interrupted."

"Amid cleaning products and paper towels were two dozen leather boxes, some large enough to hold carriage clocks, others so small they could be hidden in one's fist. Tashjian pulled out a delicious case covered in red morocco. Despite my disdain for incomplete compartments, I must confess this one was a gem. And I couldn't help but marvel at the craftsmanship of the spare hands, dials, and winding key. Tashjian had a different response. For him the leather box was the cradle of a kidnapped child."

From across the cloister came renewed tapping. Andrews was again banging against the French doors.

"What about the plan?" I pressed.

"Sorry, Alexander. I must go."

"But—"

"All in good time. The fellow who handles reservations at my club is famously unforgiving."

37

THE ANSWERING MACHINE was blinking in pentameter when I got home. I played back the messages, hoping one of them would be Jesson saying he'd had a change of heart and had canceled the match at his club.

No such luck. The first call turned out to be Nic, informing me she'd be out very late. The next was a promotional recording promising instant wealth. The third message was from my parents regarding holiday plans. There weren't any, at least none that involved me. They'd decided to visit the friends with the daughter-in-law who'd booked the lacemaker suite where Nic and I fought as newlyweds. The fourth call took me by surprise.

"Hello? This message is for Mr. Short. It's Miss Barton. From the Art Theft Archive? You might wish to come over. I have something I believe you've been looking for."

Could this be the same Miss Barton who had (almost) with-held access to the archive's proprietary files? Maybe her colleague had finally returned to work. If so, why hadn't *she* been the one to call? And how did Miss Barton know where to reach me?

The fifth and final message also came from Miss Barton. "The switchboard closes promptly at five and I have absolutely no intention of waiting for you downstairs."

Now *that* was the Miss Barton I remembered.

My initial impulse was to contact Jesson and have him meet me. But given all the earlier slip-ups, it seemed wise not to count chickens.

I made it to the archive just as the guard who loved the ponies was locking the outer gate.

"You," he said.

"Miss Barton called. I'm expected."

"Didn't sign out last time," the guard grumbled, as he let me in.

"Won't make that mistake again." I went straight to the visitor's book.

The guard locked me between the inner and outer gates of the foyer and headed for the ancient switchboard. When he returned, he was wearing an overcoat and had a *Racing Form* clutched in his hand.

"Miss B. says you're to wait here. Says she'll be right down." He waved his tip sheet at me. "And son? I don't like my Ins missing Outs, understand?"

Miss Barton wasn't in a rush, so I passed the time flipping

through the visitor's book. That cleared up one mystery: how Miss Barton had known where to reach me. (I had written down my address.) But the larger question—why it was I'd been summoned—made me incredibly antsy. I girdled some notes on two of the more unusual entries in the ledger—the Honorable Makepeace Glass-Coffin and the Heaven's Gate Elevator Repair Company—recalling as I did a Sharansky lecture on the social markers buried in penmanship. The professor had predicted the "cursive clues to class" would disappear with the rise of keyboard use. The handwriting in the log seemed to challenge his hypothesis.

A motor kicked in. An elevator light lengthened along the club's marble floor. Then, abruptly, the motor stopped. The resulting silence was soon broken by the furious jiggling of metal.

"Damn scissor gate," said Miss Barton when at last she appeared, hair in a tangle, her cameo askew.

"You have my sympathies," I said. "That thing held me hostage last time I came."

"Mr. Short, I have an urgent fax to send. I didn't come down to chitchat."

"More stolen spoons?"

Miss Barton smiled politely. "A Klimt, if you must know."

I reached for the handle of the gate.

"Don't bother. I've brought it with me."

"You have?"

"Don't sound so shocked, Mr. Short."

"How did you track it down?"

"If you must know, I tripped over it."

"You're very modest, Miss Barton."

"Not too modest to show you the bruise." She pointed at her shin.

"You hurt yourself looking for the Breguet?"

"The Breguet?" Miss Barton gave me a queer look. "I already told you. Breguets are Vivien's domain. And, by the way, she's *still* out. It's a wonder I get *any*thing done."

"So why the messages telling me to hotfoot it over?"

I felt a stab in my thigh.

"*That's* what you meant?" The stress of covert photocopying (not to mention the pressure to prepare Nic's birthday meal) had made me forget to reclaim Jesson's umbrella.

"I found it under the dormer," Miss Barton said as she slipped the thing through the gate. "Wouldn't want to be accused of theft." She let out an odd little laugh. "Now, if you'll excuse me. I've got a Klimt that needs inputting."

"Of course." I did my best not to seem disappointed.

"Next time, leave the rain gear downstairs. I'm surprised Franklin didn't tell you." Miss Barton turned and headed for the staircase.

At least I hadn't called Jesson. The misinterpreted phone messages plus the forgotten umbrella would not have gone over well. After signing out—I saw no reason to annoy Franklin further—I somehow managed to knock the visitor's book to the floor by hooking the handle of the umbrella on a table leg. As I was putting the book back, something brought me up short.

What the hell!

My stomach knotted.

The lettering grabbed my attention before I'd even read the name. The bold ascenders and tapering exit strokes were un-

mistakable. Yet the date beside the signature preceded my archive visit by a full nine months.

Calm down, I told myself. *There must be an explanation.*
I rattled the gate, but Miss Barton was long gone.

The foyer started closing in. Panicked, I ripped out the
incriminating page and fled, enraged by the deception that the
signature implied. A few blocks away, I plunged Jesson's umbrella into a trash can and headed back to the library.

38

NORTON SAW INSTANTLY that something wasn't right. "Boy, you look like shit. Dinty on your case again?"

"It's not Dinty. And do me a favor, don't mention the word *case*."

I showed Norton the page with Jesson's name.

"Isn't that Mr. Secret Compartments?"

"Look when he signed in."

"So?"

"Don't you get it?"

Norton imitated the sound of radio static and said, "That's a negative. Over."

"If Jesson was at the archive investigating the Queen way back then it means he knew about the theft before I did. If that's true, he's every bit the fake Nic said he was."

"Maybe he went there for some other loony reason."

"Doubtful, especially since he was trying to keep me away from the place. Probably got worried I'd find out about his earlier visit."

Norton ran a finger along the ripped edge of the page. "Novel method of data collection. I'm not sure Grote would approve."

"When I saw Jesson's name, I guess I just lost it."

"So it seems. What's Mr. Trinomial saying in his defense?"

"I haven't confronted him yet. I wanted to make sense of things first. Christ, I've been thick."

"Stop beating yourself up. Error comes with the territory. Besides, you still don't know what the signature means. The guy could have an honest, logical explanation."

"Logical, maybe. Honest? I don't think so."

"Okay then," said Norton. "Let's approach the question from there. Suppose he did know about the watch. Why the shenanigans?"

"Beats me. But if he *was* aware of the crime before he hired me, he also knew about *The Book of Hours*. That would mean we broke into Grote's lab for no reason."

"Red light. You can't assume Jesson had prior knowledge about a book containing an image of an object that got stolen even if he did know about the status of that object."

"I lost you there, Norton. All I know is that a lot doesn't add up. For example, why was Jesson unable to identify the engraving when I first showed it to him? He already owns a Breguet. Surely he should have made the connection. For a man with his erudition that lapse seems more than a little suspect."

"Wait!" Norton shouted. He looked at me as though he'd

hacked through the firewall of a seemingly impregnable main-frame. "Remember when the FBI came poking around Reference?"

"Before my time."

"The edited version is this. A couple of G-men showed up and tried to peddle something they called the Library Awareness Program. Major euphemism. What they wanted was for the tube clerks and reference staff to rat out researchers with suspicious-sounding names who requested sensitive material. Every time a Molotov, O'Malley, or Mohammed put in a slip for *How to Build a Better Bomb* we were supposed to call the local field office."

"I can't see that going over very well."

"Everyone went ballistic. Even Dinty objected, though less on ethical grounds than on administrative ones. He didn't see how we could do the cross-checks given the existing budget. Eventually the scheme caught the attention of the House Subcommittee on Civil and Constitutional Rights, which trashed it."

"I don't see where you're taking this."

"I'll tell you where," said Norton. "The FBI's crackpot plan may have been scary, but the logic behind it was sound. Knowing what readers read reveals what they're up to."

"I already know Jesson's private library better than this one."

"That's my point, lamebrain. We haven't checked what he looked for right here. We've been casting our net in the wrong waters."

"Cripes!" Norton's reasoning finally sank in. I said, "You take pixels, I'll take print, and we'll meet at the Blarney Stone after the final bell."

"The sonofabitch knew all along," I told Norton.

"Hold on to that thought. Let's order first. I've got news of my own."

Once we'd grabbed a spot at the bar, Norton let me vent. "You know how we've always disagreed over the utility of call slips? Well, take a look at this one." I pushed the form across the counter.

"*The Book of Hours,*" said Norton matter-of-factly.

"With Jesson's goddamn John Hancock running right along the bottom. You don't exactly sound surprised."

"I'm not. Where'd you pull it?"

"The records annex. Ever been? It's like that scene in *Miracle on 34th Street* where they prove Kris Kringle is Father Christmas by dragging in bag after bag of mail addressed to Santa Claus. If Jesson didn't have such incredible handwriting, I'd never have found this."

Norton took a swig of his beer. "My turn now?"

"Fire away."

He reached into his plastic grocery sack and pulled out a sheaf of printouts. "I believe we have been underestimating your patron by a couple of orders of magnitude. I took my search back farther than yours. To before we broke into the lab. To before Jesson even asked you about *Secret Compartments.*"

"But that was his first query."

"Correction. That was the first query he made to *you.*" Norton slid a printout toward me. "Read 'em and weep. A list of every book called up by Henry James Jesson III."

"So much for Dinty's confidentiality guidelines." I scanned

the list. "Jesus! He knew about *Slips of Love* before we met?"

"You got it. That intellectual kismet you thought the two of you shared? All orchestrated. The man's been tracking you for months."

Norton was right. The reading list proved that Jesson had been studying me by studying the books I studied. He'd apparently worked through *Slips of Love* with the diligence of a graduate student. All my interests—Samuel Johnson and fore-edge painting, calligraphy and *Gulliver*—were represented in the books he'd requested.

"And to think I was impressed by his learning. 'Is that a Pitman of some kind?' That's what he asked me when I showed him my girdle book. What a phony!"

"One thing's obvious. He's used your *Slips* to seduce you."

"But why? I'd have pursued his case without the charade."

"Are you sure?" Norton drained his beer and waved for another. "Could *he* have been sure?"

The bartender, a raven-haired woman, gave me a salacious wink as she swapped our bottles. Norton must have noticed.

"And Nic?" he said. "When are you going to tell her?"

"Not until I know what Jesson's up to. I want to be ready for her French I-told-you-sos."

39

JESSON SEATED US at the chess table. "I apologize again about dashing like that. Club rules, alas, are writ in stone."

"It's almost as if you know."

"Excuse me?"

"The game board. The queens. It's all *too* perfect."

"It is, indeed," he said with a nervous smile. "Though Mother would have fined you a nickel for the faulty superlative."

I reached into my pocket and found a dime. I walked it over to the candy dish. "Keep the change."

When I sat back down, Jesson said, "I told you I'm sorry, but I did have a match." He feigned a backhand and inadvertently knocked over a pawn.

"That's not what's bothering me." I dropped the page from the visitor's book onto the chessboard.

Jesson picked it up and read through the names. At first he showed no reaction, but then he slumped, his hand still clutching the scrap, like Marat in that famous painting. Without looking at me or even lifting his head, he said, "I feared something like this. Have you only just found out?"

"I didn't come here to answer questions."

"Fair enough. I should never have signed the archive ledger. As soon as I realized my misstep, I did what I could to keep you away. Hence the call from Vienna. I didn't want you finding out what I already knew about the watch."

"You lied to me, Mr. Jesson."

"I never lied, Alexander. At worst I kept silent about certain wrongheaded inquiries made prior to our partnership."

"Give me some credit. The trip to the Art Theft Archive hasn't been your only omission." I placed the call slip for *The Book of Hours* on the board. "You knew about the later edition of the *Chronicle* long before I did. There was never any reason for me to sneak the damn thing out of the library."

"Stop right there," said Jesson. "It's true I was aware of the book's existence. But do not for a single second consider your intervention gratuitous. The book was off-limits. I'd have waited *months* to inspect it if I hadn't prompted you to intervene."

"*Prompted* me?"

"With the clumsy reference I made to *first* editions. You needed a little nudge, so I nudged. Let's be honest here—you weren't having much luck finding the book on your own."

"Why didn't you tell me what you needed instead of sending me on a wild-goose chase?"

"Fascinating phrase, that. *Stricto sensu*, the goose represents—"

"Stop!"

"No need to raise your voice. I told you from the start I wouldn't burden you with my failed investigations. You may not like that decision, but it isn't one I kept secret. As for my diversionary impulses, you knew those were part of the package, too. Could I have been more direct? Of course. But I assumed you'd prefer the risky pleasures of the corniche to the undeviating predictability of the interstate."

I replied to Jesson's tangled self-justification by slapping down my final indictment, the printout documenting his library requests.

He gave the list the once-over. "So you know I studied your work before we ever met. You should be flattered."

"Well, I'm not."

"Suppose, for the sake of argument, I had been more frank. Say I had walked straight up to the reference desk and said, 'Excuse me, young man. A watch has been stolen. Please help me recover it to satisfy a private longing.' Would you have agreed to help?"

"Stated that way, probably not."

"Nor would you have been willing to retrieve *The Book of Hours* from the clutches of that Grote fellow if I hadn't drawn you in. When I saw you taking notes near the desk—this was before we'd even spoken—I had a hunch you'd be an ideal helpmate. That hunch spurred me to ask around about you. One of your colleagues mentioned *Slips of Love*. After I'd read through it I knew I had found my Bozzy."

"Why didn't you just tell me you liked my book?"

"I worried the enthusiasm of a stranger might offend."

"What I find offensive, Mr. Jesson, is that you made me replicate your research from scratch."

"You did more than replicate, Alexander. You provided invaluable innocence. Knowing of my efforts would have circumscribed yours. Valéry was right when he said ignorance is a much-neglected treasure."

"You're joking."

"Not at all. Think back to the first time you saw the case. You told me it reminded you of a discovery box that addressed the question 'What Am I Made Of?' I could never have distilled the essence of our challenge so beautifully. And why is that? Because my perspective had turned as murky as the fluid in the jar that sits in the case."

"Nothing you're saying explains away the lies. For all I know, Mr. Jesson, *you* stole the watch!"

"Would that I had, Alexander. If only I could say, '*Voilà la Marie Antoinette!*' Unfortunately, you grossly overestimate my capacities, if not my desires. Again, I apologize if my omission and prevarication distressed you." He looked down at the chessboard and chuckled.

"Am I missing something?"

"I seem to recollect a similar skirmish between Boswell and Johnson. They, too, fought about matters of candor and influence. Do you remember how they cleared the air?"

"No."

Jesson reached for the black queen and wiggled it.

"I don't recall any mention of chess in the *Life*."

"A quick match."

"Enough games. Tell me about the plan you hatched in Jerusalem."

Jesson pushed a pawn to the middle of the board. "I'll

give you the complete rundown while we play. Your move."

Grudgingly, I advanced a piece.

"A double king-pawn opening, eh? To that I say, knight to king's bishop 3."

I again copied his move. "The *plan*, Mr. Jesson."

"Imitation is the sincerest form of flattery, Alexander, but it can be carried to extremes. I suggest you reconsider your tactics. Symmetry is a dangerous gambit."

"Fine." I knocked over my king. "Return *The Book of Hours* and I'll be on my way."

As I started to stand, Jesson yanked me back. Taking hold of my hands, he pushed them down on a king and a pawn. "We must advance to Philidor's defense."

"What the hell for?"

"Bear with me." Jesson pressed on my hands even harder.

"Stop! You'll break the table."

He ignored the warning, applying greater and greater force.

"You're hurting me and damaging the board, Mr. Jesson. Let go!"

He kept pushing.

"Mr. Jesson!"

When I finally pulled free, his eyes were locked on mine and he was smiling mischievously, the spikes of his canines poking out of his mouth.

And then the whirring started.

"What's that?"

I touched the side of the table and felt a faint vibration. Only as the top of the board lifted did I realize that our hand pressure had triggered a mechanism. Two hidden doors began to angle upward, like the spans of a model drawbridge.

Nothing in Jesson's arsenal of secret compartments had prepared me for this. As the game board opened, the chess pieces slid to the edge of the table on their green felted bottoms.

While the chessmen toppled to the carpet, Jesson recited a few lines of poetry I later learned came from Blake:

> *The cabinet is formed of gold*
> *And pearl and crystal shining bright,*
> *And within it opens into a world*
> *And a little lovely moony night.*

I tried to peer inside the table before the doors were fully upright, but a pair of thumb-notched ivory sliders blocked my view.

Jesson couldn't conceal his delight. "I love the pacing, don't you, Alexander? If the cabinetmaker had opted for a prosaic spring catch, the effect would have been too much like a jack-in-the-box. Reduction gears and flywheels are vastly superior. They calibrate the velocity of revelation to perfection."

He was still playing games, that was obvious. But the beauty of the mechanism dissolved a lot of my anger and Jesson's pleasure got rid of the rest. Winking and rubbing his hands together like a cartoon criminal preparing to divvy up loot, he said, "Go on, Alexander. I insist you do the honors."

I parted the ivory sliders. The sight of an antique brass handle accelerated the velocity of revelation considerably; I lifted the box from the hollow of the table and undid its question-mark latch.

"I know what you're thinking," said Jesson. "Another empty case. Don't dismiss the piece too quickly. Explore its lining. Touch the spare dials, the hands, the key. Do so and you will feel, as I have, the residual radiance of the Queen."

"If it's all the same, I'd prefer an explanation about how you got Tashjian to give this to you. I assume it comes from the institute."

"It does, though I must correct you on one point. Tashjian did not *give* it to me. It's only—what was that marvelous phrase you once used?—an unauthorized loan of a temporary nature."

"Even if this box did house the Queen, who's going to care? Certainly not a thief."

Jesson frowned. "Do not presume thief and current owner are one and the same. There's a chance the person now in possession of the watch doesn't even know of the crime. Whatever the circumstances, putting the box up for sale will stimulate talk—that much is certain. The only thing collectors like better than an object in mint condition is one that is mint in box."

"You just said Tashjian loaned it to you."

"He did—with the understanding that it would be used to revive the search. I told him I'd float a rumor that the Mayer is selling off some of its holdings. Buyer discretion essential. That should stir things up."

"Neither one of us knows a thing about selling a watch, let alone a watch box."

"True. But we know someone who does, thanks to you."

It took a moment to figure out where this was going. "You mean Ornstein? He's totally untrustworthy."

"So much the better. As long as you provide monetary reward, greed will overwhelm judgment. It always does. Just secure approval rights, to ensure that I am the ultimate buyer. That way we get the box back, plus we learn who's interested in it and why."

"Say I go along with this. How would it look? First I tell Ornstein I'm interested in the Marie Antoinette. Then I return and tell him I want to sell a box that once housed her?"

Jesson mulled over my qualms. "You have a point. Still, from what you've told me about Ornstein, he seems predisposed to suspend ethical consideration for the right price."

"This is getting awfully complicated. And you haven't addressed the most obvious question."

"That being?"

"There is this box, which belongs to the institute." I wiggled the brass handle. "And there is the case, which belongs to you. Two enclosures, one watch. What happens if by some miracle we do find the Marie Antoinette? Which throne gets her?"

"Try being a bit more positive, Alexander. *When* we find the Queen she will be returned to the institute, assuming, of course, that is where she legally belongs. But relocation to Jerusalem in no way precludes first fulfilling our mission."

"A short-term reign in the case would satisfy you?"

"If you ask an enthusiast of jigsaw puzzles to explain his habit, he'll tell you what he loves is the process. Once all the pieces are in place, the puzzle retains little interest."

"That's hard to buy coming from the man who hates empty spaces."

"I'd forfeit possession only if necessary."

"That 'if' makes me uneasy."

"It shouldn't," said Jesson. He picked up the leather box and opened it. "Take a whiff."

"Sorry?"

"Take a whiff. I want you to smell a fragrance more enchanting than the finest perfume."

I stuck my nose inside. "Mildew," I said. "With a trace of what I'm guessing is neat's-foot oil."

"Try again, only this time close your eyes and forgo the sarcasm."

As I inhaled, Jesson said, "What you are smelling is nothing less than the odor of sanctity, Alexander. And there's no need to raise your eyebrows. I'm quite serious. The Egyptologist Howard Carter got a dose of it when he drilled into King Tut's tomb and was hit by its hot dynastic air. He writes of being overwhelmed by smell even before he caught the first glimmer of gold. And that peasant boy—the one who found the Dead Sea Scrolls? He was said to have received a similarly intoxicating blast when he broke open the clay jars in the cave.

"So once more, Alexander, take a good, deep whiff. And while you do think of the treasures of Tut and Qumran."

Eyes closed, I bent over the open leather box and again breathed in through my nose.

"Do you smell it now? Do you smell the scent of a mysterious past?"

Whether it was Jesson's oration, the desire to believe, or mild hyperventilation, I did seem to get, if only fleetingly, a small but potent whiff of wonder.

40

I FIGURED SOMETHING was up when I saw the hallway free of scraps and Nic, in the distance, stretched coyly on the futon. She was wearing her bull's-eye bodysuit.

"I know," she purred. "Norton called and left a message."

"About?"

"About Monsieur Jesson and *Slips of Love* and his lying about the watch. *Quel salaud!*"

"Norton needs an update."

"*En tout cas*, I knew before we spoke. The tarot never lie."

"Well, they did this time. Jesson and I cleared the air. He's explained why he kept mum about his earlier probes."

"Was he furious you walked away?"

"You're not listening, Nic. I'm still working for him. I can tell why if—"

"*Je m'en fiche!*"

"Well, you *should* give a damn. Jesson managed to track down a leather box that once housed the Marie Antoinette. We'll be using it to bait a trap."

"You think it's the watch he is after?"

"I know Jesson's ambitions probably extend beyond time-pieces. But you want to know something, Nic? So do mine."

From there, things went from bad to worse. It may have been Nic who had the bull's-eye on her body, but I became the target. She released a torrent of French invective that, though defying exact translation, can be rendered with painful simplicity: *It's* my *interests you should be satisfying, not his. And if you can't, then get the hell out!*

Less than an hour after eviction, I parted the beaded curtain of the Crystal Palace and bought six tokens from a tout in a greasy leather apron.

There are, I'm guessing, nicer strip joints, and cleaner ones as well. But in terms of kilowatts of kinkiness, the Crystal Palace seemed the perfect place to disprove Nic's charge of *impuissance.*

"Check it out," the token man exclaimed, all but pushing me into a mirrored room dominated by an elevated runway that reminded me of the catwalk in the Reading Room—except that ours had never accommodated (not even during the wild-est of postinventory staff parties) a trio of strippers dancing to an instrumental rendition of "Superstition."

"Hey there, par'ner, up for a good time?"

The cowgirl who'd been so solicitous on my earlier visit approached, spurs jangling. She smiled broadly, put her arm through mine, guided me into a dim little booth, and disappeared from view. A moment later, her voice was squawking through a loudspeaker bolted to the wall.

"Slip in a token, and let's have us some fun." She punctuated the proposition with a down-home Texas holler.

I did what I was told and discovered that feeding the coin box raised a metal screen and revealed the cowgirl on the far side of a plateglass wall. She was straddling a gymnast's vaulting horse that had a phallus attached to its spine. A shelf of whips and branding irons reinforced the ranch motif, as did the soundtrack, an improbably high-toned and dated cast recording of *Annie Get Your Gun.*

Off came the fringed skirt and matching vest as the cowgirl performed a private act of erotic bronco busting. Just as she was preparing to remove her G-string, the metal screen came clattering down.

I fed in another token. The screen went up and the G-string flew off, only to reveal a smaller triangle of leather. Even after it and two more wedges of doeskin dropped to the floor, the cowgirl bucked on energetically, her crotch now covered only by a tin badge.

Stripped of her costume—save the strategically positioned star, the Stetson, and the boots with jangling spurs—the cowgirl galloped and yippee-ay-ayed until the metal screen again rolled shut.

"You slottin' in another, par'ner?"

The shutter rose once more and the cowgirl, having finished her rodeo show, now posed near the shelf of implements.

"How 'bout if I have some fun with this?" She reached for a leather whip.

I declined.

"This?" She held up a lasso and explained its use in a spectacle called "The Roundup."

I said no to the lasso as well.

"This?" She showed me a branding iron tipped with an XXX, part of "The Cowpoke," a six-token performance she assured me didn't hurt much.

"No, thank you."

"Par'ner, ya sure ya want what I can give?"

I shook my head and sighed. "This was a mistake."

"Hey, no problem," she said, abruptly dropping the southern drawl. "I could kind of tell before we started. Your mind's somewhere else."

41

THE JUDAS HOLE slid open.

"Alexander? This is a surprise." Jesson gazed through the small window of Festinalente's lacquered door.

"Am I intruding?"

"Andrews is off doing the marketing, but of course not."

"You're sure?"

Jesson smiled benevolently and quoted a well-known line from the *Life*: "'Come to me, my dear Bozzy, and let us be as happy as we can.'" The window slot shut and the door unlocked. "You look awfully glum. Does that overnight bag imply you're seeking asylum?"

"Nic and I are going through a rough patch."

"You poor soul. I'll have Andrews prepare a berth the moment he returns."

Jesson's take on the apartment skirmish, and my ineffectual reaction to it, wasn't what I expected. "A window girl in a crystal palace? That's certainly one for the girdle book."

The next note I took down was not about enclosure, however; it addressed the reference to a "berth." The reason for the nautical vocabulary became clear once Andrews showed me to my room. A whistle sounded as I was peering through a porthole down into the cloister.

I turned and found the butler pointing at a black tin-rimmed funnel to the left of a cleat. I cupped a hand around the mouthpiece and shouted, "Mr. Jesson?"

"How do you like the accommodations?"

"Shipshape," I said.

"The fittings were all salvaged from an ocean liner my father purchased for scrap."

"Where *are* you?" I shouted into the cone.

"In the theater. Join me as soon as you've freshened up."

The raised platform was again reconfigured. This time, the palanquin had been pushed to one side, allowing my porter's chair to face the toy stage front and center. Between the two pieces was an antique tray table set with a bowl of lumpy mush.

"Oatmeal?" I said, thoughts locking onto the library paste McCarkle kept on his desk.

"Porridge," Jesson corrected.

"Aren't you joining me?"

"No," he said, as he tinkered with some miniature backdrops. "I've had my supper. Roast duckling, braised endive, and a caramelized apricot tart." I kept quiet while he tested the pulley weights. "I thought a little performance might divert you from your marital difficulties," said Jesson. "Feel free to eat while watching."

Terrific—dinner theater. "What's on?"

"A work suitably teeming with theft. How's the porridge, by the way?"

"Reminds me of Mr. McCarkle," I said without elaborating.

"I'll take that as a compliment however you might have meant it. And incidentally, an explanation is in order. I was unable to obtain decent treacle. Had to settle for molasses, which diminishes the pleasing *twist* I wanted this show to provide."

Jesson moved around to the front of the cardboard stage and lit the tiny footlights. The room quickly filled with a nutty aroma.

"Can I do something?"

"In a moment," he said monkeying with the props. "Would you do the honors?"

I reached over and tugged the drawstring to raise the Lilliputian curtain. In the spot where the case of curiosities usually resided there was now a painted backdrop of a cobbled street filled with narrow, crooked houses.

"Very nineteenth century," I said.

"One might even call it *Dickensian*, eh?"

"Oh, of course." The allusions finally registered.

Jesson's grinning face emerged above the chimney pots. "About time."

Oliver Twist held a special place in my private library of favorite works. For years I'd fantasized that my own orphanhood would be resolved as Oliver's is—by the intervention of a kindly benefactor offering nothing short of salvation. "Do you know how much I love that book?"

"Naturally. There's an Everyman's edition of *Oliver Twist* listed in your *Slips*."

Jesson did an okay job manipulating the characters. Was he at times more sentimental than I might have liked? Sure. But it was Dickens, after all. Treacle is part of the fare. What I found less plausible was the way the puppet master struggled to tease out the flimsy connections between his theatrical ef- forts and the facts surrounding our search. When Jesson brought Fagin onstage, he made direct reference to Emmanuel Ornstein and said he hoped the watch dealer would prove to be as constructively corrupt.

Ornstein buzzed me in.

"I'm back," I announced.

"And for what?"

I removed the red leather box from my satchel and placed it on the counter. Ornstein scratched his jaw, then lowered his loupe from forehead to eye and undid the question-mark catch. His features fell when he discovered the box was empty.

"This you bring me?"

"This *this* once held the Queen, Mr. Ornstein."

His interest picked up. "And you're here because . . ."

"I want you to find a buyer."

"For the box?"

"For the box."

"Empty?"

"Empty. The Mayer has decided to deaccession it. They've given up on recovering the Queen."

"You vont I should believe that?"

"What I *want* is someone to sell this discreetly." I spelled out the conditions of sale, explaining I would need to see a list of all interested parties and approve the final transaction.

"Mister, the sign outside, it says, 'Timepieces bought and sold.' You see the verd *boxes*? You see the verd *informer*?"

"You told me you hear things. Now's your chance to prove it. My terms are nonnegotiable."

After some back and forth on the matter of the commission, we reached an agreement. Ornstein removed the key from under his yarmulke and unlocked the floor safe, placed the leather box inside, wrote up a receipt, and buzzed me out of the shop.

On the street, I stopped to take a few notes and discovered my girdle book was about full. Pleased at how I'd handled the Ornstein exchange, I stopped in at an upscale stationer and purchased a stunning octavo notebook with a binding that opened flat.

42

MONDAY—Talk about turning over a new leaf! A new journal for a new life. That's the thinking I'm trying to embrace. In truth, retiring the girdle book has been nothing if not painful. I'm still tied to it, and its creator, even though I've unknotted the bootlace and placed the thing out of view. It's a lot harder to close the book *on* Nic than it is the one *by* her, but I've decided to let things cool off and to take advantage of J.'s hospitality, which comes with fewer strings.

It's time for radical change. Hence the day-by-day entries. No more alphabetical subject headings. No more artificial rubrics. From now on, I record things as they happen.

Maybe the expression I used a few lines up should be *turning over an old leaf*, considering how amazingly time-locked Festinalente can feel. The Upper West Side samba (*Santo Do-*

mingo, Caracas, Miami, Divorce) is a world and two centuries away from the plinking of Jesson's harpsichord, which I can hear as I write this. I take these notes by the light of a spill-proof oil lantern and wait for a ship's whistle to call me down to the dinner. Tonight we're having fricassee of rabbit, a choice inspired by a coffeehouse exchange J. found cited in the *Life*. "I believe the choice commendable," J. told me. "Alas, I had to scratch the green beans from the menu. I fear flageolets incite uncontrolled iliac passion." Maybe I should write up a guidebook to the language and customs of Festinalente, complete with Jesson/English dictionary. There could be chapters such as "How Coffee Is Served," "How Baths Are Drawn," "How Wood Is Arranged in the Fireplace," and "Educating Guests." The last chapter (the longest) would detail, among other things, the proper grip of knife and fork when peeling Anjou pears, the necessity of cedar shoe trees, and the vulgar ubiquity of Kleenex.

TUESDAY—Transcription of the Ornstein visit complete. J. vets my work and bestows approval, then informs me he's convinced the watch dealer will lead us to the Queen. I'm less confident. After we exhaust the topic, J. plucks an ivory game cube the size of an orange from a side table and hands it to me for inspection. Each of the surfaces is etched with an image. There's a bell, a ring, a dagger . . . J. provides the object's whenceabouts (early nineteenth century, bought at an estate sale in Devon) and produces a nifty duodecimo copy of Hoyle, half-bound in calf and tarted up with gold-speckled endpapers. He flips to the page outlining the rules. Each player must roll the "story die" no fewer than five times and from the images tossed construct a credible tale. Ten minutes into the game I concede defeat; it's clear I'm no match for J. As Nic might say, *Quelle surprise.*

Damn! Following the principle that a new notebook should reflect a new life, I was hoping to keep Nic at bay. Unfortunately, that's not possible. Even though I've ceased to girdle, there are still three Es—eviction, exile, and estrangement—that poison my thinking constantly.

WEDNESDAY— Get back from work to find Andrews, at the fireplace, arranging kindling in a cone, like the stakes of a tepee. J. abhors the use of crumpled newspaper, and has banned all woods but cedar. (I should consider adding a chapter of "Don'ts" to the Festinalente guidebook. Objects kept from this duchy, besides pine logs, include: tie pins, money clips, television, fluorescent lighting, paperbacks, any cheese wrapped in plastic, and, as I've already mentioned, Kleenex.

We spend the evening reading by the fire. It's a scene worthy of Cruikshank. J. sits bolt upright, his face thrown into relief by the flames from the chimney and the glow of the hurricane lantern resting on a stack of books. There's a history of keyholes (2 vols., ill., 1895), a short text by Paracelsus on surgery (in Latin), a sales catalog for an upcoming auction of French music boxes, a monograph called *The Art of Fencing,* yet another treatise on secret compartments, a study of magic called *Hocus-Pocus, oder Kurtzweilige Taschen-Spieler,* and, at the base of the learned mountain, a history of the carnival sideshow bearing the beguiling title *Learned Pigs and Fire-proof Women*. And what's on *my* reading list? *Modified Keyboard Configurations for OCLC Subject Searches*.

Around ten, J. turns to me and quotes a passage from *The Art of Fencing*, which until then I've assumed concerns swordplay: "'Stolen art and antiques are often relegitimated through the conduit of the dealer/fence, an individual who, in bringing together legal and black-market goods, is able to mask illicit trade.'"

THURSDAY—While I'm not completely sure, I think someone's been rifling through my stuff. Just found this diary on top of the girdle book instead of the other way around. My best guess is that Andrews got curious while he was fluffing the pillows. Not that I'm overly concerned. Tachygraphic shorthand is almost impossible to decipher without a proper handbook.

FRIDAY—I say to J., when I arrive home from the library, "TGIF." He looks at me as if I'm speaking Urdu. "It's short for 'Thank God it's Friday.'" His mystification is so astonishing I give him a little test. I ask if he's heard of John Lennon, Mick Jagger, or Michael Jackson. "Only Jackson," he says. "Wrote a fine ethnography on African shape shifters." J. reads Latin, French, and German, quotes Valéry, Blake, and Boswell, but when it comes to popular culture he scores a perfect Dunkin' Donut. I think that's why I like him as much as I do.

I suggested a few days ago that Festinalente is a foreign country, with its own customs and language. But the tempo is also unique. Time expands around here. There are more minutes in each hour, more hours in each day. I'm not entirely sure why, but Jesson Standard Time allows greater opportunity to think and read and pun and plot. Part of the reason, of course, is money. Wealth has freed J. of an entire class of chores. I've never seen him pay a bill or shop for food. He has no dishes to wash, no beds to make—or *not* wash and *not* make, which also takes up time. In domestic matters, he does little besides press buzzers. He sees almost no one, preferring to spend his days in hushed communion with books and objects. For the rest of the world, time may be money; for J., it's the other way around.

SATURDAY—The wait is intolerable. Why hasn't Ornstein called? I get so fed up I grab a cab to the Diamond District while J. is taking his late-morning bath. As soon as I reach the gemstone-shaped lampposts on Forty-seventh Street, I know I've wasted my time. There's no commercial bustle and most of the jewelry-store windows are stripped of their glitter. I catch a cab back, furious with myself for having forgotten about the Sabbath.

  J. is still soaking when I return. He calls me in to discuss the case. I find him in the tub, squinting at an ancient thermometer chained to the soap dish. J. insists on maintaining the bath water precisely fifteen degrees above "blood heat," his phrase for what most of us call body temperature. ("How Baths Are Drawn," *op. cit.*). After fiddling with the taps, he adds some colorless oil, closes his eyes, and slides down, causing his knees, two gray, wrinkly islands, to poke up above the water level. I tell him about my impetuous cab ride and he responds sympathetically, saying he shares my impatience. When he's finished bathing he asks for help getting out of the tub. With one leg out and one leg in, J. slips. Thrown off balance, he flails and grabs for the closest thing he can reach, which turns out to be my groin. I recoil but still manage to catch him before he tumbles. It takes a split second to redirect his pruney fingers to the towel rack, but the awkwardness of the grope lingers. J. mumbles an apology, which I nervously accept before leaving the room, the obscene sucking sound of the drain accompanying my hasty exit.

SUNDAY—J. and I spend two hours planning the upcoming "sale." We decide the following: J. will go into the shop first, present himself as a prospective buyer, and coax Ornstein, if any coaxing is necessary, to show him the leather box. He will negotiate a price and leave. Then I will enter and ask for an update. Separate inquiries in that order will let us evaluate the integrity of our middleman. Only after Ornstein has given me the names of all interested parties will I allow the box to be sold.

MONDAY—From beyond the pyramidal sign, which offers a clear sight line but keeps me out of view, I watch J. enter Ornstein's shop. Obviously I can't hear what's said, but the way his body moves suggests the dealer is anxious, and that makes *me* anxious. If he hasn't had any nibbles our suspect list becomes nonexistent.

Three minutes into the meeting, Ornstein opens the safe, withdraws the box, and places it on the counter. J. controls his reactions perfectly, making sure to lift the brass handle tentatively, though he knows it's perfectly secure, fumbling with the latch as if he's never touched it, though he's done so dozens of times. When J. finally opens the box he displays the agitation of the collector who's stumbled on something rare.

As for Ornstein, all the forced grins, nervous bows, and hand wringing suggest we're dealing not with Fagin but with Uriah Heep. He focuses his loupe on the keypad of a calculator, and after a few offers and counteroffers the two men seem to agree on a price. J. leaves the shop and shuffles over to my blind. "There are no other buyers," he tells me. "The man may be willing to dispose of a leather box, no questions asked, but that appears to be the extent of his dishonesty. We've agreed on a price, but he said he needs the okay of his 'associate' before he can authorize sale."

Something amazing happens as we're finishing up the post-mortem. A man with unnaturally white skin enters the shop. Ornstein is suddenly retrieving the box. J. is beside himself: "A suspect! At last! What do you think? Collector or thief?" I take a close look. "I doubt many Breguet aficionados go in for tattoos." J. doesn't understand. "His neck, Mr. Jesson. Can't you see the dragon rising out of the guy's collar?"

We consider our options and determine that J. should immediately go back. The three men confer for only a few minutes before J. leaves the shop and rejoins me. His face is as red as the box. "It can't be *that* bad," I say. "Oh no? Four thousand dollars is a lot to pay for an item that was mine from the start." "You're only out the commission. And at least you've got a name." "Guess again," he says. "Get in there and determine the thug's identity."

By the time I enter, our suspect is gone. "It's sold, thank you very much," Ornstein announces. I ask to whom and for how much, fully prepared to haggle. But the dealer quickly gives up J.'s name, stating the agreed-upon price truthfully. The Dickens comparisons have been unfair. Ornstein's neither Fagin nor Heep. The character he most resembles is reliable, honest Noddy Boffin. His integrity even extends to the commission, which he accepts only after writing up a proper receipt. Still, when I ask about other bidders, Ornstein bristles. "Look, Mr. Curious, I got you your sale. Vot more do you vont?" "Simple. The name of the man who almost bought the box." "It's sold. Be happy." "I'll be happy when I know about the other bidder." Ornstein fiddles with one of the watches strapped to his wrist. "He didn't give his name, just the card of the man he verks for." The dealer reaches under his yarmulke and extracts the card in question. He insists, as he did during our first encounter, on lowering the jeweler's loupe over his eye and laboring through the type. "Let's see vot this says here, Mr. Never-Takes-No-For-An-Answer. The fellow verks for . . . *S* as in Sam, *T* as in Time, *O* as in yours truly, *L* as in Luck, *Z* as in—"

I'm out the door before Ornstein has a chance to say Zircon. I tell J.: "The tattoo guy, you're not going to believe this, he works for Frederick Stolz!" The name doesn't register. "The only Stolz that comes to mind is the character in *Oblomov*." "Don't you remember the library I used to identify the Queen? It's *owned* by Stolz." J. says, "I seem to recall he collects more than books." "A lot more, Mr. Jesson." I take J.'s arm and drag him to the Automat, another Stolz acquisition. As we're walking there, I remind J. about the Arcade of Obsolescence and the much-publicized plan to fill it with items of technological rarity.

Soon J. is sharing my excitement: "First the private library, now the interest in the box. What would your wife say? *Jamais deux sans trois.* Maybe the third link will be the Queen herself!"

When we reach the restaurant, we find that most of the chrome hardware has already been packed off to Stolz's arcade. "Not what *I* would call an automat," J. sniffs. He's been expecting a different kind of automat, one resembling the toys in his gallery of mechanical wonders.

The lexical confusions don't end there. While we're heading back to Festinalente, eagerly plotting ways to connect with Stolz, J. accidentally calls me "Claude." When I ask him who Claude is, he seems thrown, if only for a moment. "Just a slip," he says. "A case of mistaken identity." I press but J. refuses to be drawn out. "Trust me, Claude is no one you would care to know. You'd find him depressing." "You said that about paradise, too. *And* the note roll." "Let's drop the matter, shall we? I much prefer to concentrate on Frederick Stolz and his Arcade of Obsolescence."

43

DIGGING UP MATERIAL on Stolz presented little difficulty given the scope of the man's achievements and his penchant for self-promotion. By the end of the week, I had compiled an inch-thick dossier, which I handed to Jesson as he sat in his palanquin. Probably the most telling item was the planning brochure for the arcade. It had a head shot on the cover that showed a pudgy man in his midforties, tiny eyes floating below a massive, almost primitive brow. The domelike expanse of Stolz's skull, which baldness made all the more prominent, paid homage—presumably unintended—to the curvilinear shape of the buildings pictured inside.

The brochure provided a brief biography of Stolz that boasted of his genius as a "high-tech rebel." Whereas most scientists of his caliber would have gravitated toward a university or some industry-supported think tank, Stolz trained his intellect entrepreneurially on "filling voids in the domain of digital imaging." His inventions, and the investments he made in the inventions of others, eventually put him in charge of three publicly traded companies with satellite offices in twenty-seven foreign cities, a half dozen major charities, a football franchise, and, most famously, the Arcade of Obsolescence.

Jesson pored over the printouts and photocopies for nearly two hours, only occasionally breaking the silence to marvel out loud at a particular newspaper article or quarterly report. "The man is absolutely *fixated* on timekeepers, isn't he?"

"Plus carnival games, automats—both your kind and mine—and automobiles, especially vintage Fords."

"Every one of those objects registers the *temporal* nature of technology. Stolz has the Queen, I'm sure of it. That's why he sent his henchman for the box."

"If you're saying he'd want the watch . . . well, sure. But that's a long way from proving he actually went to Jerusalem to swipe it. Passion doesn't make a thief."

"Are you sure? I am not arguing that Stolz *personally* broke into the institute. Still, even you must admit he could easily have gotten the job done."

"Why should I admit that?"

Jesson passed the brochure through the window of the sedan chair. "Open to the map on page four. Note the location of his Middle East branch."

I looked. "An office in Jerusalem hardly establishes his connection to the burglary, Mr. Jesson."

"What about that wire report you brought me? Didn't it mention the possibility of a commissioned crime?"

"And didn't Kimmelman say that hypothesis was ridiculous?"

"Fine. Even if Stolz didn't plan the break-in, having an office in Jerusalem does position him nicely to deal with thieves after the fact. And clearly the man has no scruples or he would never have had his goon try to buy the box from Ornstein."

We argued a little longer about the culpability of Frederick Stolz until Jesson tried to bolster his point with an improvised ditty:

Motive, means, mien
Stolz stole the Queen.

"Catchy but . . . if it's all the same, I'll reserve judgment until we meet the guy."

"Then let's work on doing just that."

"You've read the dossier," I said. "Any chance of you two crossing paths?"

"I haven't seen him at my racquet club or the Century, if that's what you mean."

"How about the Museum of Natural History? Stolz sits on their board. I must have pulled a dozen clips about the fundraising he's doing for them."

"Perfect. I'll have Andrews phone."

44

THE PHOTOGRAPHER FIDDLED with a knob, turning it one way, then the other, as he struggled to center four hominids—Jesson, Frederick Stolz, and a pair of diminutive wax-model Neanderthals—in the frame of his camera.

"You sir, with the yellow vest? Try putting your arm around Mr. Stolz. And can you loosen up just a wee bit?"

Jesson did his best to appear relaxed, but proximity to the man he believed had the Queen made him tense. The photographer played with his camera and eventually managed to situate the improbable quartet within the crosshairs of the viewfinder.

The largest of the upside-down group, Frederick Stolz, was a good deal bigger than I'd expected, all but dwarfing Jesson and the Paleolithic couple. And his head! Nothing—not even the picture on the cover of the arcade brochure—prepared me for the way Stolz's brow cantilevered over his face.

The unlikely photo session took place in one of the Museum of Natural History's fabled halls. When Andrews reported back that Stolz was hosting a benefit there, Jesson authorized a donation sizable enough to guarantee a personal meeting. Six days later we were listening to our suspect work a small crowd of donors.

"Folks. Thanks for coming tonight . . . and for bringing your checkbooks along. Stolz Industries—that's me, Fred Stolz—decided to help these guys out because we're always looking for ways to push the past into the future." He waved down the obligatory applause.

"This hall is just one of our projects. The Frederick R. Stolz Arcade of Obsolescence is another. And if I can give ourselves a plug, we expect my arcade to do for industrial history what this place has done—and, with your help tonight, will continue to do—for the natural world. Our motto at the arcade is simple: No cases! We will tolerate nothing coming between object and observer.

"To give you a small taste of what we have in mind, the Museum of Natural History, after a bit of arm-twisting, has agreed to pop open one of its world-famous dioramas. That buzz you're hearing"—Stolz paused and touched his earlobe—"that's the sound of the glass getting removed. Once everything's safe, we'll set up for photographs. So please join me, and that couple with the saggy tits over there, for a portrait to commemorate your wonderful donation and your devotion to the idea that objects *can* come alive."

Before the photographer had even finished securing the legs

of his tripod, guests were crowding around the open case, checkbooks in hand.

After his brief photo op with Stolz, Jesson was unceremoniously urged along by one of the entrepreneur's handlers.

"A costly meeting, but worth it," he told me under the skeletal remains of the knock-kneed Turkana Boy.

"You got Stolz to talk?"

"Didn't have to. He raised the matter himself. First words out of his mouth were, 'Hope you're happy with that friggin' leather box.' Apparently, his tattooed henchman, who by the way is named Emery Kucko, recognized me from the watch shop."

"What did you say?"

"I told Stolz that, yes, I *was* happy but would be happier still if I had what the box contained. That prompted a satisfied smirk I consider tantamount to confession. Believe me, Stolz has the Queen locked up somewhere in that arcade of his. I'm sure of it. Five minutes alone with the man and I know I'd have a confession. His type is immune to discretion."

We planted ourselves at the south exit of the museum, beneath a forlorn Haida fisherman, and waited for Stolz to finish with his guests.

"Funny," said Jesson, glancing up at the native in the dugout. "I remember a fierce Iroquois warrior, not this docile youth."

"Cardinal rule of reference, Mr. Jesson. Never rely on memory."

"Indeed. If anything, his expression seems to be saying, 'What am I doing here? I want to go home.' And who can blame him? Imagine having to watch over all these concession stands and push-button displays. What's happened to the quiet exhibition spaces I loved as a child? The kind that educated through good old-fashioned mnemonics? Camels often sit down carefully. Perhaps their joints creak."

"Sorry?"

"The geologic periods, Alexander. *Camels* for the Cambrian, *often* for the Ordovician, *sit* for the Silurian, I believe."

Before Jesson could complete his travels through time, Stolz and his entourage appeared from behind the dugout. Jesson tried to approach, but his legs failed him. Stolz's Gullwing was accelerating toward the Central Park transverse as we got out to the street.

"Follow Kucko," Jesson barked.

"I make a lousy snoop. Dinty once had me tail a reader suspected of stringing prints. I bungled the whole thing."

"I'm sure you've learned from your mistakes. Now get going!"

There was no point arguing. I followed Kucko into the subway and onto the southbound C. At West 4th Street, he changed for the F, so I did too. A half hour later, I found myself somewhere in Brooklyn, tailing Stolz's sidekick down a residential street seasonally personalized with saluting Santas, abject Madonnas, and a platoon of adjectival dwarves.

Kucko stopped at the only undecorated door on the block and rang the bell. A bearded man wearing a black robe let him in. Once the two of them disappeared, I scrambled over to the mailbox and peeked inside. A business card taped to the lid read, MARKS OF DISTINCTION, TATTOOS BY APPOINTMENT.

I planted myself in a polystyrene manger that faced the house and waited, crouched between the Infant Jesus and a Wise Man holding Day-Glo myrrh. Ten minutes later, an interior door opened. Through the picture window I saw Kucko perched on a swivel stool, his back exposed. And what a back! It was covered with snakes and dragons and Japanese warriors. I made a sketch of the design, which I then took to the library. What I discovered there sent me running to Festina-lente, where Andrews greeted me with a note:

Meeting Stolz has agitated me greatly so I have gone to my club to swat a few balls. If you return with news, which I certainly hope you do, why not join me?

Yours,

H.

45

I SHOULD HAVE known that the game Jesson played wasn't tennis—at least not as I'd ever seen it played—but rather a royal precursor known formally as *jeu de paume*. What I had no reason to anticipate based on everything I'd seen was the old man's vicious serve and agile return.

It's as if there were two Jessons: the reflective shuffler and the reflexive athlete, the latter being the one I now observed moving nimbly around the court. He defeated his adversary, who couldn't have been more than half his age, with a series of feints and returns so efficient that a physics teacher could have used the tactics to explain the conservation of energy. But once the game had ended and the players were done exchanging compliments ("Brilliant chase fours!" "Stunning giraffe!"), the Jesson from Festinalente reclaimed the athlete's body.

He was toweling down when I called out his name. It took him a moment to locate me under the banked penthouse of the archaic court. He flashed a broad smile and hobbled toward the gallery. "Does this mean you've got something?"

I nodded.

"Excellent."

"I tracked Kucko to a tattoo parlor. Now what, you might ask, does a tattoo parlor have to do with the Queen?"

"I might ask that, yes."

"I stopped at the library and did some digging. The place Kucko visited is called Marks of Distinction. It's run by a man named Mark Donatello. Donatello is pretty famous in the world of body art. His specialty is Japanese *irezumi*. Apparently, he's so good he's done designs for the *yakuza*, the Japanese Mafia. Talk about bringing coals to Newcastle."

"Forgive me," said Jesson. "I'm sure it's me. But the link between gangsters and the Marie Antoinette is what?"

"I'm getting there. The *yakuza* are known to select body designs that document their illicit activities. They'll sometimes tattoo themselves with a kind of visual rap sheet."

Jesson froze. "You're suggesting Kucko may have recorded the break-in . . . *on his body*?"

"Can't be certain since I only saw his back. But it is a possibility."

Jesson started to spin his racquet. "Have you spoken to Donatello about Kucko's design?"

"Somehow I doubt he'd talk about a client."

"He might if you were getting yourself tattooed."

"Sorry, Mr. Jesson. There's no way—"

"For goodness' sake, Alexander, use your imagination. You need only *pretend* to want one. You don't have to follow through."

"I suppose I could manage that."

"Splendid." Jesson confirmed his pleasure by smacking a tennis ball into a small, netted window at the far end of the court, which caused a bell to ring. "Finally, score one for us. I can hardly wait for your update."

"You want me to see Donatello *now*?"

"Can you give me a compelling reason not to go straight back?"

"For starters, Donatello only works by appointment. Besides, I'm completely wiped out. I think I'm coming down with something. Squatting in a crèche in subfreezing temperature was not a great idea."

"How can you say that? You've managed to learn so much. Come with me."

Down in the changing room, Jesson opened his locker and removed a thick cashmere scarf. "Now hurry," he said, tying it around my neck. "We're running out of time."

46

IT WAS WHILE seated on an overheated F train as densely packed as Jesson's shelves that I blacked out. The next thing I knew, my plastic seat had become a prisoner's dock in a crowded, noisy courtroom.

Dinty, presiding as both judge and jury from a bench that bore a distinct resemblance to the reference desk, asked the prosecutor, his ally Irving Grote, to review the charges against me.

"Defendant stands accused of tardiness, theft, excess sick leave, and two counts of mutilation. Count one: abuse of an unopened hymnal. Count two: tearing a page from a visitor's book."

The trial was short, the verdict inescapable. Dinty decided to throw the book at me, metaphor notwithstanding. He had

Mr. Singh march me up the spiral staircase to the loge of the Reading Room. There the guard unfurled his turban, one end of which he tied to the iron banister of the catwalk. After fashioning a hangman's knot from the loose end, he tried to collar me. When I resisted, he withdrew his parcel probe and began to poke me into submission.

"Doze off, buddy?"

It was the nightstick of a New York City transit cop, not a pinewood dowel, I felt jabbing my ribs.

"Train's outta service. Wait on the platform for the next one."

I loosened Jesson's scarf, which had tightened around my neck during the ride, and stumbled off the train, wondering if I'd have the strength to face Donatello.

He made it easier than expected.

"Come on in," the tattoo artist said when he opened the door. "It's usually by appointment, but I'm waiting for my seven-thirty, so let's squeeze in a consult. You like that, do you?" He must have noticed me staring at the elaborate mural covering one entire wall of the waiting room.

"Very much," I said.

"I worked that up when I first opened. Folks in my line tend to hang a lot of flash in their studios. Not me. If you're looking for a flag or a swastika you've come to the wrong guy. That's not my thing."

"Mine either."

"My take, you can probably tell, is different—more ethnic." He tapped the flattened head of a tribesman at the center of the mural. "Of course, I don't do cradle-boarding here. And the Department of Health frowns on foot-binding and Nuba scarification." His hand moved a few inches down. "But Mesoamerican tooth filing isn't a problem. I've done two of those this month alone. And if you want, we can discuss genital ventilation or Aboriginal subincision, depending, of course, where you want to take things. But just so you know, I can't do any of the tricky stuff here. I'm a stickler for hygiene. Have some articles on the table that'll pretty much show you why."

"That's okay. I'll be steering clear of genital ventilation." I felt the dizziness starting to return.

"What about a South American cheek plug or some *moko*?" He traced the geometric pattern covering the face of a Maori elder.

"I'm actually more keen on the Japanese stuff over there, next to those women with the plates in their lips."

"Come to the right place. I trained outside Kyoto. Hold on and I'll bring out some samples." Donatello rummaged around in a coat closet and handed over a three-ring binder with the word *irezumi* brushstroked across the spine. Then he settled me into a beanbag chair and excused himself.

The binder contained dozens of Polaroids grouped anatomically: Scalps and Necks, Arms and Legs, Backs and Chests. The Back section depicted nothing nearly so complex as what I'd viewed from the manger.

I waded through countless schools of carp, past river gods and sunbursts, lightning bolts and lotus thrones, in an exercise strongly reminiscent of the one Jesson had forced on me when he first presented the case and engraving. Back then, I had to locate an iron nail that would send me in pursuit of the Queen; now, I was trying to find a match for the design I'd seen on Kucko; unfortunately, the only tattoo featuring a fire-breathing dragon, snakes, and warriors had been applied to a body that very obviously belonged to a woman. To distract myself while waiting for Donatello to reemerge, I thumbed through a small stack of magazines and ended up reading a reprint from the *Journal of Dermatologic Surgery and Oncology*. This was not a good idea given how I was feeling. The article, which detailed complications associated with improper tattooing, hardly served as endorsement for body art, however safe Donatello's methods. The gruesome photos were accompanied by a couple of captions that demanded transcription:

> An infected penis tattooed with corkscrew design. (We doubt it helps.)

And:

> A female suprapubic design bearing the legend 'Admission 50¢.' (Note that the tattoo was done in the depth of the Great Depression.)

Before I could pull out my diary, the dizzy spells returned. I managed to put my head between my legs—no simple feat in the protozoan bag that enveloped me—and took a couple of deep breaths. The door to the back room opened.

"Everything okay?"

I grunted.

"You're sweating bullets. Maybe we should postpone."

"I'm fine, really. I'm sure if I—"

And then, as I had on the subway, I blacked out.

47

I WOKE FACEDOWN near the paws of the terrestrial globe.

"Alexander?"

"I'm not feeling well," I said as I dragged my body to a lounging chair.

"That's quite obvious," Jesson said. "A cabby had to bring you in. I should never have sent you off to Brooklyn. Obsession got the better of me. What happened?"

"All I remember is getting sick on the head of a plastic lawn dwarf and hailing a taxi. Where's the book, Mr. Jesson?"

"What book?"

"The one I took from Grote's lockup. The first time I conked out, when I was riding downtown, I had this nightmare about getting hanged for removing the book from the lab."

"The sentence seems a little harsh."

"If it's discovered missing—"

"Try to relax, Alexander. The book is quite safe."

"But it could mean my job!"

"Nonsense," said Jesson. "That's the fever talking." He touched the back of his hand to my forehead. "Just as I thought. Your blood heat is ghastly. I'll have Andrews help you upstairs."

"I can't move." Another wave of chills hit and the next thing I knew the butler was lugging a large ribbed trunk toward the fireplace. The trunk opened into a wood-and-canvas cot. Jesson tried to soothe me with talk of the bed's use during some Napoleonic campaign, but I was too out of it to listen. Once or twice he tried to question me about Donatello.

I turned on my side and pulled up the cover. "Could we talk when I'm feeling better?"

"You're right. This can wait. Is there anything I can bring you? Another blanket? A tisane?"

"All I really need is sleep . . . and *The Book of Hours*."

The fever broke during the night, leaving me achy and parched. Still fixated on returning the borrowed book, I tossed off the blankets and swung my legs over the crossbars of the camp bed. I hobbled to the mantel and retrieved a hurricane lantern perched between two decaying apples. As soon as I lit the wick, which presented little difficulty thanks to Jesson's fetishistic devotion to foot-long wooden fireplace matches, I set to work.

Naturally, I started my search in the library. After checking the lectern where Jesson originally had stored the volume,

I turned to the actual shelves. About halfway into the second alcove, with my head beginning to feel like the carriage return on a manual typewriter, I realized I didn't have to read the spine titles, that I could instead look for the distinctive label applied by my library's bindery. That accelerated the process but didn't improve the results.

Everything in Jesson's holdings appeared perfectly ordered: the whaling treatises, the numerology texts, the calf-bound gatherings of Grub Street doggerel, the quarto Johnsons and octavo Boswells, the shelves of unfinished works. In fact, the arrangement was so rigorous I had a hard time imagining anything getting put anywhere inadvertently, which forced me to consider the possibility of *intentional* misplacement. I had to ask myself: Where would Jesson keep something he didn't want found?

One spot immediately came to mind—the shelf marked SE-CRETS & SOLANDERS. Several minutes of probing failed to produce *The Book of Hours*, though there was an unexpected discovery. I found, nesting inside one of the nicer solander boxes, an early edition of Lindsley's *The Note-Taker, or Elements of Tachygraphy*, the same manual on which my own shorthand is based.

It didn't take much to figure out why Jesson had the book, and why he was keeping it from view. He needed Lindsley to decipher the annotations in my girdle book and diary.

Well, best of luck! That's all I had to say. Given how I'd reworked the word-signs and letter clusters (not to mention the tweaked el-hooks), he wasn't likely to get far; my writing was much too idiosyncratic to be "broken."

Seemingly isolated facts started to cohere in nasty ways. The rearrangement of my notebooks in the berth and Jesson's questions about my annotational methods, in light of the hidden manual, suggested that I'd grossly underestimated his curiosity about, well, me.

I briefly considered bursting in and confronting my sleeping host. But I resisted that impulse, tempting though it was, since it might have made retrieving *The Book of Hours* that much tougher. Returning the Lindsley to its enclosure, I continued my search in the salon.

It's in here, I told myself. *It has to be.*

I ran my hands over the baseboards, wainscot, and tables, careful to avoid the ubiquitous buzzers. I dug behind cushions and popped open the secret compartments (in the *Knorpelwerk* bureau, the lounging chair, the chess table), but all that uncovered was a monogrammed handkerchief, some sucking candies, and a gold-nibbed lettering pen.

No *Book of Hours*.

I pushed onward to the cloister, doubtful though I was that Jesson would have put the book in an open space, then doubled back to the gallery of mechanical wonders. Ten feet in, I came across an object I hadn't noticed before: an enamel-dialed schoolhouse clock. It struck me as oddly pedestrian, a poor relation to the rest of the contraptions arranged on the baize. I looked at it more closely.

The lid was locked, so I had to scout around for a key. That's how I discovered the following notice lacquered to the underside:

A Brief Account of the Roll-Player
In the history of invention few figures are as striking as M. D. Calvocoressi, one of the greatest makers of

mechanical devices living today. Known initially for his work on violin pegs (Patent No. 473,347) and his Apparatus for the Manufacture of Gas (Patent 473,350), Professor Calvocoressi has, since losing twin sons in The Great War, dedicated himself to the advancement of prosthetic innovation and the betterment of the damaged, neglected and infirm.

Both right- and left-handed models of the Roll-Player are available. Treadle, crank and electrically activated versions of the invention are planned, although not at present available.

With its patented nickel-plated mechanism and easily accessible storage containers, the Roll-Player is no simple case of curiosity; it is an efficacious, elegant solution to the needs of the amputee.

The Roll-Player library includes novels, shorter fiction, poetry, works of history and drama, each selected by our Honorary International Committee.

Blank rolls for annotation purposes may also be purchased. A booklet in which the origins of the Roll-Player is fully explained can be obtained free of cost upon request.

The text, confusing as it was, made me all the more eager to get inside the "clock." I tested various keys from the nearby automats and music boxes until I found one, in the rump of a silver elephant, that unlocked the catch on the clock case. I raised the lid, and there, on a wooden platen in the center of the device, a second paper notice provided instructions:

Directions for Use

1. Raise & secure cabinet lid with brass rod located on inside wall. (Rod fits in aperture on underside of lid.) 2. Once lid is secured, remove platen to expose take-up spool (at top) and roll-holder (at bottom). 3. Remove crank from compartment on left of case and insert in gear-train slot on right-side exterior. 4. Insert roll into roll-holder. (A note on roll insertion: left flange has *dimpled* recess, right flange has *slotted* recess. Place right flange into gear-train drive slot, then pull left-side chuck release to insert left-hand flange.) 5. Once roll is inserted, pull leader 4" to 6" off spool. 6. Reposition platen and lock at 45-degree angle, using brass rod. 7. Pull leader over lip of platen and affix reinforced roll ring to brass hook of take-up spool. 8. Push gear lever to "READ" position. 9. Turn crank *COUNTER-CLOCKWISE*. (Any infelicities in tracking may be remedied by adjustment of the patented brass lever mounted on inside wall of platen support.) 10. To remove roll: Push gear lever to "REWIND" position, and turn crank. Roll will disengage from take-up spool hook without encumbrance.

NOTA BENE: Gear lever must be in "REWIND" position before top can be closed.

I removed the platen on the off chance that *The Book of Hours* was hiding underneath. It wasn't, so I lowered the lid, locked the case, and returned the key to the elephant's rump, unsure where to go next.

Indecision soon swelled to fitful desperation as I tiptoed aimlessly from one room to the next. I'd spent enough time with Jesson to know that he'd probably resorted to some Poe-like trick of concealment. No doubt he had even fed me clues about the locus of the purloined volume.

I gave the paw-footed globe an angry spin and once more considered rousing my host. But an inexplicable sensation suddenly interrupted that line of thought.

Something in the room seemed different, off kilter. Looking about, I had a feeling bibliographers are said to experience when they perceive a significant undocumented typo even before they consciously *see* it.

The globe tottered to a halt, its wobble more exaggerated than usual. Another twirl revealed a definite imbalance. When I stopped the sphere with my palm I heard a rattle inside.

I inspected the equator, hoping to find an open seam. No such luck. A slight bulge near the compass points provided another burst of wishful thinking, but after a few pokes I had to accept that the bump was merely a bump.

Next my finger traveled to the kidney-shaped island Jesson had shown me during that first, punch-drunk tour of the salon. I didn't need to check my girdle book to remember what he'd told me the sages said about paradise. *It can depress, oppress, and sadden—and has even been known to betray.*

I understood in an instant that the cryptic aphorism contained the needed clue.

Of all the sounds I have registered none has offered as much satisfaction, however brief, as the *click* that came when I depressed *Pairidaeza*. Did the world open up in my hands? Hardly. If anything, it unhinged.

The globe wasn't hiding *The Book of Hours*. The wobble and rattle had been caused by a cardboard box housing a roll of paper the size of a small ear of corn. The roll had a leather tongue and a tiny brass ring, and looked like it belonged inside a player piano. Only instead of perforations, the paper was covered with notes written in Jesson's hand.

The moment I saw the roll I knew it was supposed to be "played" on the device I'd just inspected in the gallery of mechanical wonders.

48

AT FIRST, IMPATIENCE got the better of me; I tried to read the roll by unfurling it like so much paper toweling. But after creasing an edge, I took the thing into the gallery, retrieved the elephant's winding key, and opened the "clock" case. The directions were relatively idiot-proof. I inserted the crank and the roll, then fed the paper over the platen and—this was the only tricky part—onto the take-up spool.

Jesson's notes were split down the middle by a thin oxblood rule. The left column of text, composed in formal French, was a dense historical narrative that appeared to warrant little attention. The right column, written in English, proved almost as hard to decipher but was packed with enticing facts.

What a hodgepodge! There were snatches of dialogue between Jesson and me, ditties arranged by theme (some clearly copied from songbooks, others wholly original, to judge from the cross-outs and corrections), a collection of archaic phrases accompanied by their modern-day equivalents (for example, "blood heat~temperature; iliac passion~fart; Paracelsian~old-fashioned"). The synonyms were followed by the Jerusalem itinerary, a bibliography of theft, a roster of book titles culled from my *Slips of Love*, and a lengthy diatribe on Frederick Stolz's guilt in the matter of the missing Queen.

And what proof accompanied the charge? None, from what I could tell. Jesson's accusations were tenuously tethered to a "template of criminality" composed from a mix of documents, some of which I had found, others provided by the author himself. The latter group included definitions of theft among various indigenous peoples (with special emphasis on Trobriand Islanders) and random quotations from Johnson, Herodotus, and *The Moonstone*, that bloated Wilkie Collins mystery about the search for a stolen diamond.

Part rant, part register, the note roll was often so obscure that it reminded me of a dance instruction booklet, with Jesson's exacting, if frenzied, marginalia substituting for the silhouette of shoes. Sometimes annotational arrows would launch into the French Territory, only to shoot back across the English Channel a few inches down. I ended up cranking through the roll with no overriding logic except to dig up those passages that included my name. The first one appeared four or five revolutions in:

Ask Alexander: Might I steal a moment of your time.

This line was followed by the exact date Jesson had presented me with the call slip that precipitated our collaboration. I found the verb tense especially disturbing. The "ask" con-firmed what I'd already begun to suspect—that Jesson had been scripting his comments. The note roll, I concluded, functioned as both promptbook and journal.

An arrow traveled from that initial reference-desk query to a cluster of temporal clichés Jesson had periodically injected into his speech: *Time is of the essence, Running out of time, All in good time . . .*

Why the deception? What would explain such an elaborate ruse? Another turn of the crank pulled up four lines of light verse bearing the title "The Timepiece":

> *To steal a golden pocket watch*
> *Does not change the time*
> *It does not halt the tower bells*
> *Or make the dull sublime.*

Whatever respect I might have mustered for Jesson as a poet was obliterated by the quatrain that surfaced two cranks later, under the name "The Pageboy":

> *Plaything, puppet*
> *Pageboy, pawn*
> *My dainty, doubt-filled*
> *Troubled fawn.*

So that's how the bastard saw me. He'd been so damn amused to learn that I'd started my professional life as a library page. I was beginning to understand why. An arrow shot out from the humiliating poem and made a sharp turn, crossing the oxblood median and landing in a thicket of French.

I had hoped to ignore the foreign stuff, but that proved impossible once I recognized the link between "The Pageboy" and the Gallic narrative. With a Larousse propped against one side of the roll-player and a Littré on the other, I picked my way through a work of fiction, evidently a novel in progress, titled *Le Coffret*, or, as it was rendered on the English side of the channel, *A Case of Curiosities*.

Le Coffret was substantially less garbled than the notes, but no easier to read. After a dozen or so cranks, I realized I hadn't so much stumbled onto a tale as *into* one. The novel appropriated my thoughts, my aspirations, my interests, my words, and transported them backward in time.

My love of books, my passion for sounds, my observations on enclosure—all got packed into the imagination, actions, and speech of a character named Claude Page, an autodidact as wooden as the manikin in that other (three-dimensional) case of curiosities. The writing dredged up memories of Jesson's essay "Contemporary Roots in Historical Fiction: A Case Study of the Eighteenth-Century French Novel." Suddenly the article acquired unsettling relevance, as did the passage its author had lifted from his namesake, Henry James. The historical novel was, as *Le Coffret* proved at every turn, damned to fatal cheapness, and with it so was I. Jesson seemed as keen to hang me in his empty tale as he was to hang the Queen in the vacant compartment.

I rewound the crank until the paper disengaged from the take-up spool, then nudged the sprocket wheel to one side and freed the paper roll. I carried the roll back to the salon and slipped it inside the globe. After retriggering the secret compartment, I gave the globe a vigorous spin to make sure its wobble was right. Then I went back to the gallery of mechanical wonders to tidy up and over to the alcoves to reshelve the French dictionaries.

My options were limited to fight or flight, and I quickly chose the latter. Using the lettering pen I had found while searching for the book, I composed an innocuous one-sentence note that avoided direct mention of the roll. But that seemed too mild so I added a second line:

I'm off to work but still feeling ill. No time to spar, no time at all.

In my haste I dropped the *e* from the word *spare*, but I let the mistake stand as a prelude to more direct confrontation.

Leaving Festinalente, I was certain of only two things. First, that *The Book of Hours* had to be returned fast. And second, that once it was, I would reclaim my life from Claude Page.

49

THE FOLLOWING AFTERNOON, I foisted myself on Norton and Speaight at the Automat, now stripped of its very last bits of chrome.

"You have it again," said Norton, pressing a fist against his forehead. "That look that says 'Damaged and Withdrawn.'"

"And this time it's stamped in big fat letters," added Speaight.

"The bastard's been playing me from the start."

Norton removed his tuna sandwich from its cellophane cocoon. "Start downloading."

I told my friends about poking around for the borrowed book and listed what I'd found instead: the shorthand manual in the solander box, the roll-playing mechanism in the clock case, the notes in the globe.

As I was explaining Jesson's bizarre and unsubstantiated accusations against Stolz and his twisted appropriation of me, Speaight began to nod.

"This roll you were reading, was it about so big?" He stretched his hand an octave. "With Bakelite flanges and a hook on the end of the paper?"

"Actually, the paper has a ring on the end. The hook is part of the take-up spool. Why?"

"My center accessioned one of those a couple of years ago. It was part of an erotica collection from the twenties. If memory serves, the motto of the roll-player is 'Volumes of higher learning operated by a crank.'"

Norton smirked and said, "No wonder Jesson has one."

"He's worse than a crank. He's a plagiarist, a thief, every bit as guilty as the crooks who ripped off the Queen. The roll proves that he's been stealing large chunks of my life. Lengthy passages of 'his' work come directly from my girdle book and diary."

"So much for the gentleman scholar," said Norton. "What I find interesting is that he obviously picked you with a huge amount of care."

"He selects everything that way. Coffee, biscuits, books, watches. Why not the protagonist for some pathetic novel that has zero hope of ever getting published?"

"Maybe the roll is his way of honoring you," suggested Speaight.

"Try again. This is about lust for a stolen watch and for the librarian hired to help find it. No, correction. It's about lust for a watch and the *story* of that hired librarian."

Norton shook his head. "You got it right the first time, my friend."

"Whatever. All I know is, it's seriously clouding his judg-ment. How else could he be so convinced that Stolz has the Queen?"

"Is there a chance he's privy to info you don't have?" asked Speaight.

"After reading his whole miserable note roll, I tend to doubt it."

"The only thing that matters right now," said Norton, "is getting the book back. If Grote realizes it's missing, he'll haul your sorry butt before the Leadership Council faster than you can say bibliokleptomania."

"Don't you think I'm aware of that? Why else would I be talking to you guys? You know that Horace quote chiseled over the exit of the Reading Room?"

"The one about all books having their fates?"

"That's the one. I want Jesson's *Case of Curiosities* to meet the fate *it* deserves. Call it a pawn's gambit."

"You know the person you should be partnering up with, don't you?" said Speaight.

I shrugged.

"Hint: who does revenge better than the French?"

"Nic did have him pegged," I admitted. "The tarot cards warned her and she warned me. And I didn't listen."

"I'm guessing there's a phone in the back," Norton said.

"I've tried her a dozen times since I hightailed it out of Jesson's. All I get is the machine."

Speaight pulled a quarter from his pocket and pushed it across the Formica.

What composure I had disappeared the moment I heard her *Allô* at the other end of the line.

"Nic? Nic, it's me, Zander."

"*Oui?*"

"I . . . I . . ."

"What do you want? I teach at Paper House in twenty minutes."

"Can I come home, Nic? You were right about Jesson. Can we try to work things out?"

There was a pause. "*Pas ce soir*. We are doing half-circle full dissolves."

"What about tomorrow? I've been a jerk. We really need to talk."

"*D'accord,*" she said, reluctantly accepting my plea. "*On fera le point demain.*" Before I could ask for a translation, Nic had ended the call.

Both Speaight and Norton offered to put me up, but I declined, knowing that I needed time alone to sort things out. But as it happened, I had to spend the better part of the afternoon phoning hotels. Holiday bookings in New York being what they are, I struck out everywhere.

"Now there's a grim picture if ever I seen one." Mr. Paradis was emptying wastebaskets and must have heard me slam down the phone.

I told him about my problems with Nic.

"Got a brother who left his wife," he said. "Can't recommend it. The fella's been boardin' around two whole years."

"I'm hoping I'll need a place only for the night."

The janitor gave me the once-over. "One night, that's it? Come on then." He started wheeling his cart toward the door.

"Where to?"

"The stacks."

"Why?"

"You want to ask questions or you want a place to sleep?"

"Ever been this low?" Mr. Paradis asked after we'd spiraled down to a section of the library's subbasement devoid of shelving or books.

"Never," I told him.

He led me through a half dozen fire doors and stopped in front of the massive generator that powered the zip tubes. A security fence with a no-nonsense warning protected the ancient machinery:

DANGER! HIGH VOLTAGE! 50,000 VOLTS!

"You sure this is okay, Mr. P.?" The lightning bolt that replaced the final *S* didn't inspire confidence.

"Only risky thing around here is the heatin' coil I use for my cocoa. Think you can steer clear of that?"

"But the sign says—"

"Stop your worryin'. Pulled that off an old electric station near Bangor. Does a fine job scarin' away the stack crew. Wouldn't want them to find my little glory hole, now, would I?" Mr. Paradis unlocked the security fence and brought me to the door of a utility closet. "Go on. Ain't big enough for us both."

I poked my head inside.

"This is incredible! No wonder you're always in the library. You've got your very own pied-à-terre!"

The janitor's hideaway, which was roughly the size of my cage, came complete with a narrow foam mattress, supported on some old catalog cabinets, and two bookshelves fashioned from card trays fixed against a wall. In addition to the janitor's private library, the shelves accommodated a jar of golf pencils, a tin of cocoa powder, and a mug. Directly opposite hung a calendar from a distributor of institutional cleaning supplies, plus the aforementioned heating coil, which the janitor had draped over a nail.

"Not exactly the Trustees Room," he said. "But it works."

"Where will you stay?"

"Don't worry about me. Got another spot above the Rotunda." He turned to leave.

"Mr. P., is there a subject class for 'Thankfulness'?"

He considered my question. "Nearest I can get is 'Gratitude'—248.3. Same number as for 'Peace of mind,' which is what you seem to be needin'—that and some rest. The sink and head are around the corner."

"What should I do if someone catches me down here?"

"You'll be out long before anyone punches in."

"I could oversleep. Haven't gotten much rest lately."

The janitor chuckled and, giving the zip tubes a pat, said, "I'm pretty sure you'll be up by 6 A.M."

Mr. Paradis's bookshelves contained repair manuals (for the zips, the Reading Room's electronic number board, the hydraulics) and works devoted to classification. I can't say what influence the studies of hierarchy and subordination (the top shelf) or the guides to fixing things (the bottom shelf) had on my thoughts, but they seemed to focus on Nic.

Ever since fleeing the apartment, I had done my best to deny eviction by evicting Nic from my notes. The rationale was simple: keeping her out of the diary would minimize the pain of estrangement, an out-of-cite-out-of-mind approach to dealing with emotional turmoil.

Unfortunately, the method was far from foolproof. Each time a pair of harem pants billowed past the desk, I'd think of her. Whenever a book related to one of Nic's interests got requested, she'd jostle her way into my head. She'd appear, smiling coyly, winking, dispensing one of her classic shrugs. It seemed inconceivable to me now that I had abandoned her for the likes of Henry James Jesson III.

I turned and stared distractedly at Mr. P.'s wall calendar. An appointment a week away caught my attention. The janitor had penciled the words *Postinventory Party* and *Grote* to remind himself of the upcoming Class Struggle competition, which would pit his knowledge of Dewey against that of the conservator.

Inventory!

My apprehensions shifted. I'd completely forgotten that the books in Grote's lab, all of them, would be undergoing end-of-year inspection. That meant I had to return *The Book of Hours* pronto or keep my date with the hangman.

I was still wide-awake when, at precisely 6 A.M., the zip tubes kicked in. The force of the motor clarified why Mr. P. had chuckled at my worry about oversleeping; the vibrations were so strong they rattled the pencils in the jar.

As I was getting my things together, I heard a pneumatic

thunnk. I looked about and found a zip canister in a catch basket near the danger sign. I unscrewed the top and extracted a note wrapped around a slightly compressed Twinkie. "Gulp this down and get yourself home. That girl of yours is a keeper."

Before leaving the library, I made one quick stop at the reference desk to look up the phrase Nic had used before she'd hung up the phone. *On fera le point*: "To take a reading." Given how Jesson had stolen my words for his roll, the phrase seemed particularly apt.

50

THIS IS WHAT I wished for: that Nic would greet me at the
door in her harem pants or her funky tights (say the red ones
with the thick black stripes) and that she'd say something
tender, preferably in French. Then she'd wrap her arms
around my waist and, without rancor or reproach, ask how
she could help. A maudlin hope, I know, but I wanted her to
be what she'd been briefly early on: a lover, a partner, the
images to my words.

So much for wishes. Nic didn't even answer the bell. I
climbed over the Brobdingnagian-sized sneakers, dealt with
the police lock, and took a few tentative steps down the corridor.

I poked my head into the cage. The room was just as I'd
left it, call slips neat and tidy, books lined up at attention.

Yet it was the scraps of paper covering the carpeting that provided the greatest relief; Nic's mess was an unexpectedly comforting counterexample to the world I'd just escaped.

I entered the studio. Nic swiveled around to face me. "So what happened? No more little chocolates on your pillow?" She swiveled back to her drafting table and focused on a paper butterfly she was mounting onto oaktag.

Why should she make this easy?

"Nic, I was wrong about him, about me, about *us*. And the birthday dinner? That was a big mistake, too. It was stupid not to see that I was itemizing your faults. I now know how that feels. Also, I was wrong to ignore your opinion of Jesson. He's exactly what the cards said he was. I shouldn't have gone back to work for him after I learned he knew about the *Slips*. And you were right to kick me out when you found out that I had."

As I made a case for forgiveness, Nic fussed with the strut of the butterfly's wing until eventually it fell apart in her hands. She looked up at me and said, "It is over with the Hermit?"

"Almost. There's just one small glitch. He still has *The Book of Hours*. You called that one right, too. I should never have lent it to him."

Nic hopped off her stool and put a hand on my cheek. She abruptly crinkled her nose, as if smelling something unpleasant.

"I was sick two nights ago and spent last night in a utility closet."

"*Pauvre petit minou,*" she said.

Nic drew her poor little pussycat a bath and, after I'd stripped off my grubby clothes and soaked for a while, she kneeled next to the tub to wash my back. As I was drying off, Nic scooped up some bubbles and applied them coyly to my breast. Doing so prompted two competing memories. The first was of the regrettable incident when Jesson slipped in the tub and squeezed my groin. The second, no less awkward, recalled the topographic map Nic had drawn of her body. After unfurling the artwork, she had positioned my hand on her breast to provoke a reaction. When none came, she had hurled a snow globe at my head.

With the placement of our hands reversed, the results proved more gratifying. Our sudsy explorations moved rapidly from bathroom to loft, where Nic and I, for the first time in months, spoke openly about our wounds and how we might heal them. Suddenly Nic started to giggle.

"What's so funny?"

She climbed down from the loft. "Grab your Jesson files and follow me," she said.

"All of them?" I'd amassed half a dozen document boxes since the start of the inquiries.

"*Non. Juste un ou deux.*"

I carried a sheaf of early transcriptions into the studio. Nic said, "The Hermit, he likes the eighteenth century, *non*?" Her question seemed incongruous inasmuch as she was standing stark naked next to a paper cutter.

I gave a perplexed nod. "It's where he's imprisoned my alter ego."

"Well then?" She winked and drew a thumbnail across her neck. "Hand me a page."

I watched as she placed some notes about the Art Theft Archive under the blade of the paper cutter. She then pulled me over and wrapped my fingers around the plastic grip.

"*Vive la Révolution!*" Nic cried.

The initial cuts were tough, but soon my arm was working with measured—I'm tempted to say clockwork—regularity. Nic fed the pages to me one at a time and I shredded them with gusto.

A few minutes into the scrap operation, I scooped up some strips of transcript and draped them over Nic's naked body. Then I sliced a little more and draped a little more until I'd transformed my wife into a seaweedy siren from an X-rated version of *The Land Before Time*. When at last Nic was completely covered, I urged her to the floor, where, amid the ribbony remains of Jesson's convoluted stratagems, we made simple, straightforward love.

51

NIC AND I had so much fun plotting a way to reclaim the library book that we decided to test our idea on Norton and Speaight to make sure it wasn't too wacky. While my friends were answering phones in Tel-Ref, I slipped an envelope between a couple of *Peterson Field Guides* and twirled the multi-tiered lazy Susan of reference works.

"What's this?" said Speaight, when the envelope came spinning by his carrel.

"What's *what*?" Norton asked.

"A letter," I said. "Read it out loud. I want to hear what you guys think."

Speaight cleared his throat. "'Dear Mr. Jesson,'" he intoned, "'I would rather tell you what follows in person, but the sickness that cut short our Brooklyn campaign has returned with a vengeance. I'm suffering a nasty case of laryn-gitis, which makes speaking impossible. Hence this letter.'"

Norton butted in: "Your voice sounds fine to me."

"Quiet," said Speaight. "Let me read. 'I had hoped to re-cover fully before getting back in touch, but extraordinary developments make delay impossible. The facts are these. Be-fore losing my voice, I took another trip to Donatello's estab-lishment. (I felt guilty about bungling the earlier visit.) It's a good thing I did! As soon as I described the body design I wanted, Donatello fetched a binder I hadn't seen called "Full Body Commissions." Two clients in, I hit pay dirt. Staring straight at me, fork-tongued and alert, was the fire-breathing dragon I'd observed from the manger. It's part of a larger work that makes clever use of Kucko's torso, arms, and legs.

"'I examined the Polaroid carefully and found something pretty unbelievable clasped in the claws that curled around Kucko's right (actually it may be left) buttock. This is what we've been looking for, Mr. Jesson—an indelible link between Stolz (via his assistant) and the theft of the Queen.'"

Norton couldn't stand the suspense. "What did you see on the guy's ass?"

"Shhh!" said Speaight. "We're getting there. Where was I?" It took him a moment to find his place. "'Rather than waste time with a lot of description, I am enclosing an actual photo. Donatello gave it to me without a fuss, saying he could easily get a duplicate since Kucko is still a client. (There's an unfinished upper thigh.) I'll get back in touch once my voice returns. In the meantime, please give some thought to how we should proceed. Fondly, Alexander.'"

Speaight dropped his reading voice. "The letter ends with the word *Enclosure*, but there's nothing enclosed."

I slipped a copy of the incriminating Polaroid between the A–K and L–Z of a boxed German dictionary and gave the lazy Susan another heave. This time it was Norton who got lucky.

"What do we have here?" he said. "A dimpled buttock and lower back tattooed with a dragon clutching a watch . . . How does *this* connect to the heist?"

"Notice anything peculiar about the face of said watch?"

By now Speaight had made his way over to Norton's carrel, eager to inspect the photo for himself.

"Is it the roman numerals? Shouldn't the 'IIII' be the letter V with an *I* before it? That's what they taught us at school."

"The roman numerals are fine. Look again."

"Is it the motto underneath the claws?" Norton asked.

"No, the motto's irrelevant."

"The hands!" Speaight shouted.

"There *are* no hands," said Norton.

"That's the point! Don't you remember what Short told us about the crime scene?"

"Remind me."

Speaight rolled his eyes. "You tell him, Alexander."

"The thieves vandalized the collection by ripping hands off the clocks and watches. Kind of a calling card."

"You're saying this Kucko guy had incriminating evidence tattooed on his butt? Give me a break."

"Look, Norton. It doesn't matter if *you* buy the story, as long as Jesson does."

"How did you get Kucko to do that to his body?" Norton asked.

"I didn't."

"Then whose behind are we looking at?" Speaight demanded.

I stood up and locked the door.

"Show time," I announced, as I dropped my drawers and mooned my dumbfounded friends.

"It's only temporary," I explained as I tucked in my shirt. "Should fade in a few weeks. Nic knows this place that sells special dyes and transfers. All the hotshot makeup artists go there when they've got to give their squeamish rock musician clients body designs that'll last the length of a tour."

"She drew that thing from scratch?" said Norton admiringly.

"Pretty much, though I did call up an illustrated ethnography of Osaka gangster culture. Once Nic had that, all she needed to do was stick a clock face without hands in the talons of the dragon."

"Painful?" Speaight asked.

"Actually, it tickled—especially when Nic was dusting me with cornstarch so I'd match Kucko's complexion."

Norton spun the lazy Susan and said, "If this doesn't get under the guy's skin, nothing will."

"Very funny. I just hope Jesson hands over the book. He'll have to if he wants to hear the next installment."

"Which you provide when?"

"This evening. I stuck copies of the letter and the Polaroid through the mail slot of Festinalente last night. Jesson called back right away—promised to double my pay if I rose from my sickbed."

52

JESSON POSITIONED HIMSELF at the chessboard, my letter and photo in his lap.

"So all this time Kucko's been sitting on the evidence? Cheeky bastard."

I smiled.

Jesson picked up the Polaroid and waved it at the chessmen. "The end game approaches, Alexander. Symmetry or aggression—which do you propose we use?"

"Aggression," I said. "Definitely."

"Agreed. But it must be *psychological* aggression. Force has no place where there is need of skill."

"Herodotus, isn't it?" It felt good to quote from Jesson's roll without attribution.

"Yes," he stammered, dropping the snapshot of the pallid buttock onto the board. "Time to compel the white knave to sacrifice his Queen."

"Are you proposing blackmail?"

"Crudely put."

"Wouldn't it be better to inform Jerusalem that we've found the thieves and leave the rest to them?"

"Why on earth would we do that?"

"The watch *is* theirs, Mr. Jesson."

"*Was* theirs."

"Theft has never been part of my job description," I said.

"Nonsense. What about *The Book of Hours*?"

"*The Book of Hours* was only borrowed."

"But without authorization. How would Grote react knowing it was gone?"

I countered the implied threat with one of my own. "Grote would make sure I got fired, which is why you'll return the book right now and guarantee my continued assistance."

Jesson mulled over the demand. "Of course. As soon as it comes back."

"Back from where?"

"Did I forget to tell you?" he said, doing a lousy job of sounding casual. "When I finally unearthed the volume—this was while you were sick and incommunicado—I noticed the boards got loose. I had Andrews send it out to my binder."

"You're joking. Grote keeps a detailed condition log. He's bound to notice."

Jesson tittered at the unintended pun until he saw I wasn't amused. "Don't worry," he said. "The book will look just as it did when you brought it here. I gave explicit instructions."

"We can't put off returning it. The library does a year-end inventory. Grote's probably going through his materials as we speak."

"I would think you'd be more concerned about the watch now that it's within reach."

"Sorry, I'm not. Besides, do you really believe Tashjian will sit around jingling his watch keys if he discovers you've located his child?"

"He won't find out, and even if he does, what could he do, sue for custody?"

"Why not?"

"The Queen would be here and Tashjian would be there, which makes for all sorts of, forgive me, *complications*. If an object that gets stolen is itself a stolen object and if the loci of the two criminal acts implicate the laws of two nations—in this case, the United States and Israel—said object enters a domain of statutory ambiguity that makes reclamation nearly impossible."

"I find that hard to believe."

"And *I* find it hard to believe," said Jesson frostily, "that you possess the legal expertise to challenge what I say." Again he pointed to the chessboard. "As a lover of enclosure, you should appreciate this. Pick up that rook."

"Why?"

"Just do it."

I picked it up.

"Now, look below the turrets. See how long and thin the windows are? Why do you think that is?"

"For protection?"

"Quite. Castle fenestration narrows toward the exterior to

shield the archers inside. Those apertures have a special name, Alexander. They are called *loopholes*."

I put the rook back on the board. "My love of enclosure does not extend to prison, Mr. Jesson."

"You will not be going to jail," he said as he grabbed two pieces—a Jesson-featured king and, suggestively, a queen—and pushed them onto the squares that released the secret draw-bridge. As the spans were lifting, he sang one of the ditties I had seen in his roll:

> *To steal a golden pocket watch*
> *Does not change the time*
> *It does not halt the tower bells*
> *Or make the dull sublime.*

"What's it called?" I asked.

"'The Timepiece,'" said Jesson. "Comes off a broadside engraving by an anonymous Fleet Street printer, circa 1800."

Liar! I wanted to shout. *You're the goddamn author.* "I can see why the writer kept his name off it."

"You find it weak, do you?"

"Yes." I gave the knife a twist. "Weak, cheap, simple-minded. *Make the dull sublime?* Let's face it, either one of us could have done better."

Jesson squirmed. "I rather doubt that." He parted the ivory sliders of the table and withdrew some sheets of paper held to-gether with a silver clip. "Perhaps this will interest you more."

I leafed through the document. "A Senate bill?"

"Enacted to pacify American museum curators terrified of

foreign governments laying claim to plundered—what's the technical term I'm looking for?"

"*Goodies*?" I suggested.

Jesson smiled. "Close enough. The 'Goodies Bill' imposes strict time limits on international theft claims, and happily the Queen's date of disappearance falls outside those limits. As the bill makes clear, it doesn't matter whether the object in question is a Tang horse, a cache of Greek gold coins, or a pocket watch stolen from a small Israeli institute."

"It's hard to imagine this legislation was intended to protect private individuals."

"Do us both a favor, Alexander. Examine the document before proffering legal judgment. So-called private individuals, to use your pleonasm, receive the same protections museums do." Jesson made a gesture with his hands as if loosing an arrow at my chest. "Voilà our loophole."

"None of that will stop Tashjian from trying to get the watch back."

"Let him try. I've read of one case that dragged through the courts for thirty-eight years. And remember, I am rich and the institute is not."

"And you know that because . . ."

"Have you already forgotten that the institute's insurance had lapsed at the time of the break in? That the alarm system was disconnected and that the guards were amateurs? Clearly, the Mayer is, at best, a shoestring operation. It could never afford to sue."

"Just so we're clear on this. Say we do find the watch, do you intend to return it?"

Jesson chose his words with care. "My principal concern is the completion of the case. No more, no less."

"And *my* principal concern is getting the book back to Con-servation."

After a long moment, Jesson broke into a broad, strained smile. "Tell you what. I guarantee the book will be in your hands by the time you've met with Kucko. You have my word."

53

NIC GREETED ME that evening in the harem pants, her face aglow with a lusty conspiratorial hunger.

"*Raconte,*" she said, pushing me down on the futon.

"The photo and letter worked their magic. He gobbled the story up whole."

"*Parfait.* Just as we always wanted. My images, your words."

"Jesson's so busy laying his traps he doesn't notice ours."

"What is he doing?"

"He's come up with this bizarre legal rationale for why he'd be allowed to keep the Queen if and when we were to find her. Take a look."

I produced the document Jesson had given me and read out its poetic title. "'Senate Bill 1523. To amend title 28 of the

United States Code to set up a regime of repose for certain archeological and ethnological materials and cultural property.'"

"He could keep her?" Nic looked concerned.

"Of course not. The resolution was never enacted."

"Does he know that?"

"Sure. But he's assuming I don't. It's just another ploy to keep his troubled pawn in play. I'm sure he'd be only too happy to add a legal case to the wooden one he keeps in his theater, especially if it meant complicating my life."

"So what is pawn's next move?"

"To avoid getting captured."

"Can't you do better? Isn't there an attack where the pawn becomes a queen?"

"That's way beyond me."

Nic shook her head. "Maybe you just need a little encouragement?" She reached behind the futon.

"What's that?"

"The mop broke while I was cleaning up around the studio. I decided to use it to make you something."

"A flail?"

"I had the handle and I had the sliced up transcript."

"So you put them together?"

Nic nodded and gave me a teasing swat.

54

JESSON AND I were walking around the cloister when I sprung the news.

He stopped abruptly. "Kucko's agreed to help?"

I counted three Mississippi before answering. "Yes."

"Does he know where it is?"

"The Queen? He says he does."

"And you'll be seeing him again?"

"I suppose."

"You *suppose*?" Jesson started quivering. "Alexander, did you or did you not confront Kucko? Did you or did you not show him the photograph? Did he or did he not confess a connection to the crime? And do you or do you not have a bona fide plan to recover the watch?"

"Let's see. That would be: yes, yes, yes . . . and *maybe*."

"Can you try being more expansive?"

"Sure. As soon as we resolve the matter of a certain quarter-bound octavo with loose hinges that requires immediate relocation to the conservation lab of my library."

"Ah, so that explains the reticence. I said I would get the book back to you shortly."

"No," I corrected. "What you said was, you'd return it once I'd spoken to Kucko." I unlinked my arm and issued an ultimatum. "Well, Kucko and I *have* talked. Hand over the goods."

Jesson seemed for a moment to falter. "Wait in the porter's chair," he barked.

I was already on the raised platform when I heard the noises in the library. I tiptoed toward the shutters to see what was up and spied Jesson dragging the rolling ladder in and out of the alcoves. He parked between VOYAGES OF DISCOVERY and UNFINISHED WORKS and climbed up to the top shelf. He pressed a finger against one of the lacquered blocks used to keep the books aligned. The action triggered a panel to pop. *So that's where it was!* While Jesson withdrew *The Book of Hours* from the secret cavity, I slipped back to the platform and reclaimed my chair.

Jesson pitched the book into my lap without comment. I immediately checked for the engraving and, finding it intact, inspected the binding and spine. Nothing appeared out of order. I leafed through the gatherings to confirm that the missing front matter was still missing. (I wouldn't have put it past Jesson to insert a fake frontispiece or some similarly damning marginal note.) Page 49 offered particular comfort; its chipped corner documented the three-fold test Grote had performed in his lab. Relieved nothing had been damaged or doctored, I closed the book.

Jesson took that as his cue. "Perhaps you might now provide an unabridged account of Mr. Kucko's confession."

"Like I said, he's agreed to help. If you take your seat I'll tell you all about it."

Disconcerted by my irreverence, Jesson gave me a stern, if puzzled, look. He seemed all set to say something but checked himself and shuffled over to his sedan chair.

"All set, Mr. Jesson?"

"Go on."

I consulted the notes I'd drafted with Nic. "Emery Kucko. Act 2."

"Please, Alexander, no theatrics. Just tell me how you made contact."

"Simple. I called Donatello and told him that before choosing a tattoo I first wanted to meet the fellow in the Polaroid. Donatello agreed to call Kucko and Kucko agreed to see me."

"Amazing."

"More amazing was Kucko's willingness to give me a tour of his body. Of course, he had no idea I knew about the clock face in the dragon's claws. And thank goodness our paths didn't cross at Ornstein's or at that museum benefit. If we had met, he'd never have told me how he got his tats."

"How did he?"

"He came by the first one in Vietnam. Had it done to camouflage an ugly chest scar. During a week of R and R, which he called I and I—apparently that's short for 'Intercourse and Intoxication'—Kucko found a Burmese skin doctor who covered over his scar with the initials of the United

States Marine Corps. The doctor used gunpowder for pigment, explaining it would ward off attack."

"A tad late for that, no?"

"Not according to Kucko. A month later, he was in a helicopter crash. Of the nine men on board, only he survived. Kucko attributed his fate to the tattoo. Back stateside, laid up in a VA hospital outside Washington, he rubbed those four lumpy letters—this is his phrase, Mr. Jesson—like rosary beads. His appreciation for tattooing grew from there. Once he got discharged, Kucko started attending regional tattoo shows. He told me he interviewed a number of artists before he settled on Donatello."

"Don't you mean before Donatello settled on him?"

I faked a chuckle. "When I asked Kucko how many tattoos he had, he told me, 'Just one. There are lots of images, but they all add up to a single story.' Naturally, I asked him *what* story. His response: 'Not *what* . . . *whose*.' That's when I went for the kill. I stuck a copy of the Polaroid under his nose and said, 'How about filling in this chapter?'"

"How did he react?"

"He grabbed the picture and tore it in half. But I came prepared. I pulled out another copy and told him I had a whole bunch more. Kucko demanded to know what I was planning to do with the photo. 'Nothing,' I said. 'If you help me rescue the Queen from your boss.' I used that word, 'rescue,' to lessen the adversarial tenor of the meeting."

"And did it?" Jesson was now straining out of his sedan chair.

"To a point. Kucko made his help conditional. He's so worried about the photo, he's demanding that we implicate ourselves. He figures our involvement will guarantee silence."

"You just said *our* involvement, Alexander. You did keep me out of it, I hope."

"How could I? The man's not stupid. He must know we work together. He saw you at Ornstein's and at the benefit. What's the likelihood two individuals with no relationship to each other would approach him about the Queen?"

"If he's that smart, what prevents him from getting rid of the tattoo? There must be some kind of acid or surgery available."

"The design covers his entire body. And what good would it do if he effaced the incriminating part? We still have the photo. That's enough to link him to the burglary in Jerusalem."

"So where did you leave matters?"

"Kucko's calling as soon as he's arranged things at his end. If all goes well, your case might actually get completed by Christmas."

"Marvelous," said Jesson, sounding less than thrilled.

55

WHEN TO RETURN the book?

Norton and I compared schedules and quickly determined that our best chance to execute "Operation Reinsertion" coincided with the postinventory staff party. That was the single moment we knew of when Grote would be out of the lab, defending his title in Class Struggle, the competition he had won the previous two years.

Our plan was simple. We'd sneak into Conservation at the start of the celebrations, basing our timetable on the bookmark-shaped program Dinty had thumbtacked to the schedule board:

STAFF PARTY

1. Call Slip Race
2. Indicator Board Battleship

3. Class Struggle
4. Investiture of Lord of Misrule
5. If-You-Were-A-Book

But our plan hit a snag when Grote failed to show for the first event. As my colleagues were plucking call slips from a basket and dashing out of the Reading Room to retrieve their books, I imagined the absent conservator down in his lab, working his way, flap by flap, toward the phase box that would end my career.

Mr. Abromowitz crossed the finish line first, an oversize history of the Brooklyn Bridge suspended between outstretched hands. A member of the stack crew, carrying a slim volume of Symbolist verse bound in the poet's skin, and Mr. Singh, who submitted *Seven Weeks to a Settled Stomach*, took the silver and bronze, respectively.

The rest of the contestants trickled in soon after, with Speaight pulling up the rear. He created a minor scandal by presenting a study of pederasty in lieu of the book he was supposed to locate. Even after the commotion surrounding the tawdry submission died down, Grote was still a no-show. Norton and I tried to weigh our options but there weren't any. We couldn't do a thing until we knew for certain that the lab was clear.

Things only got worse. Mr. Paradis announced that an electrical malfunction put the kibosh on the second event, Indicator Board Battleship. "Jizzicked," is how he characterized the breakdown of the ancient number board. That seemed a fair description of my state as well. Then, just as I was despairing of ever returning the book, in walked Irving

Grote, a crib sheet of Dewey numbers poking out of his pocket.

The beauty of the DDC—and I'll confess once again to finding it beautiful despite the prejudice it engenders—resides in its adaptability. The system lets the well-trained librarian synthesize a hierarchy of people, places, and things, of ideas and phenomena. What's more, it encourages that hierarchy both to grow and to be remembered. Familiarity with classes, divisions, and sections means this: that if a reader walks up and requests, say, *The Study of Arab Women: A Bibliography of Bibliographies*, a librarian who knows the system can direct the inquirer with confidence to 016.016305488927.

Class Struggle emerged from the numerical razzle-dazzle of such compound composition. What sounded like a parlor game actually became one at our institution early in the 1940s, before Library of Congress classification horned in on Dewey.

Dinty waved his clipboard overhead and asked the contestants—a guy from Technical Services, someone from Collection Development, Grote, and Mr. Paradis—to approach their lecterns, each of which had been fitted with a reception-desk bell.

Class Struggle, Dinty explained, would be divided into two rounds. The first, or "analytic," round required the players to identify subjects on the basis of Dewey numbers. The second, or "synthetic," round reversed the challenge by requiring the conversion of subjects and titles *into* decimal classification. The first half would include bonus questions, the second half would not. Correct answers would earn ten

points each; all errors would result in five points being sub-
tracted from a score. The cataloging department, for obvious
reasons, was barred from play, as were reference librarians
with specialized training in classification. (My graduate
work on Dewey disqualified me.)

All questions and answers would follow the guidelines of
the most recent edition of the DDC, as adjudicated by Dinty,
who would serve not only as judge but as scorekeeper and
emcee, as well. Finally, the winner of Class Struggle would
garner the title Lord of Misrule and would receive, with that
title, the right to run the library for the remainder of the
party. Dinty ended his remarks with an admonition:

"Last year, most of you will recall, there was a fracas over
the use of moribund phoenix schedules and reclassed subjects."
He paused to glance at Mr. Paradis, the victim in the dispute.
"Let me make myself clear. Decisions of the judge shall be
final and binding. Is this understood?"

After each of the contestants acknowledged his authority,
Dinty extracted a catalog card from the rubber-banded packet
clipped to his board. "Let's begin with a relatively simple
classification: 577."

BING!

A white-gloved hand darted out and tapped a bell.

"And we're off," said Dinty. "Mr. Grote, are you able to
identify the number?"

"I am indeed," his ally affirmed. "As any page knows, or
should know, 577 is ecology."

"Quite right. 577 is ecology. Ten points for you." Dinty
consulted his pack of cards. "Now for the bonus question, Mr.
Grote. Please provide the subject field for 577.68."

"The point 6 narrows our focus to aquatic ecology and the

8 narrows things down further to wetlands ecology. That is my answer for 577.68—wetlands ecology."

"Once again you are correct. That brings your score to twenty."

Lukewarm claps from around the room confirmed I wasn't the only one who found Grote insufferable.

Dinty pulled another card. "629.134. I repeat—"

Ting.

Mr. P.'s leathery hand tapped a bell plunger. "Jet engines?"

"Jet engines is correct," said Dinty crisply. "But I caution you to wait to be called upon. I shall give you points this time. I won't be so generous in the future. Now for the bonus, Mr. Paradis. 629.134 . . . 3537. To repeat: 629.1343537."

Mr. Paradis tugged on a strap of his overalls. "May I?"

"Go on."

"That'd be *fan-jet* engines."

"Correct again."

Amid raucous cheering, Norton and I ducked out of the Reading Room to repatriate *The Book of Hours*.

We knew restitution would be almost as hard as removal. There were no exit-desk sensors to bypass on the return trip, but we still had to get through the lab's padlocked fencing. While I retrieved *The Book of Hours* from my locker, Norton stopped in at Periodicals for a newspaper rod.

At first glance, everything in the lab appeared as it had the last time we'd broken in, right down to the bronze book louse resting on Grote's log. But when we reached the lockup, we received a rude shock. The materials inside had been entirely rearranged. The phase box we needed was now located two shelves up, rendering access, even with our trusty rod, next to impossible.

As I was contorting my body to reach the box, Norton, at the other end of the lab, identified yet another snafu. "Christ! The Tattle-Tape."

"We got rid of it," I huffed, my face pressed against the fencing.

"That's the point. Grote mentioned it in the treatment schedule. We'll need to come up with a replacement."

"Handle it, please."

Norton managed to find a similar strip of tape inside one of the lab's dictionaries. A few gentle scrapes—this time he used a microspatula instead of his credit card—yielded a serviceable substitute. The strip covered the incriminating ghost mark perfectly.

I wish I could claim my part of the operation produced similar success. I can't. After several minutes spent jamming a newspaper rod through commercial-grade fencing, I was forced to concede defeat.

The "analytic" round of Class Struggle had ended by the time I stashed *The Book of Hours* back in my locker and took a seat near the lecterns. Dinty announced the gloomy news that his friend Grote had taken the lead, then launched into round two.

"An anthology of mathematical poetry. To repeat: an anthology of mathematical poetry."

A white glove slapped a bell.

"Mr. Grote, do you have an answer?"

"808.819356."

"That is correct, Mr. Grote. Well done." Dinty had by now abandoned all pretense of impartiality. "Next card. A bibliography of Arabic typography."

A callused hand tapped a plunger.

"Yes, Mr. Paradis?"

"016.68621927."

"Correct," said Dinty. "Next card: an English-Sicilian dictionary."

The white glove darted out. *BING!*

"Do you have an answer for us, Mr. Grote?"

"423.51."

"Bravo."

By the middle of the second round, the questions got tougher and the pace slowed. The fellow from Collection Development gave up after misidentifying the classification for the upholstery trade in Georgia. The stack runner was done in two cards later by *Know Your Czechoslovakian Pistols.* That left Mr. P. and Irving Grote.

"Treasures of Ukrainian religious art during the sixteenth through eighteenth centuries."

Grote pounced. "Seven-oh-four point nine-four-eight . . . two-oh-nine . . . four-seven-seven-oh-nine-oh-three."

"Excellent, Mr. Grote! That puts you in the lead by"—Dinty consulted his clipboard—"five points. One more correct answer wins you the championship and with it the title Lord of Misrule. That means, of course, that you will be able to run the library as you see fit for the remainder of the evening."

Dinty's comment gave me an idea. If Mr. P. could beat out Grote, I might just possibly get one last crack at returning the book to the lockup.

"Are the finalists ready?" Dinty asked.

The two rivals nodded and the room suddenly mimicked the proverbial silence of the library. Dinty extracted a card and stared at it longer than necessary, blatantly attempting to heighten the tension.

"Listen closely, please. The rules only allow me to say the title twice." He paused. "*Depression among Unmarried Southern Yemeni Mothers.* . . . I repeat . . . *Depression among Unmarried Southern Yemeni Mothers.*"

For an excruciating interval, during which only the sound of pencil scratches could be heard, Grote and Mr. P. worked through the final challenge. The cite, everyone in the room knew, would be littered with booby traps. Neither player wanted to mess up through hasty composition.

BING!

"You have an answer, Mr. Grote?"

"I do," said the conservator, barely able to contain himself. "We begin with 157 for abnormal and clinical psychologies. From there we need to narrow our scope. Unmarried mothers are designated 306.8743. Yemenis are 927533. However, one must be careful. *Southern* Yemen demands an additional 5. That brings us to"—he frowned over his pad and enunciated the numbers with the precision of a Henry Higgins— "157.30687439275335."

Dinty stared at his friend, then down at the card, then back at his friend once more. "I'm so sorry, Irving. Your number doesn't conform."

"That makes the two of them even Steven," someone in the audience shouted.

"Silence!" bellowed Dinty. "Does the other contestant wish to venture a correction? If not we—"

Ting.

All eyes settled on the janitor, who waited to be called on, knowing he could lose the match for the most minor of in-fractions.

"Mr. Paradis?"

The janitor rubbed his jaw. "Seems to me they vacated the 157s, though heaven knows 'abnormal and clinical psychologies' is a pretty darn useful category for folks working in libraries."

Everyone laughed.

"Anyway, I got a whole bunch of problems with the way Mr. Grote is tryin' to build his numbers. Can't just run 'em together that way. And besides, he's forgotten all about put-ting those poor Southern Yemeni mothers *inside* their country. No wonder they're depressed."

"Do you have an answer, Mr. Paradis?"

"Yes I do. You ready, Emil?" The janitor paused. "*Depression Among Unmarried Southern Yemeni Mothers* would be . . . 616.85270086947095335."

Dinty scowled and, double-checking his clipboard, forced himself to say, "That is correct."

Silence was abruptly replaced by stomping and whistling. In the pandemonium that followed, Norton ran up to one of the lecterns and smacked its bell. *BING-BING-BING-BING-BING-BING!*

"All hail Mr. Paradis, Lord of Misrule," he cried out. "Master of Merry Disports, Interim Director of our august institution."

Dinty slammed his clipboard on a table. "Quiet! And get away from there. Before *anyone* gets crowned, I am duty-bound, for the benefit of our recent hires, to provide a brief history of misrule, a concept with roots stretching back to the festival of the Roman Saturnalia, a custom in which—"

Hissing and catcalls forced Dinty to suspend his speech. Within minutes, the janitor, hand resting on a copy of the *ALA Handbook*, took the royal oath of office.

From a makeshift throne—a Windsor chair liberally wrapped in aluminum foil—our lord issued his first edict: immediate cancelation of If-You-Were-A-Book. The Maine-born janitor said he was tired of being reincarnated as an L.L.Bean catalog. "See no point gettin' slapped with that wet brush."

I pushed toward the throne. "All lords need a scepter," I said, handing my friend the newspaper rod I'd used so ineffectually in the lab.

"Mighty fine of you, Alexander."

I bowed and asked for a private audience. Mr. P. smiled after he heard what I had in mind. "A few snedricks can't hurt now and then." He aimed his scepter at the back of the room.

"*You* there."

All heads turned.

"Yes, *you*."

Snickers circulated.

"Bring that fella forward," the lord demanded. "This ought to take the starch out of him," he said as an aside.

Grote was drowning his sorrows in eggnog when two of the janitor's cronies grabbed him by the arms and marched him to the throne.

"It's been brought to our attention," said the lord, "that the cleanin' staff's got smaller by one since we were crowned. So it is our royal wish that this man here"—the rod targeted Grote—"fill the vacated post."

Norton, on cue, parked the cleaning cart next to Grote.

"But milord," I said, "who will take over this man's tasks if he is to polish and dust?"

Mr. P. pretended to deliberate before announcing, "It is our desire, young sir, that his position become yours."

"As you command," I said, bowing once more before turning to Grote. "Seems I'll be needing your keys."

Norton started a chant that the rest of the room quickly joined: "Keys! Keys! Keys!"

Grote had no choice but to comply. "Be advised, Short. Touch anything in my lab, *anything at all*, and trust me, you will *never* see that book you've been so desperate to get your hands on."

"You can keep it."

Once out of sight, I tore down to my locker and grabbed *The Book of Hours*. I then raced it into the lab, opened the lockup, and pulled down the phase box. Extracting the bibliokleptomania monograph, I replaced it with the borrowed volume, making sure to close the protective case in the precise order mandated by Grote: bottom flap up, top flap down, side flap over. I wound the string around the grommet *counter-clockwise*, got the box back on the shelf, and clanged shut the gate maybe thirty seconds before the conservator burst in and demanded his key ring.

By the time I made it back upstairs, the kingdom was hopping. The Lord of Misrule, having consumed royal quantities of eggnog, seemed to be enjoying the perks of benign despotism.

"Bring Nortie to us!" he hollered. "Bring him to his lord!" When Norton approached, the janitor said, "You once told us you wanted to have a chariot race in the library. Always did like the idea. Reminds me of the ice dashes we had in grade school, when the Mooselookmeguntic froze over. How were you figurin' on it?"

"Thought we could use the book trucks."

The janitor grimaced. "You don't know beans about racin' if you think book trucks will do the trick."

"What do you suggest, milord?"

"Lords don't *suggest*, Nortie. Lords decree. And I decree that you get us four garbage skips and set 'em up near Delivery."

Dinty tried to overrule the plan, but his objections were squelched by the lord's faithful subjects, whose devotion increased precipitously with the unexpected arrival of some single-malt scotch, compliments of Speaight and his center. The revelers soon congregated at the brass grille of Delivery, where charioteers paired off and laid claim to the vehicles Norton had secured.

Speaight coaxed a petite cataloger whose name I can never remember into being his mount. Mr. Abromowitz harnessed the director's administrative assistant to his canvas bin. Norton and I took a third skip, and two members of the stack crew grabbed a fourth.

With a sweep of his scepter, Mr. P. started us off on a six-lap race around the perimeter of the Reading Room.

Speaight and the cataloger were the first to roll across the finish line, their victory boisterously toasted by everyone save Messrs. Dinty and Grote. The partnership of the victors continued long after the cheers died down. In fact, as I was leaving the party, delighted to be free of the borrowed book and the headaches it had created, I caught the couple pressed against a range of medical texts, an embrace aptly captioned by the words printed on the cataloger's back. LIBRARIANS, her T-shirt announced, DO IT BY THE BOOK.

56

WITH *THE BOOK OF HOURS* snug in the phase box, I was finally off the hook and Jesson, at last, was on it—or would be soon enough. His comeuppance, Nic and I decided, should play on as many of the man's defects as possible: his blinding lust for the Queen, his obsessive suspicion of Stolz, his breach of faith with me. But we also agreed that the retaliatory adieu, whatever shape it took, should be less about payback than about the reclamation of the life Jesson had tried to plunder.

Which is why, after a few days of research and planning (and some serious coaching from Nic), I presented myself at the world headquarters of Stolz Industries, with Jesson none the wiser.

Stolz never would have agreed to see me if I hadn't embel-
lished the reason for the meeting. When I called his offices I
left the impression I was selling the leather box that his assistant Kucko had failed to obtain. I made clear to various go-
betweens that the sale was dependent on my sussing out the
buyer. To my amazement this precondition was accepted,
though not with much grace.

"You," Stolz said gruffly. "Sit."

He had his feet propped up on a desk the size of an airplane
wing, a pose that offered a fine view of the bottoms of his
shoes, which had disks of plastic affixed to the heels and toes,
evidence of a frugality Jesson would have despised. Before I
could begin my pitch, Stolz planted an egg timer on the edge
of the desk. "It was Thomas Edison's," he said. "The guy
who sold it to me claimed he kept it handy to keep meetings
brief. So do I. You've got three minutes."

Suddenly I felt the absurdity of the encounter and fumbled
as a result. "I—I work for Henry James Jesson III."

"Not the clown from the photo op with the Neanderthals?
Why's he selling?"

"He isn't."

Stolz's eyes narrowed. "Then we're done," he said, reaching
for the timer. "You've just saved me two and a half minutes."

"Hold on. Don't you want to know the real reason I'm
here?"

"Go on."

"Mr. Jesson has deluded himself into believing you've got
the contents of the Breguet box."

Stolz made a face. "The Queen? You're joking, right?"

"Nope."

"Where'd he get that idea?"

"Your interest in watches, for one thing. Your net worth, for another. Also your brief conversation with him at that fundraiser. It convinced him your personality meshes with—and I know this sounds crazy—something he calls a 'template of criminality.'"

Stolz roared with laughter, which caused his eyes to disappear. "The jerk has one hell of an imagination. And you say you work for him?"

"Worked—and trust me, his imagination isn't all it's cracked up to be." The bitterness in my voice must have registered. Stolz dropped his feet to the floor and looked me square in the face.

"Okay, so we're on the same page about the bozo. What's that got to do with the box? Or me?" He glanced at the timer. "You've got maybe another minute."

I took a deep breath and summarized the events leading up to our rendezvous. Stolz followed the ins and outs without comment until I got to the Polaroid that falsely implicated Kucko in the Jerusalem burglary.

"Wait a sec. You're telling me you had your wife paint your butt and photograph it just to convince what's-his-face that one of my employees stole the Queen?"

"That pretty much sums it up, Mr. Stolz."

He chuckled. "This I got to see."

"Be happy to send you a print."

"Not good enough."

"It's pretty faded. Maybe—"

"Time's up, kid. But tell you what. A look-see buys you another three minutes. Otherwise you can haul your polychrome ass straight out of my office."

Stolz was still laughing when I zipped up my pants. Apparently, I'd made an impression.

"You interest me, kid. Now tell me, really, why are we talking?"

"Jesson betrayed me, Mr. Stolz. He misdirected my research, pilfered my notebooks, and gave my life to a fictional eighteenth-century character."

"Sounds like you need a lawyer."

"I don't want to sue. I'm looking for a different kind of settlement. I want to take back from Jesson what he took from me."

Stolz drummed his fingers on the desk. "Steal from a thief?"

"Exactly. And what better place to do that than at the Frederick R. Stolz Arcade of Obsolescence?"

"News flash, kid. The watch isn't there."

"True. But let's not overlook the genius of Stolz Imaging Systems. I'm no expert on convection kernels and advection lengths, but it seems, from what I've read, your development team could easily recreate the Marie Antoinette."

Stolz smiled. "You flatter me. Think you could get your ex-boss over to the arcade?"

"He'd climb a greased pole naked if it meant completing his case."

"The problem is good visuals. To do this up right, we need a high-res image of the Queen."

"Which you've got," I said. "Your curator very generously gave me a copy."

"Really?" Stolz was clearly warming to the proposal. "I'll have it pulled. Though I better warn you, the arcade isn't finished yet."

"I'm not worried."

"Anything else I need to know about Project Two-Time?"

"There's this." I placed a binder on the edge of Stolz's desk. As soon as he started leafing through the sketches Nic and I had done, he shoved the egg timer into a drawer. "This is wonderful stuff, kid."

"So we're on?"

"You bet. I'll call when we're ready to offer the clown a taste of Stolz's prestidigital hocus friggin' pocus."

57

"IT'S NOW OR never, Mr. Jesson."

"Now or never *what*?" came the reply from deep inside the sedan chair.

"Kucko called. Guess who's out of town at a shareholders meeting?"

"Splendid. I'll expect a full and timely report."

"You'll be getting more than that. Kucko's exact words were, and I quote, 'the both of youse.'"

"Well, you can tell Kucko *my* exact words are 'Out of the question.'"

"He's the one calling the shots. I've got the rental car double-parked."

"That's absurd," Jesson sputtered. "We need time to prepare."

"And in a perfect world that might happen."

The door of the sedan chair flew open. "How can we even be sure Stolz is away?"

"All I know is what Kucko told me. We're supposed to drive to the back of the arcade's central hangar and flash our headlights twice."

"The man's cinematic flourishes are not what concerns me. I worry this might be a trap."

"Don't fret so much. You're pretty good at finding loop-holes."

Jesson's agitation intensified in the car. As a devotee of roomy sedan chairs, he was none too pleased to have his body squished into the vinyl bucket of a subcompact. (I'd made a special point of renting a Ford to provoke distasteful memories of his Dearborn namesake, Henry.) Of course, his harangue against the car seat—"an ignominious abuse of orthopedics"—masked an uneasiness that had little to do with the deficiencies of American automobile design. What bothered Jesson was his sudden loss of control. Staring at the warehouses we passed on our way to New Jersey, he undoubtedly felt himself de-moted to a role previously held by me: that of troubled pawn.

We reached the ring road of the Arcade of Obsolescence just as the sun was setting. Floodlights scalloped the walls of the complex, adding a sense of drama to the work site.

I parked and flashed my high beams. And while we waited for a response, I surveyed the compound. "That structure off to the side, that's the library, Mr. Jesson. It's where I learned the watch was a Breguet. As for the three buildings directly in front of us, that's the arcade proper. The hangar on the right is the preindustrial wing, the one to the left is the postindustrial—"

"And let me guess," Jesson sneered. "This tin whale that looms before us will house the industrial portion of Stolz's collection. Do we know in which of these Quonset huts the Queen is held?"

"Kucko didn't say."

"Of course he didn't. And where the devil is he?"

"Probably deactivating the perimeter alarms. Apparently, the compound's sensors are supersensitive. They incorporate land-mine technology."

Jesson slumped. "How reassuring."

The floodlights shut off. A moment later, a single beam, from a theatrical spot mounted to the central hangar, tracked across the dirt road and hit our windshield. By the time I'd hopped out of the car and made it to the passenger side, the light had started retreating.

"Stick close," I said. "And make sure you stay inside the beam."

The light guided us to a wooden pallet some forty feet away.

"Jump on, Mr. Jesson."

My passing reference to land mines clearly had made an impression; Jesson clambered up without a word. An engine sputtered to life while he was still struggling to steady himself on the slats. His grip tightened on my arm.

"Look!" he croaked.

Out of the darkness, a forklift rumbled toward us at a ferocious clip. Jesson fell to his knees, taking me down with him, just as the tines of the machine scooped us up.

"Hold on," I shouted over the noise of the motor.

"I assure you," Jesson screamed back, "I have no intention of letting go."

The forklift deposited us on the hangar's elevated loading dock.

"Over there," I said, pointing to a shoebox illuminated by another spotlight.

Jesson shuffled toward the box and glanced down but was fearful enough to let me do the honors. "What the hell are those?" he asked, after I'd removed the lid.

"Moleskin innersoles," I said.

"For what possible purpose?"

"Tell you in a second. There's a note." I unfolded the paper. "Says we're supposed to stick the innersoles on the *bottoms* of our shoes. Probably another security measure. Seems the place is multiply alarmed."

"That makes two of us," said Jesson, as he watched me apply the green felt pads to the soles of his walking boots.

With our feet felted like chessmen, we milled about, waiting for the next signal. To bide the time, Jesson approached a massive iron blade mounted above the entrance of the industrial wing.

"The caption says this thing was used to decapitate seventy-nine aristocrats during the final months of the Terror. I only hope we aren't numbers eighty and—"

Jesson jumped back, managing to avoid the descending blade only moments before it abbreviated a lot more than his words.

"Close shave," I said. The wordplay wasn't appreciated. A spotlight directed us to a leather pouch resting on the floor. I snatched it up, knowing Jesson wouldn't, and shook the contents into his hand.

"What are we supposed to do with these?" He jingled the dozen or so tarnished silver coins that had fallen out of the pouch. His question was answered by yet another beam of light. This one pointed us to the central corridor of the wing.

"What the—"

The view silenced Jesson, as it did me. We found ourselves in the middle of a warehouse filled with vintage carnival games, mechanical apparatuses, and (I'm particularly pleased to report) a fully restored, though as yet nonfunctioning, Automat, complete right down to the dolphin-head spigots on the gleaming coffee urns.

The light zeroed in on a magnificent player piano. Jesson approached it and deposited a Liberty dime. The instrument wheezed to life.

"Bastard," he said after the piano had sounded a few notes.

"What's wrong?"

"Haydn's Symphony no. 101 in D."

"So?" It was getting tough to appear ignorant.

"Also known as the *Clock*. Surely you noticed I have a reduction of the work at home. It's obvious he's mocking us."

"Kucko?"

Jesson sighed. "Not Kucko, Alexander. *Stolz*."

While the piano plinked away, a light directed us to a "Mechanical Talking Turk," a life-size wooden fortune teller promising "Prescient Prognostication for a Fee of Five Cents." Jesson placed a buffalo nickel on the Turk's tongue and turned a heavy crank. The eyes of the automaton rolled back behind leather lids and the jaw began to move.

"*Veeeee-vuuhhh-laaa-Rennn!*"

"Long live the Queen?" I said.

Jesson swung around and started yelling at an overhead surveillance camera. "*Enough!* You've made your point, Stolz. Reveal yourself!"

The challenge was acknowledged by a beam of light that led us to a cordoned-off space at the far end of the hangar, where a message had been tied to one of the stanchions. It said, TIME'S UP.

However observed (whether through the eyes of the cataloger, the collector, the liar, or the thief), the empty quadrant soon radiated an image of palpable beauty. How exactly Stolz managed the special effects eludes me to this day. Even after boning up on laser technology and optical imaging, I still don't know what he did. From a simple photo, he generated a three-dimensional timepiece, a ticking, gear-driven Queen that sparkled with the fire and flash of a flawless gemstone.

She materialized some eight feet above the roped-off space and hovered, just out of reach, like a glass egg bobbing on an invisible plume of water. Now, staring at a ticking timepiece may not sound like much. But if you talk to a research chemist specializing in pigment, he'll tell you that even observing paint dry can be exciting if what you care about is paint.

Jesson stood motionless, awestruck by the watch's internal movement. His face betrayed rapture, tinged with a mounting sense of fear. After a minute or so, he stretched his hand over the velvet braid, and by doing so made the watch tick more loudly and more ominously, like a time bomb set to explode.

"Maybe we'd better hold off," I cautioned. "Who knows how the motion detectors work."

Jesson wasn't listening. He seemed spellbound by the object needed to complete the case. Nothing else mattered. Suddenly, he lifted one leg, then the other, over the cord and began lunging for the watch. Yet each time his fingers were about to close in, the Queen bobbed to safety, inches out of reach. Eventually his arms grew weak and fell to his sides. Then, as if sensing the defeat of her pursuer, the Queen floated over the velvet cordon and disappeared behind the canvas top of a Model T.

"So, fellas. Want to explain what you're doin' here?"

With his foot resting on the bumper of the Ford and a remote control in his hand, Stolz was looking more than a little smug.

"The watch, where is it?" demanded Jesson.

Stolz responded by aiming the remote at a TV fixed to a robotic arm. The television lowered and began to flash snippets of surveillance footage showing us moving through the arcade. Freezing on an image of Jesson lunging for the watch, Stolz shook his head and said, "Wouldn't have pegged you for the break-and-entry type."

"We violated no laws. The gates to the compound were open."

Stolz gave us a skeptical look. "In the middle of the night? With no staff on duty? We'll let the police decide that one."

"Wait just a minute," said Jesson. "Surely we can resolve this matter privately. I am prepared to offer—"

"Sorry, my fossilized friend. You saw the sign. Time's up." And with that, Stolz gave the remote another click.

At first the only thing visible on the video screen was the massive guillotine we'd observed at the entrance to the industrial wing. But this was no longer surveillance footage we were watching. The camera zoomed in to reveal the Queen resting on a chopping block positioned under the guillotine blade.

"Stop!" Jesson shouted.

The magnified gears of the watch ratcheted around on sapphire pallets. A tiny gold hammer recoiled and struck, releasing a haunting series of chimes.

"Please," cried Jesson. "Can we discuss this?"

A black-hooded figure approached the block and adjusted the position of the timepiece to make sure it sat directly below the blade. As he did, his sleeve bunched up, revealing a pale, tattooed wrist.

Then, without warning or fanfare, the knife began to drop.

Three very long seconds later—Stolz slowed the film to intensify the effect—iron kissed crystal with gruesome results.

As the blade struck, I watched Jesson's face closely; it locked into a wrenching G-force rictus, a grimace of pain and helplessness that made me suddenly, and unexpectedly, sad. I wondered whether I'd taken things too far.

Stolz had no such reservations. "Now that, old man, is what I call cutting-edge technology."

The destruction, more potent than the joke, owed as much to Brueghel and Buñuel as to his so-called prestidigitalization.

Stolz kept the film looping on the monitor. And with each execution, Jesson seemed to die a bit more.

Close-up of the hooded figure, close-up of the tattooed hand realigning the watch on the block, close-up of the blade, close-up of the blade's slow-motion descent. And then . . . a fitting end for the Marie Antoinette.

58

ONLY THAT WASN'T the end.

I'd been all set to enjoy the betrayal of my betrayer. That, after all, was the reason for the humiliating game of spotlight tag. So why did Jesson's horological mugging make me feel as though I was the one beaten up? Why, when I glanced over at the old man muttering to himself in the passenger seat as we drove out the compound gates, did I think the whole charade had been a mistake?

Payback presumed that upping his misery would make mine disappear. But my reaction wasn't that tidy, and neither, it turned out, was his.

By the time we got back to Festinalente Jesson seemed much improved. He was by no means cheery, but the defeat suffered in the arcade appeared to have been supplanted by a stubborn desire to make sense of what he'd seen.

"The light show, the floating Queen, plus the film of her putative execution . . . We seriously underestimated Mr. Frederick R. Stolz."

I gave a cautious nod and, though tempted to ask why "putative," said nothing.

"I can't help feeling something about the whole spectacle rings false. He would never destroy the Marie Antoinette simply to humble me."

"Sure looked like he did."

"I'm not convinced." Jesson's suspicions seemed, to my amazement, focused solely on Stolz. He buzzed for some biscuits but jumped up from his chair before they arrived. "Follow me," he commanded as he took us into the gallery of mechanical wonders.

I had a strong urge, as he was shuffling past the hidden roll-player, to grab the tieback of his vest and shout, "I found your goddamn roll!" But I kept myself in check.

"I know what doesn't ring true!" Jesson exclaimed.

"You do?"

"I do. We may have seen a watch get destroyed, but I'm certain it was not a Breguet." He was standing in front of his precious *pendule sympathique* when he made the announcement.

"How can you tell?"

He removed the dust cover and pointed to the master clock and the pocket watch slave that it cradled. "The chimes we heard in the film," he said.

"What about them?"

Jesson reached out and tinkered with the hands of the

larger timepiece. "Do you recall how they rang just before the Queen was . . ." He drew a finger across his neck.

"Hard to forget."

"How would you describe the sound?"

"I don't know. Eerie? Plangent?"

"But not at all like this." Jesson triggered the clock to ring. It did so with none of the musicality heard in the film.

"There you have it. Proof of Stolz's fraud. Breguet's com-plicated watches possess a host of virtues, but they all share one significant flaw. A flat-sounding *sonnerie*. That dullness is a hallmark of Breguets. The gong and *à toc* system of the Marie Antoinette never could have sounded so beautiful. Ergo . . . the chimes were faked. And if the chimes were faked we can dismiss the rest of Stolz's concocted encounter. He's ob-viously enraged by my possession of the leather box."

"Which brings us where?"

Jesson draped the dust cover over the *sympathique*. "Back to square one."

It took me a moment to comprehend his about-face. "You're saying you think Stolz *doesn't* have the watch? But you were sure. In your roll you said—"

I stopped midsentence. I had had enough. "It's over, Mr. Jesson."

"What is?"

Pointing at the timepiece, I said, "Master and slave are no longer in sync."

"What's that supposed to mean?"

"Follow me." I marched out of the gallery and planted myself in front of the globe. "Stolz isn't the only one who's been making up stories, is he?" I spun the globe; its wobble confirmed that the note roll was still inside. "You want to discuss taunts and rage? Let's begin with that crack you made about my finding paradise *depressing*."

The globe came to a stop.

"That's right. I know all about my incarnation as a *page* in your bogus case of curiosities." I located the kidney-bean island and pushed down hard on the catch. The globe cleaved in two.

"How?" Jesson sputtered. "When?"

"Stumbled on it looking for *The Book of Hours*."

I extracted the incriminating roll. "If you'd resisted the bonehead puns about *depressing paradise*, I would never have discovered that you've been stealing my thoughts for some humbug piece of historical fiction."

"You've been reading too much Henry James. If I might interject a word in my defense, you're as guilty of thievery as I. True, I maintain a secret roll, but at least it's not coded. And I have never run around with my notes tethered to the lapel of my coat!"

"I've moved beyond the girdle book, Mr. Jesson."

"Have you? What am I to you, Alexander Short, besides an opportunity to annotate, fodder for your abecedarian lust? The parasite living in my gut lives in yours as well. Make no mistake: all scribbling is theft. And at least *I* pay for what I steal. Plus I put the product of that appropriation to some practical use."

"That being?"

"I have endeavored to write a novel, Alexander. What have your cryptic scrawls yielded?"

The attack flustered me. "Why do you always deflect?"

Jesson released a rueful laugh. "Alexander, when have you ever admitted *your* errors? Who was it who tried to argue that librarians have no use for emotions?"

"Go to hell! You never had the slightest intention of working with me, Mr. Jesson. I was *never* your Boswell."

"Y-yes, you were," he stammered. "And, I hope, still are."

"Not a chance. I've read the notes. I'm not interested in being your doubt-filled, troubled pawn."

"I believe it was the fawn that was doubt-filled. Nevertheless, I admit those lines were harsh. There's little about you that is pawnlike—not anymore. At the risk of sounding patronizing, I'd have to say you have grown."

"That's right. I now recognize the virtue of deceit."

"Meaning what?"

"Meaning, do you really think the events at Stolz's arcade were his doing alone? Don't you find it odd that he put Haydn's *Clock* on his player piano?"

Jesson glanced over at the harpsichord. Sheet music for the piece was in view. He returned his gaze to me. The implications of my question soon hit.

"You ungrateful flyspeck."

"Is that any way to talk to your Bozzy?" I drop-kicked the note roll, still holding onto the ring, and watched it unfurl across the carpet.

Jesson stopped the spindle with his slipper, picked it up, and began twisting the caps in opposite directions to rewind the paper. As the roll started lifting off the carpet, forming a precarious bridge between author and subject, I was faced with a choice. I could move closer, in an act of rapprochement, or hold firm and force Jesson's hand. In the end I chose a third option. I let go, quoting a line from Johnson before fleeing Festinalente: "'Of all the griefs that harass the distrest, / Sure the most bitter is a scornful jest.'"

59

"*ALORS?*" DEMANDED NIC.

"Out with it," Norton pressed.

"Did he buy it?" Speaight wanted to know.

"Might as well have been *his* head on the chopping block," I said.

"You get to use the moleskin?" said Norton.

"Yep."

"And the stuff about the land mines?"

"*And* the stuff about the land mines."

"How did the whole floating watch thing go over?"

"Like clockwork."

I made my way down the hallway, wife and friends nipping at my heels, and flopped onto the futon. "Can we shelve the update till tomorrow? I'm exhausted."

"Hey," said Norton. "We've waited all night for this. We want full text and we want it now!"

Nic joined me on the futon. "The Hermit divined nothing?"

"He got that Stolz doesn't have the watch and that the videotape of the Queen's destruction relied on digital trickery. Stolz went overboard with the chimes. But Jesson never suspected us. I finally broke down and told him, which is why I'm burnt out. Things got a little ugly."

Nic shot me a nervous look. "It *is* over?"

"Definitely."

"How did you leave things?" Speaight asked.

"The short entry is . . . from now on, Henry James Jesson III pursues his complications solo. Case closed."

"Great," said Norton. "But can we backspace to Stolz and his arcade? How did the final ka-boom look? I read this entirely excellent paper on the stuff he's doing with parallel projection."

"There was plenty of that, and not just on-screen. As I say, Jesson and I didn't exactly part on the best of terms."

"And the resolution?"

"Mine and Jesson's?"

"No," said Norton. "The film's."

It seemed hopeless to try putting him off. "You know the famous shot of the A-bomb explosion? Wed that mushroom cloud with a snippet from a documentary on the human heart—the kind we used to sit through in biology—and you might begin to get a sense of what the watch looked like when the blade came crashing down."

Speaight said, "I'm still having a hard time believing Stolz was able to turn a still photograph into a film of a ticking timepiece."

"Believe it," Norton interjected. "The guy practically invented volume visualization."

Before he pulled the conversation still deeper into the technical aspects of Stolz's achievement, I said, "The only volume *I* need to visualize is the one I'm determined to write."

Speaight perked up. "Can the center expect another of your artist's books? A sequel to *Slips of Love*?"

"Definitely not," I said. "What I have in mind is more ambitious, an extended counterargument."

"To?" Norton and Speaight asked in unison.

"Jesson, obviously. When the gloves were off, he accused me of failing to produce a single sentence of consequence despite my constant scribbling. He said that my habit of making lists was a form of petty theft."

"Give me a break," Norton said.

"Actually, I think he has a point. I'm beginning to see that invention trumps inventory."

"Hey, if you *do* write this up," said Speaight, "we could get Nic here to print it on a paper scroll and feed it into the center's roll-player."

I quickly rejected the idea. "Let's leave the mechanical devices to Jesson. I'm more interested in producing an *uncomplicated* chronicle. No bells or whistles, no chimes, and definitely no cranks."

"I guess that excludes Mr. Secret Compartments," said Norton.

"No, he'll find a place."

"When you're done writing," said Speaight, "I'll arrange an exhibition that will bring together this work and the rest of your stuff—the girdle book and *Slips of Love* and maybe even the pop-up *Kama Sutra*."

"I don't think displaying the *Kama Sutra* in public is going to win points with the director," Norton said.

"Might be right," admitted Speaight.

"Guys, I don't mean to sound ungrateful, but I've had my fill of objects under glass. Right now, Stolz's battle cry about no more cases sounds incredibly attractive."

"Fine," replied Speaight, slightly wounded. "Would you at least consider letting the center sponsor a reading? We've got the funds."

"That's awfully kind, but it'll be a while."

"No problem," Speaight responded. "No one's watching the clock."

After years of meticulous list making, I found it thrilling to sit down and write without concern for the shape of the lettering or the category of the note. Unconstrained by rubric, I worked quickly, pencil flying across paper at near zip-tube velocity.

My method was simple. I gathered together all the call slips I'd accumulated while working with Jesson and arranged them chronologically. I then used those slips as cue cards. Six months to the day after leaving Jesson's employ, I had a rough draft of a book describing my search for the Queen. Nic gave the pages a close reading, corrected my lousy French, and then dragged me into the loft to improve the scenes of seduction.

She brought similar zest and diligence to the book's layout. After rejecting a half dozen typefaces for their lack of charm, Nic selected a Goudy Modern with whimsical acute hyphens and ornamental italics. When I mentioned in passing that the numbers on a watch dial were known as "chapters," Nic designed the whole book to summon up the overlapping vocabulary of watchmaking and typography, even going so far as to tweak the pagination to come full circle on page 360. She further reinforced the watch motif by including a tiny line drawing of a gear from the Marie Antoinette, explaining that the escapement was as essential for the movement of my "timepiece" as it was for the Queen.

60

MY FIRST READING as a *professional* writer—I feel comfortable stressing the qualifier since the event was advertised in the library newsletter and Speaight did have his research center pay me an honorarium of $150—had been planned for the spacious precincts of the Trustees Room. But those arrangements were quashed by Dinty, who was still outraged by the chariot race and the scotch-fueled bacchanalia that followed. So Speaight improvised, rustling up some folding chairs that he arranged in the coatroom underneath the grand staircase.

The setting, though cramped, was just fine, since only a dozen or so of my colleagues—plus Nic, Christopher Lyons, and Emmanuel Ornstein—came to hear me speak. Speaight had popped announcements in the mail to everyone involved with the search, Stolz and Jesson included; only Stolz bothered to send regrets. (The opening of the Arcade of Obsolescence prevented him from attending.)

And the other major no-show? Frankly, the absence of the chamois vest with the purple ribbon tieback came as a relief. I doubt I could have done the reading if Jesson had been in the audience. It was hard enough to ignore the cyclopic gaze of Mr. Ornstein, who for some inexplicable reason decided to wear his jeweler's loupe.

Speaight joined me at my makeshift podium—one of the library lecterns last seen during the Class Struggle competition—and tapped a reception-bell. *Bing-bing-bing!*

"Welcome all. The Center for Material Culture is pleased to sponsor the literary deflowering of my dear friend Alexander Short. Most of you know Alexander as the Level 2 reference librarian whose curiosity always has him poking around the Reading Room with a notebook tied to his coat. But a few months ago, he put that so-called girdle book aside in favor of—well, I can't say what exactly. He's kept me entirely in the dark about tonight's presentation. So, without further ceremony or delay, I'll pass the reins to him."

I thanked Speaight for his goofy intro and, to allay my growing panic, dove straight into the pages I'd arranged before me:

The search began with a library call slip and the gracious query of an elegant man.

"I beg your pardon," said the man, bowing ever so slightly. "Might I steal a moment of your time?"

He deposited his slip on the reference desk and turned it so that the lettering would face me. And if

this unusual courtesy wasn't enough to attract attention, there was also the matter of his handwriting—a
gorgeous old-fashioned script executed with confident
ascenders and tapering exit strokes—as well as the title
of the book he requested. *Secret Compartments in
Eighteenth-Century Furniture* played right to my fascination with objects of enclosure. . . .

I read for thirty minutes and was surprised when Speaight
jumped up and, over mild applause, demanded that I read some
more, a kindness loudly seconded by the T-shirted cataloger
he'd befriended at the staff party. After a twenty-minute en-
core, several hands shot up.

"Fact or fiction?" Speaight's petite playmate asked.

The classificatory bent of catalogers being what it is, I said,
"Definitely 900s—the realm of recorded memory—insofar as it's
possible to be factual when the memories in question involve
a deceitful man."

"You tellin' us that the pocket watch doesn't even exist?"
said Mr. Paradis from behind his cart of cleaning supplies.
"That the old guy made the whole thing up?"

"No, Mr. P., the Queen exists."

"So where is she?"

"Couldn't say. Ever since the Jerusalem heist, she's joined
an elite community of objects—the Maltese Falcon and the treasure of the Sierra Madre come most quickly to mind—defined
more by pursuit than by possession."

"I still don't understand something," Abromowitz said. "Is
this *your* book or his?"

"That's another tough one. There's a ditty that Mr. Jesson

once recited that addresses the issue of influence better than I ever could:

> *The viewer paints the picture,*
> *The reader writes the book,*
> *The glutton gives the tart its taste,*
> *And not the pastry cook.*

"Following the logic of those lines, you could argue I became a writer the moment I read Mr. Jesson's fiction."

"So what do we become," Norton called out, "once we've read *yours*?"

"Vot do you think?"

All eyes turned toward Ornstein.

"There's a midrash that says pretty much the same thing. Reading spurs writing, vich spurs reading, vich spurs writing." The watch dealer spiraled his finger toward the ceiling.

Nic cleared her throat and tugged discussion away from paradox. "Why did Jesson compose his *histoire* in French?"

"You know, I never thought to ask. Could be rooted in a desire to satisfy his mother's Francophile passions. There are actually a number of such unanswered questions."

"Like vot, for instance?"

"Like was it kismet or calculation that brought the two of us together? And *why* did he seek me out? It must have been more than the Queen he was after."

Lyons was the first to approach after the Q&A. "Thanks for the invite."

"Happy you could come, Mr. Lyons."

"*Christopher!*"

"Christopher. That pinpricked note about the completion date gave my work a real boost, even if the watch never was recovered."

"Let it stay stolen. If you ask me, that dumb old watch doesn't deserve her name. Anyway, you tell a great story. I've already cast the film. Robert Morley would have made a top-notch Jesson, but we'll have to settle for that guy who was in *Amadeus*. And I won't even *say* who I have playing you. Might swell your head." Lyons laughed and made one of his endearing dip-and-pivot exits.

Mr. Paradis approached in his wake. "Mighty entertainin', Alexander."

"Stop your soft-soapin'," I said.

"No, your friend here is entirely correct," Finster Dapples interjected. "I must confess to finding the account not entirely unamusing, though I would make some refinements to the discussion of heraldry."

Mr. Singh joined the group. "Very good, Alexander. Most pleasurable indeed. I must protest on one matter, however. I am thinking it is not accurate to say that I bob my turban this way and that way. No, my friend, it is not accurate."

"I'll tone down the bobbing."

"I would be most grateful if you did so." The guard held out a letter. "A gentleman is asking me to give this to you. I believe he may be the same gentleman described in your tale. He, too, is wearing a vest the color of ghee."

The emblem on the envelope, a book within a book, confirmed Mr. Singh's suspicions. Turning away from my colleagues, I lifted the flap and read the card inside. It said only, "Might I steal a moment of your time?"

A tightness grabbed my chest, and not solely because of the message. The handwriting was still exquisite: ascenders strong, exit strokes perfectly restrained.

"Mr. Singh, the man who handed you this, is he here?"

"Yes indeed, Alexander. He is wishing to meet you in Reference at your earliest possible convenience, which must be now since the library is soon closing."

Jesson had positioned himself in the glow of the neon question mark mounted above the reference desk. Shirt crisply ironed, cheeks shaved as smooth as fine-grain morocco, he was, like his damn lettering, a flawless specimen of proportion and grace. And like the lettering, he was leaning slightly backward, in anticipation, I sensed, of a fight.

"Seems you've evened the score," he said.

"You were there? You heard?"

He gave a nod. "I put myself behind a display cabinet, though I might as well have been inside it for all the attention I received."

"Now you know how I felt reading *my* words in *your* roll!"

"Please, Alexander. I didn't give the guard that note to provoke further recrimination. I won't try to excuse what I did. But I do wish to clarify something. Ditties aside, I have never considered you a plaything or a pawn."

"Fine. What have I been? The dutiful hire?"

"Not a hire. Never that. Transpose the letters and you'd be closer to the mark."

It took me a moment to catch what he meant. "Heir to what, Mr. Jesson?"

"To everything I have and to a good deal that I lack. I suppose what I'm saying is, the empty compartment in the case of curiosities isn't the only void I wanted to fill." Jesson tapped his chest. "Your narrative succeeds where my notes and poems fail. You've made the dull sublime."

The final bell rang.

Mr. Singh approached. "Closing time, gentlemen. It is most imperative that you are leaving the premises." The guard passed through the swing gate and extinguished the neon question mark. Jesson reached for my arm.

"Can you take a bit more Johnson?"

"Always."

"I'm reminded of what the great man said about libraries."

"You mean about their serving the vanity of human hope?"

Jesson nodded.

"Sharansky chalked those words across the blackboard the very first day of class."

"And he was right to have done so. I bring up the phrase because I sense my own vanity and hope shifting."

We walked toward the exit in silence, our arms linked. "And the Queen?" I asked. "Do you think she'll ever resurface?"

"If you had asked me that question when we started our work together I would have said she *must* be found."

"And now?"

"And now that imperative has been tempered. I'm beginning to see that a completed case is a journey ended, and that I wish for ours to continue."

As we left the Reading Room, I lifted my gaze and pointed to the quotation chiseled on the wall.

"'*Habent sua fata libelli,*'" Jesson read.

"Horace got that one right," I said. "All books do have their fates."